Rick was struggling to get the cap off the bottle. "It's stuck."

"Give it to me." Barbara tried turning the bottle cap. She was two years older than Rick. Her hands were stronger. But she couldn't open the bottle either.

Barbara took a metal paperweight off the top of her desk. She used it to bang the edges of the bottle cap. Still the cap wouldn't budge.

"I've got a pair of pliers in my room." Rick ran to get them.

Barbara fitted the pliers on the bottle cap and twisted. Now the cap turned. She lifted it off and stuck her thumb and forefinger into the bottle.

Suddenly Barb͟ ͟ ͟͟'t cold all over. "Rick!" she whisp ͟ ͟ ͟ ͟ ͟ ͟ has hold of my finger ͟ ͟ ͟

RUTH CHEW

THE TROUBLE WITH MAGIC

with illustrations by the author

A STEPPING STONE BOOK™

Random House New York

Copyright © 1976 by Ruth Chew
Cover art copyright © 2014 by David Hohn

All rights reserved.
Published in the United States by Random House Children's Books,
a division of Random House LLC,
a Penguin Random House Company, New York.
Originally published in the United States in hardcover
by Dodd, Mead & Company, New York,
and in paperback by Scholastic, Inc., New York, in 1976.

Random House and the colophon are registered trademarks
and A Stepping Stone Book and the colophon are trademarks
of Random House LLC.

Visit us on the Web!
randomhouse.com/kids
SteppingStoneBooks.com

Educators and librarians, for a variety of teaching tools, visit us at
RHTeachersLibrarians.com

Library of Congress Cataloging-in-Publication Data
Chew, Ruth, author, illustrator.
The trouble with magic / Ruth Chew, with illustrations by the author.
pages cm. — (A stepping stone book)
Summary: Harrison Peabody, a very pleasant wizard, demonstrates that
a great deal of trouble often accompanies a little bit of magic.
ISBN 978-0-449-81379-9 (trade) — ISBN 978-0-449-81380-5 (tr. pbk.) —
ISBN 978-0-449-81381-2 (lib. bdg.) — ISBN 978-0-449-81382-9 (ebook)
[1. Magic—Fiction. 2. Wizards—Fiction. 3. Brothers and sisters—Fiction.
4. Family life—Fiction. 5. Humorous stories.] I. Title.
PZ7.C429Tr 2014 [Fic]—dc23 2013004951

Printed in the United States of America
10 9 8 7 6 5 4 3 2 1

To the memory of
Rick Foels

"Pew!" Barbara ran out onto the front porch.

Her brother came out of the house after her. He slammed the door behind him. "If *you* won't tell Mrs. Cunningham to stop cooking cabbage, Barb, I will."

"Don't you dare, Rick Benton! Mother told us to be good to Mrs. Cunningham. She's such a nice old lady. Remember the woman who took care of us the last time Mother and Daddy were away."

Rick made a face. "Miss Henry wouldn't ever let us go anywhere. She made us stay in the house all the time or else play on the front walk."

"Mrs. Cunningham even gave us a front door key," Barbara said. She sat down on the porch steps. "Oh, I wish she didn't like cabbage. It smells so awful."

Rick scratched his head. "Hey, Barb, I've got an idea. Do you have any money?"

"I still have my allowance from last week." Barbara took two quarters out of the pocket of her jacket.

"Come on, then. We can buy a spray can to get rid of the cabbage smell." Rick started down the steps.

Barbara stood up. She wanted to save the quarters to buy a birthday present for her mother. But, "First things first." That's what her mother always said.

Barbara followed Rick down the Brooklyn street. The maple trees were clouded over with pale green blossoms. The children walked to the supermarket on Church Avenue.

Rick found a shelf stacked with spray cans. He read the labels. "Do we want the house to smell like a tropic garden or a South Sea isle?"

Barbara looked at the price. "Sixty-nine cents."

Rick took a green bottle down from the shelf. "These are cheaper than the cans. There's a wick in them that you pull up. This one is marked down. It only costs a quarter."

"Maybe there's something wrong with it." Barbara looked at the bottle. The cap was rusty, and the label was blurred. Otherwise it seemed to be all right.

After Barbara paid for the bottle at the checkout counter, the two children went out of the supermarket. "It's raining," Rick said.

"Come on, then. I've got to get started with my homework," Barbara told him. "We can open the bottle and put it in my room for a while."

"What about my room?" Rick asked.

"I paid for the bottle," Barbara said. "And I always have more homework than you do. You can borrow the bottle later."

The rain was coming down harder. Rick and Barbara began to run. By the time they got home, it was pouring. Mrs. Cunningham opened the front door. "I thought I heard you come in before, children. You're late getting home from school. Give me those wet jackets."

Barbara took off her jacket. "We did come home before, Mrs. Cunningham. We had to go to the store for something."

"Would you like some milk and cookies?" Mrs. Cunningham asked.

"Yes," Rick said. "But not right now." He handed her his jacket. "We have to do something first." He ran up the stairs with the bottle and took it to Barbara's room.

Barbara came in after him and shut the door.

Rick was struggling to get the cap off the bottle. "It's stuck."

"Give it to me." Barbara tried turning the bottle cap. She was two years older than Rick. Her hands were stronger. But she couldn't open the bottle either.

Barbara took a metal paperweight off the top of her desk. She used it to bang the edges of the bottle cap. Still the cap wouldn't budge.

"I've got a pair of pliers in my room." Rick ran to get them.

Barbara fitted the pliers on the bottle cap and twisted. Now the cap turned. She lifted it off and stuck her thumb and forefinger into the bottle.

Suddenly Barbara felt cold all over. "Rick!" she whispered. "Something has hold of my fingers!"

2

Barbara was shaking so much she could hardly pull her hand out of the bottle. Something small and black clung to the end of her finger.

As soon as Barbara's hand was out of the bottle, the black thing began to grow. At first Rick and Barbara couldn't tell what it was. Then they saw it was a man. He was wearing a black suit and holding a black umbrella over his head. The man got bigger and bigger and bigger until he blocked the light from the window. The room was getting dark. In a minute Barbara and Rick would be squashed.

"Stop!" Barbara cried.

At once the huge shape began to

shrink. It got smaller and smaller. Then it stopped.

The man closed the umbrella. "How do you like this size?"

Barbara was still shaking. She opened her mouth, but she couldn't say a word.

Rick swallowed. "It's a nice size," he said. "You're just about as big as the man who runs the bakery on Church Avenue."

Barbara stared at the little man. He was short and tubby. His eyes were bright blue in a round pink face. When he took off his tall, wide-brimmed black hat, Barbara saw that the top of his head was bald. He had a ring of gray curls around the back and curly gray sideburns. His black suit seemed a little too tight for him.

Suddenly Barbara wasn't afraid any-more. "Are you a genie?" she asked.

The little man's face became even pinker. "Oh my goodness, no." He smiled shyly. "I'm a wizard. My name is Harrison Peabody, but you can call me Harry." He gave a little bow. "What's your name?"

"I'm Barbara Benton. This is my brother, Rick."

"If you're not a genie," Rick said, "what were you doing in the bottle?"

Harrison Peabody coughed. His face turned bright red. For a minute he didn't answer. Then he said, "It's a long story. I went into the bottle just for a minute. And then some busybody came along and put the top on. And I couldn't get out."

"If you're a wizard," Barbara said, "you ought to know enough magic to get out of a bottle."

Harrison Peabody lowered his voice. "Bottles," he said, "are very bad for magic. Don't ever go into one."

"I won't," Barbara promised. Then she said, "Why did you grab my fingers?"

"I wanted to be sure I got out of the bottle before you put the cap back on. Once before somebody opened that bottle to smell it and then shut it so fast I got banged on the head."

Rick looked into the bottle. "No wick," he said. "We wasted a quarter."

"What do you mean?" Harrison Peabody asked.

"Barbara bought the bottle to get rid of the awful smell around here," Rick told him.

The little man sniffed the air. "It smells good to me."

"What did you eat when you were in the bottle?" Barbara asked.

"There was nothing to eat but the wick," the wizard said. "I used to bite off little bits and pretend it was different things. One time I'd make believe it was roast beef. Another time it would be ice cream. Yesterday I finished the last piece. It really wasn't bad."

"Well, I guess Rick and I are stuck with the smell of cabbage," Barbara said.

"What kind of smell would you like?" Harrison Peabody asked.

"Roses." Barbara put the cap back on the bottle.

The little wizard walked to the window and looked out. It was raining hard. "Roses, please," he said, and opened the umbrella.

3

Little pink roses began to grow out of the lamp on Barbara's desk. She bent over to sniff them. "They're real! How lovely, Harry." Barbara turned to look at the wizard.

Harrison Peabody was dancing around

the room, holding the black umbrella over his head. A climbing rose covered with bright red blooms crawled up one wall. "I haven't had so much fun in a long time. You've no idea how boring it was in that bottle."

Suddenly Barbara saw that there were roses everywhere. They grew from under the bed, twined around the mirror, and crowded out of the dresser drawers. "Stop!" Barbara said.

The wizard stopped dancing. He closed the umbrella. "What's the matter? I thought you liked roses?" The little man looked sad.

Barbara didn't want to hurt his feelings. "I do, Harry." She stood on tiptoe to sniff a huge white rose that hung down from the light fixture. "They're lovely. Thank you."

Rick was feeling the petals of a yellow rose. "You're terrific, Harry."

The wizard beamed.

"It's late," Barbara said. "I'd better go get the cookies. Mrs. Cunningham doesn't like us to eat right before supper. Do you want some, Harry?"

"Yes, please," the little man said.

Barbara wondered how long he'd been shut up in the bottle, nibbling on the wick. She ran downstairs.

Rick called after her. "Don't forget me."

Mrs. Cunningham was in the kitchen peeling apples. She looked up when Barbara came into the room. "The cookies are in the cookie jar in the dining room, dear. Get yourself a glass of milk."

Barbara took a container of milk out of the refrigerator. "I'll take some up to Rick." She pulled three paper cups from the dispenser in the kitchen and went to load her pockets with cookies.

When Barbara got to the top of the

stairs, she found Rick and the wizard waiting for her. They both had big grins on their faces. Barbara was sure they had been up to something, but she pretended not to be interested. She filled the paper cups with milk and divided the cookies into three parts. Barbara took her milk and cookies into her room and sat down at her desk to do her homework.

4

Barbara was trying to read her social studies book. The roses on the lamp cast dark shadows on the page. She twisted her chair to get in a better light. "Ouch!" Her

leg had touched a thorny vine that poked out of the kneehole of her desk. Barbara tried to move it out of the way. A thorn stabbed her finger.

Barbara sucked her finger for a minute. Then she went to look for Harrison Peabody.

Rick had gone downstairs to put the milk container back in the refrigerator. The wizard was sitting on the top step finishing his last cookie. He looked up at Barbara and smiled. "Delicious!" He licked the crumbs from his fingers.

"Harry," Barbara said, "please would you take away some of the roses. There are too many. I don't have room to work at my desk."

The little man got to his feet and picked up the umbrella. He followed Barbara into her room. It had stopped raining. The late-afternoon sun was shining through the window. It brought out all the different colors of the roses. They looked even more beautiful than before.

The wizard rubbed his chin. "Wonderful job, even if I say it myself. It seems a shame to spoil it."

"I know," Barbara said. "But I have such a lot of homework. And I can't even get started."

"Couldn't you do your homework somewhere else?" Harrison Peabody asked.

"If I did it downstairs, Mrs. Cunningham would want to know why. She knows I have my own desk," Barbara said. "She might even look into this room. What would I tell her if she saw all the roses?"

"Don't you have a key to your room? You could lock it up," the wizard suggested.

Barbara looked around the room. She wondered if the roses would have to be watered. That would be pretty messy.

"Harry," she said, "maybe you ought to take away all the roses."

"But the room would smell like cabbage again," the little man reminded her.

Barbara had a feeling that he was stalling. She looked him straight in the face. "I know I said I wanted the room to smell like roses. But I never meant anything like this. Please will you take them away?"

"Magic," Harrison Peabody said, "is easier to do than to undo."

"You mean you *can't* take the roses away?" Barbara said.

The little man wouldn't look at Barbara. Instead he gazed out of the window at the bright sunshine. "Well," he said, "not right now."

At this moment Rick came into the room. His eyes were shining. "Hey, Barb, come with me. I've got something to show you."

Barbara picked up her schoolbooks. She took a notebook and pencil off the top of her desk. Maybe Rick would let her use his room to study. He never spent much time on his homework.

Rick grabbed Barbara's hand and pulled her down the hall to his room. He looked at her and grinned. "Open the door, Barb."

Barbara turned the handle, and the door swung open. It was very dark in the room. Barbara felt for the light switch. She touched something rough and hard like the bark of a tree. Barbara peered into the gloom. As her eyes became used to the shadows she saw that there was a fat tree growing out of the floor between Rick's bed and his dresser. The branches stretched right across the room. One of them was jammed against the light switch. Smaller trees were growing around Rick's desk.

Underfoot there was a thick carpet of pine needles.

For a minute Barbara just stood in the doorway. Then she said, "I suppose you told Harry you wanted your room to smell like a pine woods."

Rick nodded. "How did you guess?"

Barbara lay on her stomach on the tile
floor of the bathroom. She propped her
social studies book against one of the legs
of the sink and spread her notebook open
in front of her. It wasn't as easy as working
at her desk. But there was plenty of light
for reading. And by the time someone

banged on the door, Barbara had finished most of her homework.

"Who is it?" Barbara asked.

"Me," Rick said. "Mrs. Cunningham is calling us to come to supper."

"Where's Harry?" Barbara wanted to know.

"In my room," Rick said. "Why?"

Barbara got up off the floor. "We have to take him something to eat. He's only had cookies and milk. I think he's hungry. And we ought to find a place where he can sleep. There isn't room for both of you in your bed."

"Oh, he says he'll be leaving soon," Rick told her.

"We can't let him go," Barbara whispered. "He has to unmagic those rooms. They can't stay the way they are."

"Of course," Rick said. "I've been having fun in my room, but Harry has a bush growing out of my pillow. I'd have trouble sleeping in the bed. We can tell him to change the rooms back before he goes."

"Didn't he tell you?" Barbara said. "He says he *can't* change the rooms back now. I don't know if he's forgotten how. Anyway, we'll have to keep him here until he does change them."

They heard Mrs. Cunningham's voice. "Barbara, Rick, come along. Supper will get cold."

"Go downstairs," Barbara said to her brother. "Tell Mrs. Cunningham I'm coming."

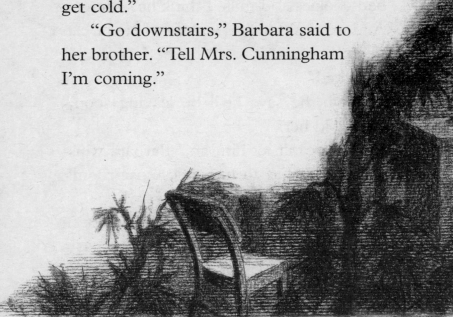

She ran down the hall to Rick's room and opened the door. Harrison Peabody was sitting on the low branch of a tree. He was swinging his legs and gazing through the pine boughs out of the window.

"Harry," Barbara said in a low voice, "just wait here. We'll bring you some supper."

Mrs. Cunningham had made stuffed cabbage for supper. Neither Rick nor Barbara had ever tasted it before. Barbara was about to eat her second helping when she remembered the wizard. She poked Rick under the table. "Save some for Harry," she whispered.

Barbara looked around for something to put the stuffed cabbage in. She had not yet poured any milk into her glass. When Mrs. Cunningham went into the kitchen to take the pie out of the oven, Barbara filled the glass with stuffed cabbage. She wedged it between her knees under the tablecloth.

Rick crammed a load of cabbage into the butter dish. He fitted the lid over it.

When Mrs. Cunningham came back from the kitchen, she saw the children's empty plates. She smiled. "Who would like some hot apple pie?"

Harrison Peabody picnicked under the trees in Rick's room. They still hadn't figured out how to get to the light switch. But Rick had a flashlight that his father had given him. It gave just enough light for the wizard to see his supper. He sat cross-legged on the pine needles. Rick and Barbara sat one on each side of him and watched him eat.

He liked the stuffed cabbage just as much as the children had. The little man said the apple pie was the best he'd ever eaten. He didn't at all mind eating it out of a sugar bowl. "I never had any silverware in the bottle either," he told them.

When supper was over, Barbara said, "I've been thinking, Harry. You could live in our attic. There's a mattress up there for you to sleep on. And Rick and I could take food up to you."

"I didn't see any attic stairs," the wizard said.

"There aren't any stairs." Rick opened the door of his room and pointed to a trapdoor on the hall ceiling near the bathroom. "You have to use a stepladder. We've got one in the basement. I'll go get it."

Rick went downstairs. Mrs. Cunningham had finished the dishes. She was sitting in the living room watching television. When Rick came up from the basement with the stepladder, he had to walk past the living room to get to the stairs.

"What do you want the ladder for, Rick?" Mrs. Cunningham asked.

"I have to put something in the attic," Rick said.

"Well, bring the ladder right down when you've finished with it, dear," Mrs.

Cunningham said. "I know your mother wouldn't want it cluttering the upstairs hall."

Rick took the ladder upstairs. He set it up in the hall under the trapdoor. The little wizard waited while Barbara climbed up and pushed the trapdoor open. She stood on the top step and looked into the attic. "It's awfully dark in there, Rick. You'd better lend Harry your flashlight."

"What will I use in my room?" Rick asked. "It's dark too."

Barbara thought for a moment. "Mother has a little flashlight on her night table," she said. "Harry could use that."

Rick got his mother's flashlight. He handed it up to Barbara. She climbed into the attic and beamed the light all around.

The attic ceiling was low and slanting. Barbara saw the mattress rolled up in a corner. A chest of clothes stood against a wall. Next to it were three cardboard boxes full of files from her father's office. There was a baby carriage covered with a plastic dropcloth, a broken television set, a pile of dusty phonograph records, and stacks and stacks of old magazines. Everywhere she looked there were spiderwebs. The one window of the attic was covered with them. When a fat gray mouse scurried across the floor, Barbara almost dropped the flashlight.

Rick held the ladder steady while Harrison Peabody climbed up. The tubby little wizard scrambled into the attic.

The two children cleared a space on the floor. They unrolled the mattress on it.

"I'm afraid it's not very fancy," Barbara told the wizard.

"It's much better than living in a bottle," Harrison Peabody said.

"How are we going to get food to you, Harry?" Rick asked. "Mrs. Cunningham told me not to leave the ladder upstairs."

"Don't you have a rope?" the wizard wanted to know.

"There's some clothesline in the basement," Barbara said. She handed the flashlight to the little man and backed out of the attic onto the stepladder. Rick followed her. Harrison Peabody closed the trapdoor.

"Take the stepladder down if you're going to the basement, Barb," Rick said. "I'd better get busy with my homework."

"There's a good light in the bathroom," Barbara told him. She picked up the aluminum stepladder and carried it down to the basement.

The clothesline was on top of the washing machine. There was a broom beside the freezer. Barbara decided to take the broom upstairs too.

Mrs. Cunningham was watching an old Greta Garbo movie on television. She never even looked up when Barbara passed the living room door.

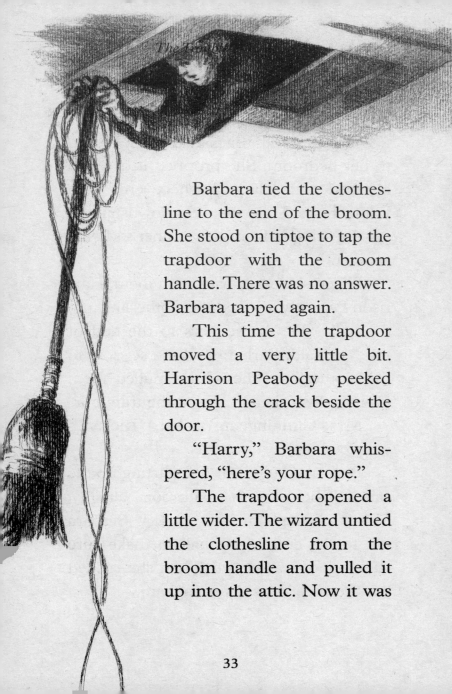

Barbara tied the clothes-
line to the end of the broom.
She stood on tiptoe to tap the
trapdoor with the broom
handle. There was no answer.
Barbara tapped again.

This time the trapdoor
moved a very little bit.
Harrison Peabody peeked
through the crack beside the
door.

"Harry," Barbara whis-
pered, "here's your rope."

The trapdoor opened a
little wider. The wizard untied
the clothesline from the
broom handle and pulled it
up into the attic. Now it was

his turn to whisper. "Barbara, do you have a pair of scissors?"

"I'll get some." Barbara took the broom to her bedroom. She propped it between her bed and a large bush covered with yellow roses. Then she went downstairs to get the scissors from her mother's sewing cabinet.

When she came back with them, Harrison Peabody lowered the clothesline into the hall. "Tie the scissors to the end of this," he said. Barbara tied the scissors to the clothesline. The wizard pulled them up into the attic and closed the trapdoor.

Mrs. Cunningham called, "Rick, it's your bedtime."

Barbara could hear her starting up the stairs. "Rick's in the bathroom already, Mrs. Cunningham," she yelled. Barbara ran to the end of the hall to make sure Rick's door was closed. Then she rushed back to meet Mrs. Cunningham.

Mrs. Cunningham was carrying a tray with two glasses of milk on it. She walked over to Barbara's door. Barbara got to her before she could put her hand on the knob. "Let me help you, Mrs. Cunningham. I'll give Rick his milk."

"You're a sweet child. Thank you." Mrs. Cunningham handed the tray to Barbara and walked across the hall to her own room.

When Barbara heard Rick come out of the bathroom, she gave him the milk. "I was afraid to put it in your room," she said. "You'd be sure to knock it over in the dark."

Rick was still dressed. "Take your shower first, Barb. I've got to go look for my pajamas in that pine forest." He went down the hall to his room.

Barbara rushed to get ready for bed. She waited until Rick had finished washing and was in his room with the door closed. Then she knocked on Mrs. Cunningham's door. "The bathroom's clear. Good night. See you in the morning."

"Good night, dear," Mrs. Cunningham said.

Barbara went to sleep with the sweet smell of roses all around her. Sometime in the night she was awakened by a light shining in her face. She opened her eyes.

Rick was standing beside her bed with his flashlight in his hand. "I can't sleep with that bush in my bed," he said.

Barbara sat up in bed. "It's chilly," she said. "And we forgot to give Harry a blanket." Barbara got up, taking care not to scratch her feet on the roses sticking out from under her bed. She put on her bathrobe and slippers and went with Rick to get a blanket from the linen closet in the bathroom.

It was dark in the hall. But there was a light coming from under the bathroom door. Barbara tried the knob. The door was locked. Then something brushed against her face. Barbara grabbed Rick. He clicked on the flashlight.

"Look!" Rick pointed to the ceiling.

The trapdoor was open. A rope ladder dangled from it almost to the floor. The ladder had swung against Barbara's face.

"That's our clothesline!" she whispered. "The wizard cut it up to make a rope ladder. And we'll be blamed for it."

"I guess Harry is too fat to shinny up a rope," Rick said. "Anyway, it's a neat ladder."

There was the sound of water splashing in the bathroom.

"Harry must be taking a shower." Rick started to climb up the rope ladder. Barbara came up after him.

The wizard had folded his clothes in a neat pile on the mattress. Right on top were the black hat and the black umbrella. Barbara looked at the umbrella. She was sure it was what the wizard used to do his magic.

She picked up the umbrella and opened it.

"You'd better not mess with the wizard's things," Rick warned her.

All at once there was a crash of thunder.

Both children jumped. Now they could hear the rain. It was beating against the attic window.

Rick ran to the trapdoor. "Let's get out of here, Barb." He started to climb back down the rope ladder.

Barbara looked up at the umbrella. She might never get another chance.

"Could you please take away the roses and the pine trees and make our rooms the way they were?" she begged.

The umbrella seemed to quiver in her hand.

Barbara closed it. She laid it back on top of the pile of clothes on the mattress.

Barbara climbed down the rope ladder
after Rick. She had just stepped off it onto
the floor of the hall when the bathroom
door opened. Harrison Peabody came
out. Barbara held her breath. Suppose by
some magic the wizard knew she'd been
playing with his umbrella!

He was wearing a red velvet evening coat. Barbara remembered that her mother had packed it away in the attic. The little man's gray curls were damp. And his face was even pinker than usual. Rick could smell his father's aftershave lotion.

"What should I do with these?" Harrison Peabody asked. He handed his socks and his underwear to Barbara. "I washed them out, but I didn't think I should leave them in the bathroom. And there's no good place to hang them in the attic."

Rick took a blanket and a pillow out of the linen closet in the bathroom. He gave them to the wizard. "Go to bed, Harry," Rick whispered. "And please *stay* there. Mrs. Cunningham will have a fit if she sees you."

Harrison Peabody tucked the pillow and blanket under one arm. He wrapped the red velvet coat tightly around his tubby little form and climbed the rope ladder into the attic. Then he pulled up the ladder and closed the trapdoor.

Rick went back to his room.

Barbara looked at the damp socks and underwear. I guess I can hang them on a rosebush, she told herself.

But when Barbara opened the door of her bedroom, there wasn't a rose to be seen. She hung the socks and the under-wear over a chair near the radiator and went back to bed.

Barbara and Rick were both late getting up next morning. Mrs. Cunningham had to call Rick three times. The children rushed to get ready for school.

It was still raining. Mrs. Cunningham insisted that they wear raincoats and rubbers. Rick had forgotten that his rubbers were under the refrigerator in the back pantry. By the time he found them it was almost eight-thirty.

They were splashing through the puddles toward school.

"I slept OK after you fixed my room, Barb," Rick said. "I wonder why Harry wouldn't do it."

"Yipe!" Barbara said. "Harry's underwear and socks are still in my room.

Suppose Mrs. Cunningham finds them!"

"And we forgot to take him any breakfast," Rick said. "He might go down to the kitchen to get something to eat."

The two children turned around and began to run home. When they reached the house, they raced up the front steps. Rick pushed the doorbell. There was no answer. He pushed it again. "Mrs. Cunningham must have gone to the super-market."

Barbara remembered her door key. She fished it out of her pocket and opened the front door. Then she ran upstairs. She saw the broom on her bedroom floor. Barbara picked it up and took the socks and underwear off the back of her desk chair.

Rick hurried to the kitchen for a box of cornflakes and a container of milk. He took a bowl and a spoon and went upstairs.

Barbara was standing in the hall under the trapdoor waiting for him. She banged with the broom handle on the trapdoor of the attic. "Harry, open up!"

The trapdoor opened. Harrison Peabody looked down. "Good morning." He dropped one end of the ladder through the opening.

Rick climbed up. "We brought you some breakfast."

"Thank you, but I've already had some," the wizard said.

Rick pulled himself into the attic. Barbara followed him. The children blinked their eyes.

"How do you like it?" Harrison Peabody asked. He looked very pleased with himself.

The whole attic was changed. Not a cobweb was left. The dusty records and magazines were gone. There was no sign of the baby carriage or the boxes of files. Lace curtains fluttered in the little arched window. A pretty fringed rug was in the middle of the shiny dark floor. And on the rug stood a table and four chairs.

The table was set with a white cloth and blue dishes. The children saw a platter of crunchy little sausages. Hot cocoa steamed in a big pitcher. And a stack of waffles was ready on a plate beside a jar of honey. Harrison Peabody wore a new black-and-white checked suit and red socks.

The wizard didn't say anything about changing the children's rooms. Barbara began to wonder whether it was she or Harrison Peabody who had unmagicked them.

When the little man saw the socks and underwear Barbara was holding, he took them from her. "Thank you," he said. "Now may I offer you a waffle?"

"They sure smell good," Rick said.

"We'll be late for school," Barbara reminded him.

Rick remembered the last time he was late. "We'll have to go to the school office for late passes."

The wizard picked up the black umbrella. "Maybe I can help you." He opened the umbrella and waved it over the children. "Get them to school on time," he said, "please."

Rick and Barbara looked around. The wizard had disappeared. They were standing in line in the school yard. The last bell was ringing. And it was raining hard.

11

It stopped raining sometime during the morning. And when Rick and Barbara went home for lunch, the new little leaves on the hedges were sparkling in the sunlight.

Mrs. Cunningham had made a big pot of vegetable soup. Both children had

second helpings. Rick would have liked a third, but there wasn't time. They had to be back at school by one o'clock.

"Harry can magic up something to eat," Rick said. "We don't have to worry about him. Come on, Barb."

They left their rubbers and raincoats at home and walked back to school. At three o'clock Rick waited for Barbara in the school yard. They ran home together.

They were out of breath when they reached the block where their house was. Rick slowed to a walk. "I want to see what Harry is up to. I'll bet he's thought of a lot of magic he can do in the attic."

Barbara was quiet. She was thinking. "What I don't understand," she said, "is why we had to take him food last night."

"Maybe the umbrella doesn't like stuffed cabbage," Rick said.

When they got home, Mrs. Cunning-ham had graham crackers and milk ready for them in the kitchen. "Eat now, children," she said. "If you eat later, you'll spoil your supper." Mrs. Cunningham was stuffing a chicken.

Rick and Barbara finished their after-school snack and raced upstairs. Barbara looked for the broom. She must have left it in the hall this morning. If she asked where it was, Mrs. Cunningham might ask why she wanted it.

Rick had an idea. He told Barbara to hold a chair steady while he stood on the back of it and tapped on the trapdoor with a yardstick.

Rick only had to knock once before the wizard opened the trapdoor. "Did you bring me anything to eat?" Harrison Peabody whispered.

"Let down the ladder, Harry," Barbara whispered back.

The little man lowered the rope ladder. Rick climbed up. Barbara put the chair back in her room. Then she too climbed into the attic.

The sun was shining through the lace curtains. The attic would have looked very nice except that the table was covered with dirty dishes. There were some cold, greasy-looking sausages left on the platter. The waffles were limp, and the cocoa had a skin on it.

"Why didn't you magic away the mess?" Rick asked the wizard.

"I never had a chance," Harrison Peabody said.

"What do you mean?" Barbara asked.

The little man didn't answer her. He turned even pinker than he was before and looked at the floor.

Suddenly Barbara was sorry for him. "What's the matter, Harry?"

"I've never told anyone before," Harrison Peabody said. "You'll laugh at me."

Barbara put her hand on his arm. "No, we won't, Harry."

"I'm not really a powerful wizard," the little man said in a very small voice. "I'm not even a very good one."

"Yes, you are," Rick told him.

Harrison Peabody shook his head. "The only magic I have is in my umbrella. And I have to be very polite to it, or it won't do what I want."

"Now I know why you always say 'please' to it," Barbara said.

"You mean you were rude to the umbrella, and it got mad and wouldn't wash the dishes?" Rick wanted to know.

"No, no, nothing like that," the wizard said.

"Then what happened?" Rick persisted.

"The umbrella," Harrison Peabody explained, "only works when it's raining."

12

After supper Mrs. Cunningham wanted to watch a Rudolph Valentino movie on television.

"I'll load the dishwasher for you," Barbara told her.

Mrs. Cunningham scrubbed the pots and pans and then went into the living room. Rick went down into the basement to look for the broom. He found it in the laundry room.

"Hide it in your room after we use it," Barbara told him. She was putting leftover roast chicken and chocolate pudding into a plastic bag for Rick to take to Harrison Peabody. "He must be starved," Barbara said.

Rick hid the plastic bag under his shirtfront. He took the broom and went quietly upstairs. Barbara went on loading the dishwasher.

Barbara had an idea. She took a white garbage bag from the carton on the kitchen shelf and ran upstairs with it.

Rick was in the attic. He had pulled up the rope ladder and was just about to shut the trapdoor when Barbara came down the hall. "Rick!" she called in a low voice.

Her brother looked down at her. Barbara held up the garbage bag. "Let's put Harry's breakfast dishes in this," she said. "I'll stick them in the dishwasher."

Rick let down the ladder for Barbara to climb up. Between them they cleared the table and loaded everything into the garbage bag. Barbara backed carefully down the ladder and took her load downstairs. She stacked the blue dishes in the dishwasher and hid the waffles and sausages under the chicken bones in the kitchen garbage can.

Barbara turned on the dishwasher. While the dishes were washing, she went back upstairs. The big pitcher of cold cocoa was still in the attic. Rick and the wizard managed to carry it down the ladder. Barbara dumped the cocoa down the toilet and washed the pitcher in the bathtub. She dried it with a clean bath towel and took it back to the attic. Then she went to get the blue dishes from the dishwasher.

When Barbara had finished, the attic looked much nicer.

Tomorrow was Saturday. "We can take Harry for a picnic in the park," Rick said.

"We'd better go to bed." Barbara walked to the trapdoor. She took a last look around the attic. It really was a pretty room now.

"Oh, Harry!" Barbara said.

"What's the matter?" the wizard asked.

"You magicked away the mattress," Barbara pointed out.

"So I did," the wizard said.

"What will you sleep on?" Rick asked.

"I'll curl up on the rug." The little man smiled. "And it's still better than living in a bottle."

Mrs. Cunningham was packing a picnic lunch. Barbara was helping her. "Do you want one or two baloney sandwiches?" Barbara asked Rick.

"Three," Rick told her. He hoped the wizard liked baloney.

Rick went into the basement for the stepladder. He took it upstairs while Mrs. Cunningham was busy in the kitchen. The wizard would have to use it to get down from the attic. They couldn't leave the trapdoor open with the rope ladder hanging out of it.

Harrison Peabody backed down the stepladder. He was wearing his tall black hat and his new checked suit, and was carrying the black umbrella.

"You won't need the umbrella," Rick said. "It's a lovely day."

"At this time of year," the wizard said, "you never can tell."

Rick put the stepladder behind the door in his room. He went downstairs. Mrs. Cunningham was still in the kitchen with Barbara. Rick gave a low whistle. Harrison Peabody tiptoed down the stairs, and Rick let him out of the front door.

"Wait for us on the sidewalk," Rick told the little man.

Prospect Park is very large. Today it was crowded with people walking their dogs, riding horses on the bridle path, fishing in the lake, or just sitting on the benches in the sunshine.

Rick and Barbara took Harrison Peabody to the top of a hill called Lookout Mountain. From there they could see far out over the trees and houses of Brooklyn.

They walked across the Long Meadow
and past the boathouse and the band shell.
At noontime they sat on the rocks near the
little stream and ate their lunch. Rick saw
a crayfish in the stream. He tried to catch
it, but it was too fast for him.

When the sandwiches were all gone

and the last drop of lemonade drunk, they put their litter in a trash basket. Then they went to the lake. Barbara saw a flock of mallard ducks swimming toward the shore. She stood on the stone wall at the edge of the lake. "Look at that funny duck!"

One of the ducks had a much longer neck than the others. It was a different color too. Instead of being brown or having a dark green head, this duck was a pale silvery green all over.

Rick stared at it. "Maybe it's a goose."

Harrison Peabody turned to look at the strange duck. A gust of wind caught his hat and tore it off his head. Rick chased after the hat. Before he could catch it, the hat was blown into the water.

There were rusty cans and broken bottles in the lake. Rick didn't want to go wading. He knelt down on the stone wall and tried to reach the hat, but it drifted away from him.

Barbara saw an old man whose hat had been blown off too. She ran after the hat and caught it before it went into the lake. Barbara gave it back to the old man.

"Thank you," he said. "You'd better go home, little girl. There's going to be a storm."

Barbara looked at the sky. Dark clouds covered the sun. Two boys with fishing poles ran past her. The lake was covered with choppy waves. All the people in the

park were getting ready to leave.

Harrison Peabody still stood on the stone wall at the edge of the lake. He was looking across the water. Rick went over to him. "Sorry I couldn't get your hat, Harry."

The wizard felt his bald head. "Did I lose it? Well, never mind. It's not the first time."

Barbara remembered the duck. She could still see it swimming through the choppy waves. The water foamed behind it for quite a long time. And now and then something silvery green seemed to loop up into the air out of the foam.

The duck turned to look at them. It dived into the water and came up with something black in its mouth. Then it began to swim in a straight line toward Harrison Peabody.

As it came closer Rick and Barbara saw that it wasn't a duck at all. It had a head like a lizard's. And it was covered with shining scales.

When it reached the stone wall, the creature reared its long neck high up out of the water. It placed the black thing it had in its mouth on the wizard's head.

"Isn't this your hat, Peabody?" a husky voice said. "I'd know it anywhere."

14

All the other people in the park were in a hurry to get home before the storm. They never even noticed the strange creature who brought the wizard's hat back to him. The creature slipped back into the water as soon as the hat was on Harrison Peabody's head. Little rivers of water trickled down from the hat. The wizard was too excited to care. "George!" he said. "It's been a long time."

The creature poked its head out of the murky water. "It's been years, Peabody," the husky voice said, "but you haven't changed much."

Rick and Barbara were down on their hands and knees on the stone wall. They leaned over the water and tried to get a better view of the creature.

"It has a body like a snake," Rick whispered.

"Sh-sh," Barbara said.

By now there were no other people in the park. Harrison Peabody looked down at the two children kneeling beside him. "Barbara, Rick," he said, "I want you to meet an old friend of mine. This is George."

"How do you do?" Barbara said.

"Pleased to meet you," the creature answered.

"What is he?" Rick asked.

At this George reared up into the air. He twisted his body so that long, scaly curves of what looked like a giant fire hose looped out of the water.

"He's showing you what he is," the wizard said. "A sea serpent."

"Aren't you a bit mixed-up, George?" Rick said. "This isn't the sea. It's a lake."

"I'll have you know," the serpent said, "that Brooklyn has had sea serpents for a long time." He glared at Rick.

The wizard said, "Remember that time—a long time ago—John Van Nyse claimed he saw five great sea serpents rise out of Steinbokkery Pond?"

George laughed so hard that his whole long body shook. It churned up the lake in white foam. "I could understand if he said four. My brother Pete and I were playing in the moonlight. Van Nyse could have seen our reflections in the pond. But *five*? He must have been drunk."

"He said there were flames bursting from your head," Harrison Peabody reminded him.

"Phosphorus," the serpent said. "I glow in the dark."

"Like a firefly?" Barbara asked.

The serpent nodded.

"I never even heard of Stein-whatever-it-is Pond," Rick said. "Where is it?"

"Not too far from here," the wizard told him. "On the other side of this park, I should say."

The serpent shook his head. "Not anymore, Peabody," he said. "They drained the pond and put the old Lefferts house in its place. That's why I came here." He looked at the broken bottles and tin cans in the lake. "Steinbokkery Pond was much nicer." The serpent gave a gusty sigh. His long, scaly body quivered in the murky water.

"Let bygones be bygones," Harrison Peabody said. "What about giving my friends a ride, George?"

The serpent's mouth stretched into a smile. He looked like a good-natured alligator. "That sounds like fun," he said. "Just tell them to hold tight. I don't want them falling into this dirty water."

The serpent arched his back. A long loop
of him curved up out of the water. The
wizard pointed to it. "Climb aboard." He
stepped off the stone wall onto George's
back. Harrison Peabody hugged the ser-

pent with one arm. In the other hand he held his umbrella.

Rick was next. He crawled behind the wizard and grabbed the scaly body of the serpent with both hands.

Barbara expected the serpent's back to be slimy and slippery. But the scales were dry and hard. She seated herself behind Rick and put her arms around his waist.

"Ready?" Harrison Peabody asked.

"Yes," Rick and Barbara said together.

The serpent glided forward. His head went in and out of the water. But he kept the big curve of his back high and dry. His tail splashed behind them like a propeller.

They whizzed around the lake. Barbara was enjoying the ride. Suddenly she felt a drop of water on her nose. Then another. In a minute it was raining hard.

Harrison Peabody sat up straight and locked his legs around the serpent. He opened his umbrella. "Please," he said to the umbrella, "keep the rain off all three of us."

The umbrella didn't get any bigger, but Rick and Barbara found that even though the rain was falling all around them they weren't getting wet.

Rick was sure the umbrella could do more interesting things than just keep the rain off. He wondered if it would listen to him. He looked at the lake below. All at once he had an idea. "Please, magic umbrella," he said, "make the air warm and the water clean."

It was still raining hard, but Rick and Barbara suddenly felt much too hot in their jackets. The lake looked cool and inviting.

"We'd like to be in bathing suits," Barbara said.

Nothing happened.

"Please," she added.

Rick found that he was wearing a pair

of blue swim trunks. Barbara had on a yellow bathing suit. And Harrison Peabody was dressed in an old-fashioned two-piece, striped bathing suit. It was like the ones in the silent movies Mrs. Cunningham liked to watch on television. The wizard didn't seem to think there was anything unusual about his suit.

"Last one in is a rotten egg." Barbara dived into the water. Rick jumped in after her, but the wizard stayed where he was. He sat on the serpent's back and held the umbrella over his head.

The two children splashed about in the lake. The rain was pouring all around them, but they couldn't feel it. They could feel the sparkling clear water of the lake.

Barbara swam underwater and chased a sunfish. Then she rolled over onto her back and looked at the raindrops that never quite reached her.

"I'll race you to the island." Rick began

to swim toward a little island that was covered with trees. Barbara turned over onto her stomach and swam after him.

Barbara caught up with Rick before he reached the long brown grass that grew out of the water at the edge of the island. Her knees touched the sandy bottom of the lake. Barbara stood up. She brushed

her hair out of her eyes and looked at the sky. It wasn't so dark now. And the rain was just a drizzle.

A moment later a bright shaft of sunlight came through the clouds. The rain stopped.

16

Harrison Peabody closed his umbrella and tucked it under his arm. "An April shower," he said.

The air was still warm, and the water was clean. It was even more fun to swim when the sun was shining.

"Why don't you come in the water, Harry?" Rick called.

The little man blushed and didn't answer.

George slid through the water toward the children. "Peabody can't swim," he told them in his husky voice. The serpent turned to look at the lake shore. Now that the sun was out, people were coming back into the park.

"Hold your breath, Peabody. And hang on! We're going under." The serpent dived down into the water.

Rick and Barbara saw Harrison Peabody carried down into the lake. A line of foam told them that the serpent was swimming toward the shore. They swam after him as fast as they could.

George took the little wizard to the edge of the lake. He left him in the shallow water near the stone wall. Then the serpent sank under the surface of the water, and the children couldn't see him anymore.

Harrison Peabody was coughing and sputtering. Rick and Barbara helped him to climb out of the lake.

A crowd of curious people began to gather near them. Barbara heard a man say, "If a policeman sees them, they'll be locked up. It's against the law to swim in that lake."

"It's hotter than I ever remember for this time of year," a woman said. "But that doesn't mean you can run around like *that*!"

A police car was driving slowly along the road through the park. When the two policemen in it saw the crowd of people, they stopped the car. Rick and Barbara grabbed Harrison Peabody by the hands. They pulled him toward the gate of the park. When they saw one of the policemen get out of the police car, the children began to run. The wizard puffed along between them. They didn't stop running until they reached the front porch of the Benton house.

"Oh!" Harrison Peabody gasped. "I dropped my umbrella in the lake!"

"And I don't have my door key anymore," Barbara said. "It was in the pocket of the jacket I was wearing. There's no pocket in this bathing suit."

Barbara didn't want to ring the doorbell. She would never be able to explain to Mrs. Cunningham why they were wearing bathing suits.

Rick climbed onto the porch railing. He shinnied up the pole in the corner and swung himself up onto the roof of the porch. Barbara had left her bedroom window open. Rick slipped through it and tiptoed downstairs to open the front door for his sister and the wizard.

Mrs. Cunningham heard him open the door. She was in the kitchen getting supper ready. "Is that you, children?" she

called. "Did you get caught in the rain?"

"Yes," Barbara answered. "We're going upstairs to change."

The two children and the wizard raced up the stairs. Rick got the stepladder from his room and helped Harrison Peabody up into the attic. Before he closed the trapdoor the little man looked down and said, "I don't have anything to change into."

"What happened to your other suit?" Rick asked.

"I turned it into the new one," the wizard said in a sad little voice. Then he brightened. "Oh, yes, I do have the socks and underwear Barbara dried for me."

17

Mrs. Cunningham made beef stew for supper. Barbara was able to shovel quite a lot of it into a plastic bag. After supper the children took it upstairs to the wizard.

Rick tapped on the trapdoor with the broom handle. Harrison Peabody lowered the rope for Rick and Barbara to climb into the attic.

The little man had taken off the wet bathing suit and hung it over the back of one of the chairs to dry. He was wearing his undershirt and shorts and the old black socks.

Barbara noticed that the wizard's eyes were red. She wondered if he had been crying. His nose was red too.

"Achoo!" Harrison Peabody sneezed. "I wish I had a handkerchief."

"I'll get you some Kleenex." Barbara opened the trapdoor. She heard the roar of the MGM lion and the sound of music from the television set in the living room. Mrs. Cunningham had settled down to watch *Naughty Marietta.*

Barbara climbed down the rope ladder. She took the box of Kleenex from her room and two blankets from the linen closet in the bathroom. "Rick," she called, "give me a hand with this stuff."

Rick came down from the attic. He got the stepladder out of his room. It made it easier to carry the blankets up to the attic. There wasn't another spare pillow in the linen closet. Barbara took the pillow off her own bed and handed it up through the trapdoor to the wizard.

"Harry's got an awful cold," Rick told her. He went to his father's closet and found a threadbare blue bathrobe. Mr. Benton was very fond of it, but Mrs. Benton wouldn't let him take it along when they went for a trip. Rick put away the stepladder and then climbed the rope ladder with the blue bathrobe under his arm.

"You can wear this for now, Harry," Rick said. "But whatever you do, don't turn it into anything else."

"How can I?" the wizard said. "I don't have my umbrella."

Harrison Peabody put on the bathrobe. It was much too long for him. Barbara rolled up the sleeves so the little man could eat his supper. Rick had remembered to bring a spoon. The wizard ate the stew right out of the plastic bag.

Barbara made up a bed on the rug with the two blankets and the pillow. "Don't worry, Harry," she said. "Tomorrow Rick and I will go to the park and get your umbrella for you. You ought to stay in bed anyway and take care of that cold."

18

On Sunday morning Barbara woke very early. She could hear the rattle of rain on her windowpane. She threw off her covers and got up. Her slippers were on the floor beside the bed. Barbara put them on and wiggled into her bathrobe. Then she ran down the hall to Rick's room.

Rick was fast asleep, rolled up in the

quilt on his bed. A tuft of his hair stuck out of one end of the quilt, and his bare feet were poking out of the other end. Barbara tickled the sole of one of Rick's feet. He grunted and turned over onto his stomach.

Barbara tickled his other foot. "Rick, get up. It's raining!"

Rick sat up in bed and rubbed his eyes.

Mrs. Cunningham was still asleep. She had stayed up late the night before. Barbara made oatmeal for breakfast. Then Rick stood guard in front of Mrs. Cunningham's door while Barbara took a glass of orange juice and a bowl of the hot cereal to the wizard.

Barbara used the stepladder to get into the attic. She didn't want to bang on the trapdoor. Harrison Peabody was lying in the makeshift bed Barbara had made on the pretty fringed rug. The little man was snoring softly. Barbara shook him. The wizard opened his eyes.

"How do you feel, Harry?" Barbara asked.

"Terrible," he said. "My head is all stuffed up."

Barbara put the orange juice and the

oatmeal on the floor beside the little man's pillow. "Here's your breakfast. Rick and I are going to the park to get your umbrella. Please stay in the attic while we're away. And be careful."

Harrison Peabody looked at the rain trickling down the attic window. "You be careful," he said.

The two children put on their raincoats and rubbers. Barbara left a note on the kitchen table.

Dear Mrs. Cunningham,
Rick and I lost something
yesterday. We are going to the park
to look for it.

Yours truly,
Barbara

On the way to the park Rick and Barbara found that they were much too warm in their raincoats.

"It's your fault, Rick," Barbara said. "You asked the umbrella to make the air warm."

"But you were the one who changed our jackets and blue jeans into bathing suits," Rick reminded her.

"Now I see," his sister said, "why magic in stories always goes wrong."

"You mean like having three wishes and wishing for all the wrong things?" Rick asked.

"Yes. We ought to make a list of exactly what we want the umbrella to do," Barbara said. "Harry always makes such a mess with his magic. I'm sure we can do better."

They went through the gate of the park and crossed the road. There was no traffic. Cars were not allowed to drive

through the park on weekends.

When they reached the stone wall at the edge of the lake, they saw that people had already started throwing things into the water. Barbara saw four metal rings from flip-top cans, a piece of plastic with six holes in it to hold the cans, and

a section of Saturday's newspaper.

The rain was coming down in a steady drizzle. There were no other people in the park. The children stood on the stone wall and looked out over the lake.

Rick put both hands to his mouth. "George!" he yelled as loud as he could.

Far out in the middle of the lake there was a splash. The water churned into a line of foam. The sea serpent was swimming toward them. His head stuck out of the water.

George swam close to the stone wall. "Where's Peabody?" he asked in his husky voice.

"He's in bed with a bad cold," Barbara told the serpent. "And anyway, all he has to wear is that funny-looking bathing suit. He needs the umbrella to get his clothes back."

"If you ask me," the sea serpent said, "Peabody would be a lot better off without that fool umbrella."

"He sure would," Rick agreed. "But right now *we* need the umbrella to get our jackets. Barb left our front door key in the pocket of hers."

"Please, George," Barbara begged. "Try to find the umbrella for us."

"Well," the serpent said, looking at her with bright green eyes, "I owe you two something for cleaning up the lake. I only wish it would stay clean." The serpent scooped a sheet of wet newspaper out of the water with his mouth. He laid it on top of the stone wall. Then George swung around. "Just wait here." He dived down into the lake. The water frothed and steamed where he had been a moment before.

Rick and Barbara waited for what seemed a very long time. Suddenly the serpent popped out of the water. He tossed a beer can off his head. Rick caught it.

George was carrying the black umbrella in his mouth. He reared up and laid it on the stone wall beside the children. "I had a hard time finding it," he said. "It was stuck in the mud over by the island."

20

Barbara picked up the umbrella and opened it carefully. It was muddy. One spoke was bent. Otherwise it seemed to be all right.

"Don't forget," George said, "that's *Peabody's* umbrella."

The sea serpent swung his long body around in a huge arc. He did a double somersault in the air and streaked away from them across the lake. He left in such a hurry that Rick and Barbara never had a chance to thank him for finding the umbrella. They could see him far out in the middle of the lake, rolling and twisting and chasing his tail.

Rick put the beer can in a litter basket. "Come on, Barb," he said. "Work the magic."

Barbara had done a lot of thinking while the serpent was looking for the umbrella. She held the umbrella over her head now and looked up at it. "Pretty please, dear Umbrella," she said, "change all three of those bathing suits back to the clothes that they were before. And make the air the way it ought to be in April." The umbrella gave a little jerk and almost pulled itself out of Barbara's grasp.

Rick reached up and grabbed the umbrella with both hands. Barbara let go of it. "While you're at it, Umbrella," Rick said, "how about taking Barb and me to the zoo?"

Nothing happened.

Rick looked at the umbrella. "Oh, all right," he said. "Please, please, please!"

The umbrella began to rise in the air. "Oops!" Rick said.

Barbara caught hold of Rick's ankles before he was yanked away. The two children were pulled higher and higher. The umbrella sailed just over the treetops. Some of the trees were covered with little red buds. And some had leaves already out. The umbrella swooped up and down

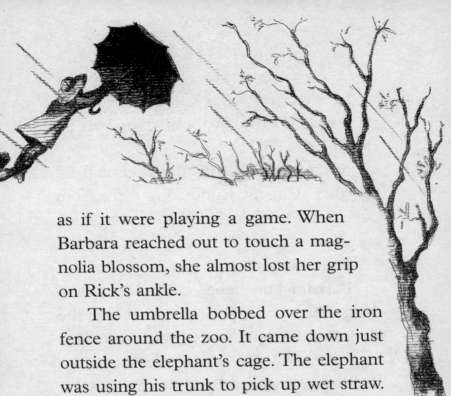

as if it were playing a game. When
Barbara reached out to touch a mag-
nolia blossom, she almost lost her grip
on Rick's ankle.

The umbrella bobbed over the iron
fence around the zoo. It came down just
outside the elephant's cage. The elephant
was using his trunk to pick up wet straw.
He raised his head to look at the children
standing under the black umbrella. Then
he snorted and tossed the straw onto his
back.

"It's a shame that the elephant has to
be shut up in a cage with nothing to do all
day," Barbara said. "And the park is so
great at this time of the year."

Rick had an idea. "He doesn't have

to be shut up." Rick looked up at the umbrella. "Please let the zoo animals go free in the park."

Suddenly the elephant was gone from his cage. A happy trumpeting came from outside the tall iron fence of the zoo. Rick and Barbara heard the roar of a lion on Lookout Mountain.

Barbara knew she had to do something. She was sorry for the animals in the cages, but it wasn't safe to have them running around loose. Barbara grabbed the umbrella away from Rick. But she was too late.

It had stopped raining.

21

Rick and Barbara heard excited voices. Then there was the sound of running feet. Two zookeepers ran past them. They were carrying nets. "Which way did the tiger go?" one keeper yelled to the other.

The men raced up the steps and out of the big gate of the zoo. They tore off down the road that led through the park.

Barbara closed the umbrella. She and Rick left the zoo. They began to walk through the woods. Now they could hear sirens. Two police cars went shrieking down the road.

A deer with a little spotted fawn leaped across the path in front of the children. Two zebras were playing in the Long Meadow. Overhead an eagle swooped.

"Hey, Barb, look!" Rick pointed to an enormous beech tree. Barbara saw a little monkey with a long tail chasing a gray squirrel. The squirrel had never seen a monkey before. He chattered in fright and climbed higher and higher in the tree.

Now that the rain had stopped, people were coming into the park. Mothers pushed baby carriages along the walks. People of all ages rode bicycles on the roadway.

Rick and Barbara joined a crowd on the lake shore. "Somebody saw an alligator in the lake," a boy with a fishing pole told Rick.

A woman screamed, "There it is!"

"What's that next to it?" a man asked. "It looks like a hippopotamus."

Three police cars and a large green van drove up close to the lake. The policemen got out of their cars. They ordered the people to move back from the water's edge.

"Just keep calm, everybody," one policeman said. "Lady, is that your little boy? Hold on to him. Alligators move fast."

There were two zoo men in the van. They both carried ropes and heavy nets. The policemen cleared a path for them through the crowd. The zoo men walked to the lake shore. One of them whistled. He held out a piece of meat.

"Here, Jenny," the zoo man called.

A fat old alligator waddled out of the water. The zoo man waved the meat and backed away.

"Good girl, Jenny," he said.

As soon as the alligator was clear of the water, the keeper threw the meat to her. The other zoo man tossed a thick net over her. The alligator thrashed her tail and struggled, but she was caught. The two keepers lifted the alligator into the van.

When the zoo men tried to catch the hippo, he swam to the middle of the lake and played submarine. "We'll have to use a dragnet," a policeman said. "Who wants to help?"

Almost everybody did. They spread a big net along one side of the lake and slowly dragged it to the other side. It wasn't just the hippo they caught in the net. There were sea lions, a beaver, a pair of otters, and a lot of fish in the net when it was pulled out of the lake. The people scooped up the fish and threw them back into the water.

Something else was in the net—all curled up into a very large ball of silvery green scales. Nobody seemed to know what it was. Rick and Barbara stared at it.

"It's George!" Barbara whispered. "They've caught George!"

22

The zoo men were looking at the sea serpent. Barbara and Rick heard one of the men say, "Wow! Look at the size of this guy! I wonder what he is. Whatever he is, he didn't come from the zoo. And we don't have room for him there."

"We could put him in the alligator pen with old Jenny," the other man said.

"We can't risk it. They might fight. I'd hate to have anything happen to Jenny. We don't know anything about this fellow. Anyway, we can't leave him here."

The men threw a net over George and hoisted him into the green van. Then they drove away down the road.

The children watched until the van was out of sight. Barbara said, "We'd better go. We have to take Harry his lunch."

Rick and Barbara walked home in silence. Both of them remembered the sea serpent doing somersaults and chasing his tail in the lake. He couldn't do that in a pen. They felt much too bad about what had happened to George to talk.

Mrs. Cunningham opened the front door when Barbara rang the bell. "Did you find what you were looking for?" she asked.

"Yes," Barbara told her.

Mrs. Cunningham took the children's

raincoats and hung them in the hall closet. While Rick and Barbara were pulling off their rubbers, Mrs. Cunningham picked up the umbrella and put it away in the closet too.

"Hurry and get your lunch, children. It turned out to be a nice day after all. I thought I'd take you to Coney Island this afternoon." Mrs. Cunningham looked excited. "I haven't been to Coney Island for years," she said.

After lunch Barbara cleared the table. While Mrs. Cunningham was loading the dishwasher, Barbara dumped the leftover tuna fish salad into a plastic bag. She gave it to Rick. "Don't forget to take Harry his

umbrella. It's in the hall closet," she whispered.

Rick tucked the plastic bag under his shirtfront and went to the closet for the umbrella. Then he ran upstairs and banged with the broom on the trapdoor of the attic.

The trapdoor opened. Harrison Peabody peeped out. When he saw Rick, he let down the rope ladder. Rick climbed up. He handed the wizard the umbrella he was carrying.

The little man was once more dressed in his checked suit. He smiled. "I knew you got the umbrella back when my bathing suit turned into this," he said. "I suppose George found the umbrella for you?"

Rick nodded.

"Good old George!" the wizard said.

Rick couldn't bear to tell Harrison Peabody what had happened. He knew it was all his fault. He pulled the bag of tuna fish salad out from under his shirt. "Here's your lunch, Harry. I have to go now. Mrs. Cunningham is taking Barb and me to Coney Island. We'll see you when we get back."

Rick backed out of the attic and climbed down the rope ladder. The wizard pulled up the ladder and closed the trapdoor.

Mrs. Cunningham and the children walked down Albemarle Road to the subway station.

Barbara and Rick were wearing their jackets. Rick had found his in the drawer where he had stuffed the wet bathing suit the day before. His shoes and jeans and underwear were all crammed in with the jacket. Rick had a hard time opening the drawer.

Barbara had no problem. Her clothes were all in her closet where she had hung the dripping suit. The front door key was safe in the pocket of her jacket.

Most of the way the train ran on elevated tracks high above the ground. The children looked out over the roofs of

Brooklyn. When the train came near Coney Island, they saw the boardwalk and the huge Ferris wheel.

"Look, children!" Mrs. Cunningham pointed.

Between two tall apartment buildings Rick and Barbara caught a glimpse of the shining sea.

The train came to the end of the line. Everybody got off. Rick, Barbara, and Mrs. Cunningham walked along a wooden platform and down a stairway to the street.

Barbara wanted to ride the roller coaster. Rick said it made him sick.

"It makes me sick too," Mrs. Cunningham said.

They walked along the boardwalk to the pier. People were fishing there. Rick watched a funny blowfish puff itself up like a balloon. Barbara and Mrs. Cunningham were happy when the man who

caught the blowfish threw it back into the water.

"If you want to see interesting fish," the man said, "you ought to go to the aquarium."

The aquarium was a long low building. The entrance was on the boardwalk. Once inside they walked down a dark hall past the brightly lit plate-glass windows of large tanks. They stopped to watch an electric eel light up a lightbulb. Mrs. Cunningham looked at the octopus while Rick looked at the sharks. And Barbara saw live sea horses for the first time in her life.

Then they all went outdoors to the open deck. A killer whale was splashing around in a tank there. "He's really very friendly," one of the aquarium men told Rick. The man reached into the tank to pet the whale.

Barbara pointed to a tank with a crowd of people around it. "What's over there?"

"It's a new arrival," the aquarium man said.

Mrs. Cunningham walked over to the crowd. Rick and Barbara joined her.

"What is it?" a man said. "Sure looks funny."

"Well," the woman beside him said, "we can't stand here all day waiting for it to do something. Let's go look at the seals."

The crowd began to thin out. Mrs. Cunningham and the children were able to get to the railing around the tank. They looked down into the water.

Curled up in the bottom of the cement tank was a very large ball of silvery green scales. The ball of scales twitched. Barbara saw the glint of angry green eyes.

It was George!

24

Mrs. Cunningham was soon tired of watching the ball of silvery green scales. "I read in the *Times* this morning that there are some baby whales here at the aquarium," she said. "I'll go look at them. Come and join me when you're through looking at Old Scaly." She walked across the open deck to where a crowd had gathered around the whale tank.

Now only Rick and Barbara were standing beside the railing. George uncoiled himself enough to stick his head out. "Old Scaly indeed!" he hissed. He glared at the children. "Something tells me you two are to blame for the mess I'm in. Well, you ought to be able to get me out of it soon. It's starting to rain." The sea serpent reared his long neck up out of the tank of water. He turned to look at the open sea. "I've had enough of that lake," he said. "You're right, Rick. I belong out there in the ocean. Now use the umbrella to get me there. And watch how you talk to it. The fool thing likes to play tricks."

"I gave the umbrella back to Harry," Rick said.

"And he's home in bed with a bad cold," Barbara told the sea serpent.

"Just my luck!" George glared again at the children and dived to the bottom of his tank.

Now Rick and Barbara felt the rain. It was beginning to come down hard. Mrs. Cunningham came running over to them. "That's how it is with an April day." She smiled. "Lucky I brought an umbrella, even if all I could find was this dirty old thing."

Barbara looked at the muddy black umbrella. Her heart began to pound inside her.

Mrs. Cunningham opened the umbrella and held it over the children. Barbara looked up. She could see the bent spoke.

"Dear, darling, sweet Umbrella," Barbara said, "please put George where he wants to be!"

Barbara heard a husky voice say, "Good girl!"

Then Mrs. Cunningham said, "We'd better go inside out of the rain, children." She looked into the tank. "Well, I see Old Scaly is gone. They must have found a better place to put him."

25

Mrs. Cunningham took the children to a restaurant for dinner. Both Rick and Barbara ordered stuffed cabbage. It was very late when the three of them got home. And it was raining hard.

It was time for the Sunday night movie

on television. Mrs. Cunningham sat down in the living room to watch it. Rick quietly went to the hall closet. He took out the black umbrella. Mrs. Cunningham had put it there when she walked into the house.

Barbara took the umbrella away from him. She gave it a little hug. Then the two children went upstairs. Rick tapped on the trapdoor with the broom handle.

Harrison Peabody opened the trapdoor. He let down the rope ladder. Rick climbed up first. Barbara came after him with the umbrella. She was still on the ladder when the little man said, "Do you think you could get me some supper, Barbara? I've had nothing since lunchtime. When it began to rain this afternoon, I tried to magic up a little something. But my umbrella is in a nasty mood. I can't get it to do anything."

Barbara climbed into the attic. She

opened the umbrella and looked up at it. "Dear Umbrella," she said, "please set the table with a dinner Harry will enjoy. And please will you clean up the dirty dishes afterward?"

At once a platter of corned beef and cabbage appeared on the table.

Harrison Peabody stared. Barbara closed the umbrella and handed it to him. "Rick gave you the wrong umbrella by mistake," she said.

The wizard sat down at the table. While he ate his dinner, Rick and Barbara told him all the adventures of the day.

The little man listened without interrupting. Then he said, "The trouble with magic is that it's terribly hard to handle." The wizard ate the last bite of cabbage, and the platter vanished. In its place was a dish of chocolate chip ice cream. "Would you like some?" Harrison Peabody asked the children.

Before Rick and Barbara had time to
answer, two more dishes of ice cream
were on the table. There were two more
spoons too.

The wizard rubbed his chin. "I've
never known this to happen before," he

said. "The umbrella must have taken a liking to you."

When they had finished the ice cream, all the dishes disappeared from the table.

Barbara had been thinking. "Harry," she said, "suppose Daddy and Mother come home and see the attic like this?"

Rick remembered something. "This is where Dad puts the suitcases when he comes home from a trip."

Harrison Peabody stood up. He walked to the attic window and looked out. It was still raining. "We had fun," Harrison Peabody said. "Didn't we?"

"Oh, yes!" Barbara and Rick said together.

The wizard opened the magic umbrella and held it over his head. "Please," he said, speaking slowly and carefully, "change everything back to the way it was before."

The children looked around the dusty

attic filled with cobwebs and old magazines. The little man whispered something to his umbrella. He smiled at Rick and Barbara.

An instant later, both the umbrella and Harrison Peabody were gone.

LET THE MAGIC CONTINUE. . . .

*Here's a peek
at another enchanting tale
by Ruth Chew.*

MAGIC
IN THE
PARK

"I hate Brooklyn! Why did we have to move here?" Jennifer threw her schoolbooks onto the kitchen table.

Her mother picked up the books and put them in a neat pile. "Daddy has a job here, Jenny," she said. "We have to live where Daddy can work."

Jennifer thought about the woods and fields near Carbondale and about the school where everybody knew everybody else. "Mother," she said, "there are *five* fourth grade classes in my new school."

"That's nice," Mrs. Mace said. "You can be in a class that's just right for you."

Sometimes Jennifer wished her mother didn't have an answer for everything.

"I hate all the big buildings," she said.

"Prospect Park is near here," Mrs. Mace told her. "Why don't you walk over there and look at it?"

She just wants to get rid of me, said Jennifer to herself, but she put on her jacket and went out of the apartment. She didn't wait for the elevator. The Maces lived on the third floor. Jennifer ran down the stairs to the lobby.

When she was out on the street, Jennifer looked around. A boy was delivering groceries to the apartment building. "Which way is the park?" she asked him.

He pointed down the street. "Just walk that way," he said. "You can't miss it."

Jennifer started walking past all the big apartment buildings. Here and there an old wooden house was sandwiched in between them. The old houses made Jennifer homesick for Carbondale.

At last she came to the park. It was

much bigger than Jennifer had expected. There were roads running through it. Jennifer went through the gate and crossed a road to get to the bank of a large lake.

A duck with a shiny green head and neck was swimming offshore. Jennifer watched him dive down into the water until only his tail feathers stuck up in the air. After a minute the duck bobbed up again. He shook the water off his bill. Just as he was about to swim away, a crust of bread sailed through the air and landed in the water near him. The duck gobbled the bread and looked to see if there was more where that came from.

Jennifer looked too. She saw an old man standing close to her on the bank of the lake.

That's funny, she thought. I didn't notice him before.

A fat pigeon sat on each of the old man's shoulders. Around his feet was a

flock of starlings and sparrows. Jennifer couldn't be sure, but she thought she saw something peeping out of the side pocket of his baggy brown overcoat. The old man was throwing crumbs to the birds.

Suddenly there was a loud whirr of wings. All the birds flew up into the air and scattered. A huge black raven flew down and landed on the old man's floppy hat. "Oh, hello, Napoleon. Where have you been?" The old man reached up to give the bird a piece of bread.

The raven stood on one foot and held the bread in the claws of the other. He cocked his head and kept a bright eye on Jennifer while he ate.

She took a step toward the bird, and the raven spread his wings and flapped away. "I must have scared him," Jennifer said. "I'm sorry."

The old man smiled down at her. His brown face was crisscrossed with wrinkles. It looked as dry and hard as the bark of an old tree. "Don't worry about Napoleon," he said. "He'll be back."

"Do you come here often to feed the birds?" Jennifer asked.

"They're my friends," the old man said. "I have to take care of them." He took a handful of nuts out of one of the many pockets of his coat. As if from nowhere a gray squirrel came running toward him. "See if you can get him to eat out of your hand." The old man gave Jennifer a little nut.

She stooped down and held it out to the squirrel. He put his head on one side. Jennifer made a chirping noise. The squirrel thought for a moment, took a good look at the nut, and slowly crept over to Jennifer. He sat up, holding his little paws in front of his chest.

"Don't be afraid," said Jennifer.

The squirrel made a quick grab for the nut, stuffed it in his mouth, and scampered up a beech tree. When he was halfway up the trunk of the tree, he turned upside down. He clung there and watched Jennifer.

"I did it!" Jennifer turned to look at the bird man. She couldn't see him anywhere.

Jennifer looked again at the squirrel on the tree trunk. The tree was enormous.

The tangled roots around the base were as big as the branches on ordinary trees. Jennifer saw a small hole in the trunk near the ground. She got down on her hands and knees and looked in. The tree seemed to be hollow inside.

I'm sure there's room enough in there for me, Jennifer told herself, but the hole is too small. The hole was too small even for her arm to reach in. She put her eye against it. There was a dim light inside the hole. Jennifer put her ear to it. She could hear faint fluttering sounds.

There must be a bird in there, she thought. But how did it get in? Maybe there's another hole at the top of the tree.

Jennifer stood a short distance away from the tree and looked up. Now she could see that the trunk of the tree had snapped off. It must have happened long ago. The branches had grown higher than the broken trunk.

A black shape flew out of the top of the tree trunk. It was the raven.

WITCHES, TIME TRAVEL,
AND A LITTLE
TROUBLE WITH MAGIC...

"RUTH CHEW'S CLASSIC BOOKS PERFECTLY CAPTURE THE JOY OF EVERYDAY MAGIC."

—MARY POPE OSBORNE, bestselling author of the Magic Tree House series

AND MORE TO COME!

RASSELAS

SAMUEL JOHNSON was born in 1709 in Lichfield, Staffordshire. The son of an impecunious bookseller, he experienced poverty throughout the first part of his life, and, in spite of his formidable mental endowments, was able to attend Pembroke College, Oxford, for only a year. After moving to London in 1737, he earned his living by miscellaneous journalism for many years, until his *Rambler* essays and the first historical dictionary of the English language brought him fame. A government pension of £300 a year relieved him from necessity, and in the later part of his life he came to be regarded as the greatest literary figure of his time in England. Among his most noted works are his poem 'The Vanity of Human Wishes', his periodical essays, his moral tale *Rasselas*, his edition of Shakespeare's plays, and his long series of *Prefaces, Biographical and Critical*, to the works of the English poets. He died in 1784 and was buried in Westminster Abbey.

J. P. HARDY is Professor of Humanities at Bond University, Queensland. His publications include a selected edition of *Johnson's Lives of the Poets* (1971), *Samuel Johnson: A Critical Study* (1979), and *Jane Austen's Heroines: Intimacy in Human Relationships* (1984).

OXFORD WORLD'S CLASSICS

SAMUEL JOHNSON

The History of Rasselas
Prince of Abissinia

Edited with an Introduction and Notes by
J. P. HARDY

OXFORD
UNIVERSITY PRESS

OXFORD
UNIVERSITY PRESS

Great Clarendon Street, Oxford OX2 6DP

Oxford University Press is a department of the University of Oxford.
It furthers the University's objective of excellence in research, scholarship,
and education by publishing worldwide in

Oxford New York

Athens Auckland Bangkok Bogotá Buenos Aires Calcutta
Cape Town Chennai Dar es Salaam Delhi Florence Hong Kong Istanbul
Karachi Kuala Lumpur Madrid Melbourne Mexico City Mumbai
Nairobi Paris São Paulo Singapore Taipei Tokyo Toronto Warsaw

with associated companies in Berlin Ibadan

Oxford is a registered trade mark of Oxford University Press
in the UK and in certain other countries

Published in the United States
by Oxford University Press Inc., New York

Introduction, Note on the Text,
Select Bibliography, Chronology, and Notes
© J. P. Hardy 1968 and 1988

First published 1968
First issued with revisions as a World's Classics paperback 1988
Reissued as an Oxford World's Classics paperback 1999

British Library Cataloguing in Publication Data

Data available

Library of Congress Cataloging in Publication Data
Johnson, Samuel, 1709–1784.
Rasselas, Prince of Abissinia / Samuel Johnson; edited with an
introduction by J. P. Hardy
p. cm.—(Oxford world's classics)
I. Hardy, J. P. (John P.), 1933– . II. Title. III. Series.
PR3529.A2H375 1988 823'.6—dc19 99–19503

ISBN–13: 978–0–19–283913–8
ISBN–10: 0–19–283913–6

9

Printed in Great Britain by
Clays Ltd, St Ives plc

CONTENTS

LIST OF ABBREVIATIONS

Anecdotes	H. L. Piozzi, *Anecdotes of Samuel Johnson*, ed. S. C. Roberts, 1932 revised edn.
Bicentenary Essays	*Bicentenary Essays on 'Rasselas'*, ed. Magdi Wahba, 1959 (Supplement to *Cairo Studies in English*).
Dict.	*A Dictionary of the English Language*, 1755, 2 vols.
Emerson	*The History of Rasselas, Prince of Abyssinia*, ed. O. F. Emerson, 1895.
Ency. Brit.	*Encyclopædia Britannica*, 14th edn., 1962 reprint.
Hill	*The History of Rasselas, Prince of Abyssinia*, ed. G. B. Hill, 1887.
Johnson, Boswell	*Johnson, Boswell and their Circle: Essays presented to L. F. Powell*, ed. M. M. Lascelles *et al.*, 1965.
Journey	*A Journey to the Western Islands of Scotland*, 1775, 1st edn.
Letters	*The Letters of Samuel Johnson*, ed. R. W. Chapman, 1952, 3 vols.
Life	*Boswell's Life of Johnson* (including Boswell's *Journal of a Tour to the Hebrides*), ed. G. B. Hill, rev. L. F. Powell, 1934–50, 6 vols.
Lives	*The Lives of the Poets*, ed. G. B. Hill, 1905, 3 vols.
Lobo	*A Voyage to Abyssinia by Father Jerome Lobo*, 1735.
MLN	*Modern Language Notes.*
MLQ	*Modern Language Quarterly.*
MP	*Modern Philology.*
NQ	*Notes and Queries.*

OED	*The Oxford English Dictionary.*
PMLA	*Publications of the Modern Language Association of America.*
PQ	*Philological Quarterly.*
Raleigh	*Johnson on Shakespeare,* ed. Walter Raleigh, 1908.
RES	*Review of English Studies.*
SEL	*Studies in English Literature.*
TLS	*Times Literary Supplement.*
Yale	The Yale Edition of the Works of Samuel Johnson, gen. ed. A. T. Hazen: vol. i, *Diaries, Prayers, and Annals,* ed. E. L. McAdam, Jr., with Donald and Mary Hyde, 1958; vol. ii, *The Idler and The Adventurer,* ed. W. J. Bate, J. M. Bullitt, L. F. Powell, 1963; vol. vi, *Poems, ed.* E. L. McAdam, Jr., with George Milne, 1964.

INTRODUCTION

THE CIRCUMSTANCES leading to the composition of
Rasselas recall Johnson's well-known saying, 'No man but a
blockhead ever wrote, except for money'.[1] Never rich, and
often poor, he found himself in need of money to send to his
dying and much-loved mother. In his letter dated Saturday,
13 January 1759, Johnson expresses deep sorrow at her
illness, adding that he has twelve guineas to send. On the
following Tuesday, in a letter to his stepdaughter Lucy
Porter, he writes that the money has been sent, and that
he expects to have more to send in a few days. On Saturday,
20 January, he wrote as follows to his friend the printer
William Strahan:

> When I was with you last night I told you of a thing which I
> was preparing for the press. The title will be
> ### The Choice of Life
> #### or
> The History of ——— Prince of Abissinia.

Then, after some discussion of the size and price of the
work, the letter continues:

> I shall have occasion for thirty pounds on Monday night when
> I shall deliver the book which I must entreat you upon such
> delivery to procure me.[2]

Since Johnson is reported to have told Sir Joshua Reynolds
that *Rasselas* had been composed 'in the evenings of one
week',[3] it can be conjectured that it was begun after he had
heard of his mother's grave illness. Unfortunately he was
unable to fulfil his further intention of journeying to
Lichfield to see her.[4] Before he wrote again to Lucy Porter
on Tuesday, 23 January, he had heard of his mother's death.
Rasselas, written within a week or so in January, was

[1] *Life*, iii. 19. Cf. ibid. n. 3.
[2] *Letters*, i. 115, 116, 117, 118.
[3] *Life*, i. 341.
[4] See *Letters*, i. 117.

published in April 1759.¹ That its author had long been familiar with the background material on which he drew is clear not only from these circumstances of composition, but also from his other published work. Having read as an undergraduate at Pembroke College, Oxford, an account of a voyage to Abyssinia by Father Jeronymo Lobo, a Portuguese Jesuit, Johnson translated it for publication several years later.² Then in 1752 he devoted two numbers of the *Rambler* (nos. 204 and 205) to an account of ten days in the life of Seged, 'lord of Ethiopia'. The name of this emperor is mentioned in various works on Abyssinia (including Lobo's); but two of Johnson's details have been shown to be derived from separate accounts by the German scholar Job Ludolf and the French physician Charles Jacques Poncet.³ Obviously he had read such authors as these long before he came to write what he modestly called his 'little story book'.⁴

Though *Rasselas*, too, contains some details from earlier accounts of Abyssinia, it is, as a 'story book', an eastern tale only in name. Unlike the popular *Arabian Nights Entertainments* and *Persian Tales*, which had appeared in English earlier in the century, *Rasselas* was intended to curb imagination rather than excite it. Putting the eastern setting to ironical use, Johnson presents not an exotic world of romance and escape, or even a succession of romantic reversals of fortune,⁵ but a searching and deliberately un-optimistic analysis of the human condition. Instead of dismissing his characters to a happiness-ever-after, he forces upon them and his reader the realization that no such happiness exists.

---

¹ Johnsonians have generally accepted Thursday, 19 April, as the date of publication. D. D. Eddy, however, argues persuasively for Friday, 20 April (*NQ*, ccvii, 1962, 21–2).

² Johnson worked from the French translation by Joachim Le Grand.

³ D. M. Lockhart, '"The Fourth Son of the Mighty Emperor": The Ethiopian Background of Johnson's *Rasselas*', *PMLA*, lxxviii (1963), 526–7.

⁴ *Letters*, i. 122.

⁵ See Mary Lascelles, '*Rasselas* Reconsidered', *Essays and Studies*, N.S. iv (1951), 40, where the essential difference between *Rasselas* and the *Persian Tales* is succinctly stated; also G. J. Kolb, 'The Structure of *Rasselas*', *PMLA*, lxvi (1951), 716.

Indeed, the difference between *Rasselas* and the more conventional eastern tale can be demonstrated from even their superficial resemblances.[1] Both, for example, make use of the device of the story-within-a-story. But this potential means of diversifying and enriching the narrative does not lead in *Rasselas* to further possibilities of fictional suspense and excitement. In recounting his 'history', Imlac paints a sombre picture of the unhappiness of the outside world—though this, ironically enough, makes Rasselas even more eager to escape from the Happy Valley and begin his own quest for happiness! And Pekuah, after her abduction, suffers in the Arab's palace no greater fate than boredom. In fact, Johnson had set his face against elements of romance right from the very beginning. Though the almost Gothic description of the palace in the opening chapter could well have provided the scene for an exciting adventure, nothing further is made of it.

Nor is the book's episodic quality at all reminiscent of the eastern tale, where the episodes exist solely for the story, and usually occur within a larger plot. Instead, Johnson's narrative style reflects what has aptly been described as 'his intense awareness of arbitrariness, ignorance, uncertainty, flux . . . his concern with that part of life which eludes prescription and planning'.[2] No artifice of plot could have made us so aware of the tentative, experimental, unpredictable quality of life itself, or of its constant and basic ironies. Early critics, who tended to complain that *Rasselas* was 'an ill-contrived, unfinished, unnatural and uninstructive tale',[3] overlooked this significant connection between its form and meaning.

By adopting an eastern setting and thereby moving beyond the constraints of a familiar, circumscribed society, Johnson could more easily invent for his characters a code of

---

[1] Some scholars have, even so, discussed their affinity. See M. P. Conant, *The Oriental Tale in England in the Eighteenth Century* (1908), pp. 140–54; E. A. Baker, *The History of the English Novel* (1934), v. 53–64; Geoffrey Tillotson, '*Rasselas* and the Persian Tales', *TLS*, 29 Aug. 1935, p. 534.

[2] Emrys Jones, 'The Artistic Form of *Rasselas*', *RES*, N.S. xviii (1967), 395.

[3] H. M. Chapone, *Posthumous Works* (1807), i. 108.

manners giving them open access to the world on terms of easy informality.[1] Yet despite their names and titles, there is nothing exclusively eastern about them. Johnson set out to capture not the exotic grandeur of eastern life, but the 'grandeur of generality'.[2] He describes not Persians and Egyptians, but men in general. Even the scenery has little that is specifically eastern about it; while Cairo is arguably described from the vantage-point of Johnson's own London.

There are, however, two eastern features—the Nile and the Happy Valley—which possess an almost symbolic significance in Johnson's narrative. Regarded by early biblical scholars as one of the four great rivers of the garden of Eden, the Nile subtly presides over the youthful travellers' search for earthly happiness. At first, curious and hopeful, they set out from the river's source on their own journey through life. But the course of life, like that of the Nile, proves to be ceaseless, unreturning, continually subject to flux.[3] Hope of happiness restlessly moves them on, but happiness, as insubstantial as flowing water, eludes their grasp. After observing life in populous Cairo, the princess, having begun to doubt the possibility of human happiness, turns to address the Nile on the banks of its lower reaches. 'Answer, said she, great father of waters, thou that rollest thy floods through eighty nations, to the invocations of the daughter of thy native king. Tell me if thou waterest, through all thy course, a single habitation from which thou dost not hear the murmurs of complaint?' The conversation between herself and Rasselas begins, while the waters of the Nile continue to flow before them. As the debate draws to a close, Nekayah, coming now to see the special lesson which the river holds for human hopes of happiness, expresses with gnomic force one of life's central truths: 'No man can taste the fruits of autumn while he is delighting his scent with the flowers of spring: no man can, at the same time, fill his cup from the source and from the mouth of the Nile.'

[1] Cf. Mary Lascelles, op cit. p. 43.   [2] *Lives*, i. 45.
[3] Cf. Emrys Jones, loc. cit.

The eastern setting of the Happy Valley, so appropriate to its luxuriance, is also significant in view of that tradition which had placed the Earthly Paradise in Abyssinia.[1] Much of Johnson's initial description is reminiscent of traditional accounts of Eden. In the Happy Valley 'all the diversities of the world were brought together, the blessings of nature were collected, and its evils extracted and excluded'. And, like Eden, in which man's first parents enjoyed a perpetual spring, the Happy Valley provided constant gratification for every kind of sensory appetite. 'The sides of the mountains were covered with trees, the banks of the brooks were diversified with flowers; every blast shook spices from the rocks, and every month dropped fruits upon the ground.' There, however, the likeness ends, and the pattern of ironies begins. The outward and visible sign of man's loss of prelapsarian Innocence is the palace 'built as if suspicion herself had dictated the plan'. Inwardly man is tormented by 'some latent sense', 'some desires distinct from sense', which, receiving no gratification from the sensual pleasures of the Happy Valley, make him dissatisfied with purely animal contentment, and urge the superiority of Experience, however bitter, to blind and unknowing Innocence.

When Johnson's story opens, Rasselas is 'in the twenty-sixth year of his age'; and some twenty chapters and six years later he is said to be still 'young'. Such a description accords with the allegorical dimension of the work, for Rasselas possesses throughout both the innocence and 'freshness of apprehension' of youth.[2] Moreover, since 'youth is the time of enterprise and hope', since 'to learn is the proper business of youth',[3] Rasselas is never more Johnson's hero than when he desires to escape from the 'imprisonment' of the womb-like Happy Valley in order to explore the outside world.

Finding his imagination stirred by Imlac's narrative,

---

[1] Cf. *Paradise Lost*, iv. 280–3.
[2] Mary Lascelles, op. cit. p. 44.
[3] *Rambler* III, 121.

Rasselas promptly adopts him as his guide and tutor. Nor can any amount of warning dampen the young hero's enthusiasm. Even though Imlac paints an uninviting picture of life outside the Happy Valley, the prince makes a telling rejoinder. 'Since thou', he says, 'art thyself weary of the valley, it is evident, that thy former state was better than this.' 'Better' in one important sense it will be in that Rasselas will learn at first-hand of the difference between hope and reality, between man's initial confidence of success in pursuing his goal and the bitter facts of experience. The irony is that Imlac, as tutor, can ultimately teach the young prince nothing.[1] Rasselas must learn for himself.

It has often been pointed out that Rasselas is a prose version of Johnson's earlier *Vanity of Human Wishes*. According to Boswell, who was obviously aware of its kinship with the outlook expressed in the Old Testament Book of Ecclesiastes, 'this Tale, with all the charms of oriental imagery, and all the force and beauty of which the English language is capable, leads us through the most important scenes of human life, and shews us that this stage of our being is full of "vanity and vexation of spirit" '.[2] It has also been rightly pointed out that *Rasselas*, like Voltaire's *Candide*, was intended as a satire on the optimistic philosophies then current—'the principles of Leibniz and the complacent view of the deists and benevolists that all is right with the world'.[3] Chapter 22, for example, is largely an attack on the doctrines of Rousseau. Yet the book's opening sentence—'Ye who listen with credulity to the whispers of fancy, and persue with eagerness the phantoms of hope . . .'—is not addressed to philosophers alone. Firmly

---

[1] Cf. Mahmoud Manzalaoui, '*Rasselas* and Some Medieval Ancillaries', *Bicentenary Essays*, p. 70, where the author fittingly relates the situation in *Rasselas* to a long line of texts stressing the importance of the education of princes. Contemporary readers would have been aware of the educational motif in this eastern Grand Tour.

[2] *Life*, i. 341–2. Boswell quotes from Ecclesiastes, 1: 14, Cf. J. W. Johnson, 'Rasselas and his Ancestors', *NQ*, cciv (1959), 185–8.

[3] J. L. Clifford, 'Some Remarks on *Candide* and *Rasselas*', *Bicentenary Essays*, p. 10. Professor Clifford notes (pp. 7, 9) that *Candide*, written during 1758, and published at Geneva and Paris early the next year, did not receive notices in the London press until *Rasselas* itself had been published.

persuaded that 'the natural flights of the human mind are not from pleasure to pleasure, but from hope to hope',[1] Johnson presses his conviction on the reader by having his travellers observe human life in all its forms and conditions.[2] They traverse both city and country, mix with philosophers and shepherds, enter the homes of the lowly as well as the courts of the great, and encounter youthful roisterers as well as men of venerable age, piety and learning. They even visit the monuments of antiquity in an attempt to understand the character of a former race of men. Yet all their searches only prove the truth of Imlac's earlier words to Rasselas in the Happy Valley: 'Human life is every where a state in which much is to be endured, and little to be enjoyed.'

The causes of human unhappiness are variously described in *Rasselas*. Least important, perhaps, is the unhappiness that arises from the unavoidable accidents of life. Yet even here, because of the perennial conflict between hope and reality, man is inclined to aggravate his own wretchedness. A cruel turn of Fortune's wheel leaves the stoical sage inconsolable; and when the princess loses her devoted maid she sees no point in pursuing happiness if it can itself so unexpectedly lead to misery. Man is also the victim of his baser passions, whether in himself or in others. The Arab chieftain who finds delight in Pekuah's company eventually parts with her because he is unable to refuse the proferred gold; while the generous host of chapter 20 surprises the youthful travellers by telling them that his 'prosperity', having attracted the notice of envious eyes, puts his 'life in danger'. Less obviously to the superficial observer, unhappiness also occurs within the same family as a result of the inevitable frictions and antagonisms that exist between people of different ages and temperament. But the most permanent threat to human happiness arises from the mind's own quixotic tendencies. Though Johnson realized that some form of wishing or questing is necessary to

---

[1] *Rambler* 2. Johnson expressed the same sentiment in conversation: 'Life is a progress from want to want, not from enjoyment to enjoyment' (*Life*, iii. 53).

[2] Cf. G. J. Kolb, op. cit. pp. 707 ff.

prevent man from being condemned to the dispiriting 'vacuity' of a Happy Valley,[1] he also realized that, in indulging hope, man often merely luxuriates in the 'anticipation of happiness',[2] allowing the mind to escape to those more seductive vistas forever opening before it. Whatever the different ends which different men pursue, the mind is continually restless in a way that is destructive of present happiness. As one critic has remarked of *Rasselas*: 'The nucleus of the subject is the perpetual, and essentially comic, psychological irony of the mind itself, always wishing, always imagining happiness even in the midst of happiness, always, by its very nature, incapable of satisfaction.'[3]

All three youthful travellers entertain dreams that are contradicted by the reality of the world around them. The princess celebrates the virtues of pastoral felicity even as she observes a group of shepherds and pronounces them 'envious savages'; while, on hearing of the astronomer's delusions, all three later admit that they have *often* given themselves up to private fantasies. Even in the last chapter, with the sobering experience of life behind him, the prince, having imagined himself the just ruler of a little kingdom, 'could never fix the limits of his dominion, and was always adding to the number of his subjects'. Nothing in the whole book better illustrates the mind's inveterate habit of building pyramids in the air; and nowhere is the reason for this explained more impressively than in the course of the travellers' visit to the Pyramids. In proposing the visit, Imlac reminds the prince and his sister that 'no mind is much employed upon the present: recollection and anticipation fill up almost all our moments'. Later, after the Pyramids have been surveyed, Imlac, discoursing on the reason for their construction, can attribute this only to 'that hunger of imagination which preys incessantly upon life, and must be

[1] See note to p. 12, l. 26.

[2] *Rambler* 2. Johnson was convinced that 'the present was never a happy state to any human being' (*Life*, ii. 350–1). Cf. *Life*, iii. 5, 53, 241.

[3] Sheridan Baker, '*Rasselas*: Psychological Irony and Romance', *PQ*, xlv (1966), 250–1.

always appeased by some employment'. 'Those', he continues, 'who have already all that they can enjoy, must enlarge their desires. He that has built for use, till use is supplied, must begin to build for vanity, and extend his plan to the utmost power of human performance, that he may not be soon reduced to form another wish.' And Imlac concludes: 'I consider this mighty structure as a monument of the insufficiency of human enjoyments.'

The 'hunger of imagination' craves 'some employment': confined to the Happy Valley, Rasselas imagines that he would be happy if he had 'something to peruse'. Yet, as one Johnsonian has pointed out, there exists a fundamental conflict between the infinite imagination and its finite 'employments in time'.[1] Man's circumstantial involvement in the temporal world inevitably limits the choices open to him. In the words of *Rambler* 162, 'it is impossible but that, as the attention tends strongly towards one thing, it must retire from another'. That things mutually exclusive cannot be reconciled within any larger scheme or 'choice of life' becomes obvious during the debate between Rasselas and his sister on early and late marriages. Since no one can enjoy the best of both, he who tries to combine their advantages is in danger of enjoying neither. Adroitly underlining the point for the youthful travellers, Imlac, at the beginning of the next chapter, interrupts them and remarks: 'It seems to me that while you are making the choice of life, you neglect to live.' The central irony of Johnson's work is here apparent. In setting out expressly to observe life in all its varied aspects, the youthful travellers are in very real danger of letting life itself slip through their fingers.

Imlac's remarks on the Pyramids serve as a fitting conclusion to those 'experiments upon life' which form the 'second movement' of *Rasselas*.[2] Thereafter the youthful

---

[1] Arieh Sachs, 'Generality and Particularity in Johnson's Thought', *SEL*, v (1965), 493.

[2] I follow here the suggestion of Mr Emrys Jones that *Rasselas* is composed of three 'movements', each of sixteen chapters, followed by a 'trailing coda' (op. cit. pp. 396–400).

travellers, from being largely spectators, become more actively involved in the life around them. Moreover, it is during this third section or movement that they witness the most frightening spectacle of the obsessive tendencies of man's seemingly infinite mind. The mad astronomer has obviously given himself 'something to persue'; but in an important sense he too has neglected to live. Indeed, his concern with one 'particular train of ideas' has, in leading him to disregard all other ends of man's existence, dangerously isolated him from that more general converse with mankind which Johnson considered requisite to an intellectual and moral being.

The choice of an astronomer for this climactic episode not only follows on neatly from Pekuah's account of her studies in the Arab's stronghold, but underlines Johnson's criticism of that habit of abstraction from daily life fostered by the vagaries of hope, a wayward imagination, or misdirected curiosity. Though curiosity was 'a passion . . . in some degree universally associated to reason', and provided strong proof of a vigorous and enquiring mind (like Rasselas's in the Happy Valley), it could also be too easily 'confined, overborne, or diverted' from its proper object or end.[1] As numerous pages of the *Rambler* show, its proper object was the study of man, 'self-knowledge' as opposed to the vain pursuit of 'star-knowledge' or things remote from use.[2] Arguably the episode of the astronomer, which makes use of this opposition, is also to be linked with the earlier visit to the Pyramids. In his initial reaction to this, the prince recognizes that 'the proper study of mankind is man'. 'My curiosity, said Rasselas, does not very strongly lead me to survey piles of stones, or mounds of earth; my business is with man.'[3] During the visit Pekuah was abducted and the

---

[1] Cf. *Rambler*, 118; note to p. 18, l. 6.
[2] See my article 'Johnson and Raphael's Counsel to Adam', *Johnson, Boswell,* pp. 122–36; Emrys Jones, op. cit. pp. 399–400; note to p. 15, l. 20. Since speculation on the source of the Nile was also traditionally used as an *exemplum* of improper curiosity, the contemporary reader might have discerned an imaginative link between the astronomer and the youthful travellers who dwelt at its source.
[3] See notes to p. 73, ll. 16, 20.

travellers, greatly distressed, 'returned to Cairo, repenting of their curiosity'. Some half-dozen chapters later, however, after Pekuah has been restored to them, this sentence is more happily echoed: 'They returned to Cairo, and were so well pleased at finding themselves together, that none of them went much abroad.' That this represents a new-found wisdom such as Milton's Raphael and eighteenth-century Christian humanists would approve seems to be obliquely suggested in the ensuing pages. When Rasselas proposes to pass 'the rest of his days in literary solitude', Imlac, citing the example of the astronomer, remarks: 'Men of various ideas and fluent conversation are commonly welcome to those whose thoughts have been long fixed upon a single point, and who find the images of other things stealing away.' Replying later to a question on the 'choice of life', the astronomer can offer no advice beyond the fact that he has chosen wrongly: 'I have passed my time in study without experience; in the attainment of sciences which can, for the most part, be but remotely useful to mankind.' Despite his acknowledged disposition to charity, his studies, like those of the other curious 'sons of learning' described in *Rambler* 180, have tended to limit his active participation in the world, thereby largely removing him from man's proper sphere of virtue. He accordingly suffers melancholy and madness, until the cheerful company and conversation of his new friends restores him to sanity.

There follows the visit to the catacombs, where the theme of the 'choice of life' is finally set within the larger context of eternity. For the youthful travellers the catacombs become a *memento mori*, warning them of the 'shortness' of their 'present state'. Rasselas, in characteristic Johnsonian fashion, ponders on the scene: 'Those that lie here stretched before us, the wise and the powerful of antient times . . . were, perhaps, snatched away while they were busy, like us, in the choice of life.' And Nekayah, in the book's last piece of direct speech, utters what is surely, in one sense, Johnson's conclusion: 'To me, said the princess, the choice of life is become less important; I hope hereafter to think only on the choice of eternity'. No one aware of Johnson's preoccupation with ultimate Judgment, of the anxiety with which he recalled the 'account' to be rendered up to man's 'Eternal Master',[1] can help but feel his whole-hearted endorsement of this sentiment. In the *Rambler* he had often complained that 'few of the hours of life are filled up with objects adequate to the mind of man';[2] and there he had also summarized the lesson his youthful travellers must learn. 'Life', he wrote in *Rambler* 63, 'allows us but a small time for inquiry and experiment, and he that steadily endeavours at excellence, in whatever employment, will more benefit mankind than he that hesitates in choosing his part till he is called to the performance.'[3] Such pronouncements by Rasselas, Nekayah and the Rambler derive particular poignancy from the fact that Johnson lamented, throughout his life, his own misspent time and lack of purposefulness in living. Many years after writing *Rasselas* he could still reflect: 'I have great reason to fear lest Death should lay hold upon me, while I am yet only designing to live'; and two years earlier, on his sixty-second birthday, he had complained: 'I have neither attempted nor formed any scheme of Life by which I may do good and please God,'[4] Even at that advanced age, when the danger of being 'snatched away' was very great, Johnson was troubled that *some* 'choice of life' was still to be made.

That *Rasselas* reflects Johnson's convictions at the deepest levels of experience accounts, I believe, for the quality of its seriousness, humour, and compassion. On hearing he had met its author, Sir David Dalrymple wrote to Boswell:

It gives me great pleasure to think that you have obtained the friendship of Mr. Samuel Johnson. He is one of the best moral

---

[1] Yale, vi. 315. Boswell, for example, notes not only Johnson's 'aweful dread of death, or rather, "of something after death"', but records that 'the solemn text, "of him to whom much is given, much will be required" seems to have been ever present to his mind, in a rigorous sense, and to have made him dissatisfied with his labours and acts of goodness, however comparatively great' (*Life*, ii. 298; iv. 427).

[2] No. 41.

[3] Cf. the advice of the hermit: 'To him that lives well every form of life is good.'

[4] Yale, i. 143, 160.

writers which England has produced. . . . May I beg you to present my best respects to him, and to assure him of the veneration which I entertain for the authour of the Rambler and of Rasselas? Let me recommend this last work to you. . . . In Rasselas you will see a tender-hearted operator, who probes the wound only to heal it.[1]

Unlike Voltaire, who set out 'to discredit the belief of a superintending Providence',[2] Johnson is never sardonic or cynical at man's expense. Indeed, the essential difference in tone between *Rasselas* and *Candide* was brilliantly suggested by G. B. Hill in his note on the would-be aviator of chapter 6. 'Johnson', he writes, 'is content with giving the artist a ducking. Voltaire would have crippled him for life at the very least; most likely would have killed him on the spot.'

Because Johnson continually looks for reassurance beyond this world to another, *Rasselas* cannot be described along with *Candide* as a pessimistic work. Indeed, as one critic has pointed out, there is 'above the ground tone of sorrow . . . a melodic line that is vigorous, energetic, vibrant',[3] and is sustained even in the 'trailing coda' of the final chapter, 'The conclusion, in which nothing is concluded'. Critics who maintain that the travellers return to the Happy Valley not only have no textual support for their view, but seem to have badly mistaken the book's tone and message. Nothing could be more pessimistic than a return to the Happy Valley, for such a conclusion would deny that the youthful travellers had realized this childhood Eden to be incompatible with the process of growing up. True, they proceed to outline 'the various schemes of happiness which each of them had formed'. But they are no longer deluded: as the text makes clear, they are now merely *talking* for their own diversion. In order that his reader should not miss this point, Johnson makes it quite explicit in his final paragraph: 'Of these wishes that they had formed they well knew that none could be obtained. They deliberated a while what was

[1] *Life*, i. 432-3.
[2] Ibid. i. 342.
[3] F. W. Hilles, '*Rasselas*, An "Uninstructive Tale"', *Johnson, Boswell*, pp. 117-18.

to be done, and resolved, when the inundation should cease, to return to Abissinia.' The youthful travellers, at least, return to live a life of their own in the world. Their journey remains parabolic in movement, not circular. They do not end where they began. Their initial optimism has been tempered by experience. They now know where unreal hopes must end.

Yet it is significant that they do not altogether relinquish their dreams.[1] The contrast between them on the one hand and Imlac and the astronomer on the other is noticeable. Youth, with its life still before it, clings obstinately to hope, refusing to be forced by experience into adopting the resignation of age. Johnson's juxtapositions are too complex to be finally resolved, but it is possible that this last chapter also implies some approval of those who go on wishing to make a positive contribution to life, whether, like Pekuah, as the 'prioress' of an order of 'pious maidens', or, like Nekayah, as the instructress of 'models of prudence, and patterns of piety', or, like Rasselas, as a wise and virtuous ruler. As a prince, Rasselas, especially, has a role to fulfil in the world, and is therefore still far removed from that unenviable state, described in *Rambler* 127, in which man 'abandons himself to chance and to the wind, and glides careless and idle down the current of life, without resolution to make another effort' to reach a particular port. It is Imlac and the astronomer who are content 'to be driven along the stream of life, without directing their course to any particular port', and for this reason it is, perhaps, the youthful travellers who are meant to have the last word. If they are, then it is the prince and not his tutor who is, first and last, Johnson's hero.

[1] In *Samuel Johnson: A Critical Study* I have argued for the importance of the final chapter as 'the point to which the whole book tends': 'The "choice" that is so immediate to this life can never bcome irrelevant or unimportant'; 'we feel how important it is that the youthful travellers should . . . continue to have the capacity of planning and hoping' (p. 146).

NOTE ON THE TEXT

THIS volume was originally undertaken as a revision of G. B. Hill's edition of *Rasselas*, first published by the Clarendon Press in 1887. My intention was to provide a new introduction and revised notes incorporating the findings of more recent scholarship and criticism. I have substituted for Hill's the text prepared by R. W. Chapman and published by the Clarendon Press in 1927. This text is based on the second edition as revised by Johnson.

In the notes I have supplemented Hill's quotations from Johnson's conversation and other writings, giving references, wherever possible, to standard modern editions. I have glossed Johnson's usage whenever it differs significantly from that commonly accepted today, usually by quoting from either the *Oxford English Dictionary* or Johnson's own *Dictionary*. Following the practice of Chapman's text, I have retained the original spelling and punctuation of works quoted in the notes.

J.P.H.

SELECT BIBLIOGRAPHY

I. BOOKS

BATE, W. J., *The Achievement of Samuel Johnson*, New York: Oxford University Press, 1955

BRONSON, B. H., *Johnson Agonistes & Other Essays*, Cambridge University Press, 1946, pp. 1–52.

CLIFFORD, J. L., *Young Sam Johnson*, New York: McGraw-Hill, 1955; *Young Samuel Johnson*, London: Heinemann, 1955.

HARDY, J. P., *Samuel Johnson: A Critical Study*, London: Routledge & Kegan Paul, 1979.

KRUTCH, J. W., *Samuel Johnson*, New York: Henry Holt & Company, 1944; London: Cassell & Co., 1948.

McINTOSH, CAREY, *The Choice of Life: Samuel Johnson and the World of Fiction*, New Haven: Yale University Press, 1973.

WAIN, JOHN, *Samuel Johnson*, London: Macmillan, 1974.

II. ARTICLES

BAKER, SHERIDAN, '*Rasselas*: Psychological Irony and Romance', *PQ*, xlv (1966), 249–61.

CULLUM, GRAHAM, 'Dr. Johnson and Human Wishing', *Neophilologus*, lxvii (1983), 305–19.

EVERSOLE, RICHARD, 'Imlac and the Poets of Persia and Arabia', *PQ*, lviii (1979), 155–70.

HARDY, JOHN, 'Hope and Fear in Johnson', *Essays in Criticism*, xxvi (1976), 285–99.

HILLES, F. W., '*Rasselas*, An "Uninstructive Tale"', *Johnson, Boswell*, pp. 111–21.

JONES, E. L., 'The Artistic Form of *Rasselas*', *RES*, N.S. xviii (1967), 387–401.

KOLB, G. J., 'The Structure of *Rasselas*', *PMLA*, lxvi (1951), 698–717.

LASCELLES, MARY, '*Rasselas* Reconsidered', *Essays and Studies by Members of the English Association*, N.S. iv (1951), 37–52.

LOCKHART, D. M., '"The Fourth Son of the Mighty Emperor": The Ethiopian Background of Johnson's *Rasselas*', *PMLA*, lxxviii (1963), 516–28.

LOMBARDO, AGOSTINO, 'The Importance of Imlac', *Bicentenary Essays*, pp. 31–49.

WASSERMAN, E. R., 'Johnson's *Rasselas*: Implicit Contexts', *Journal of English and Germanic Philology*, lxxiv (1975), 1–25.

WHITE, IAN, 'On *Rasselas*', *Cambridge Quarterly*, vi, no. i (July, 1972), 6–31

WHITLEY, ALVIN, 'The Comedy of *Rasselas*', *Journal of English Literary History*, xxiii (1956), 48–70.

WIMSATT, W. K., 'In Praise of *Rasselas*', in *Imagined Worlds*, ed. Maynard Mack and Ian Gregor, London: Methuen, 1968, pp. 111–36.

A CHRONOLOGY OF
SAMUEL JOHNSON

1709	Born at Lichfield, 18 September.
1728–9	Undergraduate of Pembroke College, Oxford.
1732	Temporarily usher (or schoolmaster's assistant) at Market Bosworth School.
1733	Translated Lobo's *Voyage to Abyssinia* (published 1735).
1735	Married the widow Elizabeth Porter; opened private school at Edial, near Lichfield.
1737	Moved to London; worked at unfinished tragedy *Irene*.
1738	Began writing for *Gentleman's Magazine*; *London*.
1740–3	Reported debates in Parliament (published in *Gentleman's Magazine* 1741–4 as 'Debates in the Senate of Lilliput').
1744	*An Account of the Life of Mr. Richard Savage*.
1745	*Miscellaneous Observations on the Tragedy of 'Macbeth'*.
1747	*The Plan of a Dictionary of the English Language*.
1749	*The Vanity of Human Wishes*; *Irene*.
1750–2	*The Rambler*.
1752	Death of his wife.
1753–4	Contributed to *The Adventurer*.
1755	*A Dictionary of the English Language*
1756	*Proposals for an Edition of Shakespeare*; contributed to and probably edited *The Literary Magazine*.
1758–60	*The Idler*.
1759	Death of his mother; *Rasselas*.
1762	Awarded pension of £300 p.a.
1763	Met James Boswell.
1764	The Club founded (other foundation-members included Beauclerk, Burke, Goldsmith, Hawkins, Langton, Reynolds).
1765	Met Thrales; received LL D from Dublin; edition of *The Plays of William Shakespeare*
1770	*The False Alarm*.

THE
HISTORY
OF
RASSELAS,
PRINCE OF ABISSINIA.

CHAP. I

Description of a palace in a valley

YE who listen with credulity to the whispers of fancy, and persue with eagerness the phantoms of hope; who expect that age will perform the promises of youth, and that the deficiencies of the present day will be supplied by the morrow; attend to the history of Rasselas prince of Abissinia.

Rasselas was the fourth son of the mighty emperour, in whose dominions the Father of waters begins his course; whose bounty pours down the streams of plenty, and scatters over half the world the harvests of Egypt.

According to the custom which has descended from age to age among the monarchs of the torrid zone, Rasselas was confined in a private palace, with the other sons and daughters of Abissinian royalty, till the order of succession should call him to the throne.

The place, which the wisdom or policy of antiquity had destined for the residence of the Abissinian princes, was a spacious valley in the kingdom of Amhara, surrounded on

every side by mountains, of which the summits overhang
the middle part. The only passage, by which it could be entered, was a cavern that passed under a rock, of which it has
long been disputed whether it was the work of nature or of
human industry. The outlet of the cavern was concealed by a
thick wood, and the mouth which opened into the valley
was closed with gates of iron, forged by the artificers of ancient days, so massy that no man could, without the help of
engines, open or shut them.

From the mountains on every side, rivulets descended that
filled all the valley with verdure and fertility, and formed a
lake in the middle inhabited by fish of every species, and frequented by every fowl whom nature has taught to dip the
wing in water. This lake discharged its superfluities by a
stream which entered a dark cleft of the mountain on the
northern side, and fell with dreadful noise from precipice to
precipice till it was heard no more.

The sides of the mountains were covered with trees, the
banks of the brooks were diversified with flowers; every blast
shook spices from the rocks, and every month dropped fruits
upon the ground. All animals that bite the grass, or brouse
the shrub, whether wild or tame, wandered in this extensive
circuit, secured from beasts of prey by the mountains which
confined them. On one part were flocks and herds feeding in
the pastures, on another all the beasts of chase frisking in the
lawns; the sprightly kid was bounding on the rocks, the
subtle monkey frolicking in the trees, and the solemn elephant reposing in the shade. All the diversities of the world
were brought together, the blessings of nature were collected,
and its evils extracted and excluded.

The valley, wide and fruitful, supplied its inhabitants with
the necessaries of life, and all delights and superfluities were
added at the annual visit which the emperour paid his child-

ren, when the iron gate was opened to the sound of musick;
and during eight days every one that resided in the valley
was required to propose whatever might contribute to make
seclusion pleasant, to fill up the vacancies of attention, and
lessen the tediousness of time. Every desire was immediately
granted. All the artificers of pleasure were called to gladden
the festivity; the musicians exerted the power of harmony,
and the dancers shewed their activity before the princes, in
hope that they should pass their lives in this blissful captivity,
to which these only were admitted whose performance was
thought able to add novelty to luxury. Such was the appearance of security and delight which this retirement afforded,
that they to whom it was new always desired that it might be
perpetual; and as those, on whom the iron gate had once
closed, were never suffered to return, the effect of longer experience could not be known. Thus every year produced new
schemes of delight, and new competitors for imprisonment.

The palace stood on an eminence raised about thirty paces
above the surface of the lake. It was divided into many squares
or courts, built with greater or less magnificence according
to the rank of those for whom they were designed. The roofs
were turned into arches of massy stone joined with a cement
that grew harder by time, and the building stood from century to century, deriding the solstitial rains and equinoctial
hurricanes, without need of reparation.

This house, which was so large as to be fully known to none
but some ancient officers who successively inherited the secrets
of the place, was built as if suspicion herself had dictated the
plan. To every room there was an open and secret passage,
every square had a communication with the rest, either from
the upper stories by private galleries, or by subterranean passages from the lower apartments. Many of the columns had
unsuspected cavities, in which a long race of monarchs had

reposited their treasures. They then closed up the opening with marble, which was never to be removed but in the utmost exigencies of the kingdom; and recorded their accumulations in a book which was itself concealed in a tower not entered but by the emperour, attended by the prince who stood next in succession.

CHAP. II

The discontent of Rasselas in the happy valley

HERE the sons and daughters of Abissinia lived only to know the soft vicissitudes of pleasure and repose, attended by all that were skilful to delight, and gratified with whatever the senses can enjoy. They wandered in gardens of fragrance, and slept in the fortresses of security. Every art was practised to make them pleased with their own condition. The sages who instructed them, told them of nothing but the miseries of publick life, and described all beyond the mountains as regions of calamity, where discord was always raging, and where man preyed upon man.

To heighten their opinion of their own felicity, they were daily entertained with songs, the subject of which was the *happy valley*. Their appetites were excited by frequent enumerations of different enjoyments, and revelry and merriment was the business of every hour from the dawn of morning to the close of even.

These methods were generally successful; few of the Princes had ever wished to enlarge their bounds, but passed their lives in full conviction that they had all within their reach that art or nature could bestow, and pitied those whom fate had excluded from this seat of tranquility, as the sport of chance, and the slaves of misery.

Thus they rose in the morning, and lay down at night, pleased with each other and with themselves, all but Rasselas, who, in the twenty-sixth year of his age, began to withdraw himself from their pastimes and assemblies, and to delight in solitary walks and silent meditation. He often sat before tables covered with luxury, and forgot to taste the dainties that were placed before him: he rose abruptly in the midst of the song, and hastily retired beyond the sound of musick. His attendants observed the change and endeavoured to renew his love of pleasure: he neglected their officiousness, repulsed their invitations, and spent day after day on the banks of rivulets sheltered with trees, where he sometimes listened to the birds in the branches, sometimes observed the fish playing in the stream, and anon cast his eyes upon the pastures and mountains filled with animals, of which some were biting the herbage, and some sleeping among the bushes.

This singularity of his humour made him much observed. One of the Sages, in whose conversation he had formerly delighted, followed him secretly, in hope of discovering the cause of his disquiet. Rasselas, who knew not that any one was near him, having for some time fixed his eyes upon the goats that were brousing among the rocks, began to compare their condition with his own.

'What,' said he, 'makes the difference between man and all the rest of the animal creation? Every beast that strays beside me has the same corporal necessities with myself; he is hungry and crops the grass, he is thirsty and drinks the stream, his thirst and hunger are appeased, he is satisfied and sleeps; he rises again and is hungry, he is again fed and is at rest. I am hungry and thirsty like him, but when thirst and hunger cease I am not at rest; I am, like him, pained with want, but am not, like him, satisfied with fulness. The intermediate hours are tedious and gloomy; I long again to be hungry that I may again quicken my attention. The birds peck the berries or the corn, and fly away to the groves where they sit in seeming happiness on the branches, and waste their lives in tuning one unvaried series of sounds. I likewise can call the lutanist and the singer, but the sounds that pleased me yester-day weary me to day, and will grow yet more wearisome to morrow. I can discover within me no power of perception which is not glutted with its proper pleasure, yet I do not feel myself delighted. Man has surely some latent sense for which this place affords no gratification, or he has some desires distinct from sense which must be satisfied before he can be happy.'

After this he lifted up his head, and seeing the moon rising, walked towards the palace. As he passed through the fields, and saw the animals around him, 'Ye, said he, are happy, and need not envy me that walk thus among you, burthened with myself; nor do I, ye gentle beings, envy your felicity; for it is not the felicity of man. I have many distresses from which ye are free; I fear pain when I do not feel it; I sometimes shrink at evils recollected, and sometimes start at evils anticipated: surely the equity of providence has ballanced peculiar suffer-ings with peculiar enjoyments.'

With observations like these the prince amused himself as he returned, uttering them with a plaintive voice, yet with a look that discovered him to feel some complacence in his own perspicacity, and to receive some solace of the miseries of life, from consciousness of the delicacy with which he felt, and the eloquence with which he bewailed them. He mingled cheerfully in the diversions of the evening, and all rejoiced to find that his heart was lightened.

CHAP. III

The wants of him that wants nothing

On the next day his old instructor, imagining that he had now made himself acquainted with his disease of mind, was in hope of curing it by counsel, and officiously sought an opportunity of conference, which the prince, having long considered him as one whose intellects were exhausted, was not very willing to afford: 'Why, said he, does this man thus intrude upon me; shall I be never suffered to forget those lectures which pleased only while they were new, and to become new again must be forgotten?' He then walked into the wood, and composed himself to his usual meditations; when, before his thoughts had taken any settled form, he perceived his persuer at his side, and was at first prompted by his impatience to go hastily away; but, being unwilling to offend a man whom he had once reverenced and still loved, he invited him to sit down with him on the bank.

The old man, thus encouraged, began to lament the change which had been lately observed in the prince, and to enquire why he so often retired from the pleasures of the palace, to loneliness and silence. 'I fly from pleasure, said the prince, because pleasure has ceased to please; I am lonely because I am miserable, and am unwilling to cloud with my presence the happiness of others.' 'You, Sir, said the sage, are the first who has complained of misery in the *happy valley*. I hope to convince you that your complaints have no real cause. You are here in full possession of all that the emperour of Abissinia can bestow; here is neither labour to be endured nor danger to be dreaded, yet here is all that labour or danger can procure or purchase. Look round and tell me which of your wants is without supply: if you want nothing, how are you unhappy?'

'That I want nothing, said the prince, or that I know not what I want, is the cause of my complaint; if I had any known want, I should have a certain wish; that wish would excite endeavour, and I should not then repine to see the sun move so slowly towards the western mountain, or lament when the day breaks and sleep will no longer hide me from myself. When I see the kids and the lambs chasing one another, I fancy that I should be happy if I had something to persue. But, possessing all that I can want, I find one day and one hour exactly like another, except that the latter is still more tedious than the former. Let your experience inform me how the day may now seem as short as in my childhood, while nature was yet fresh, and every moment shewed me what I never had observed before. I have already enjoyed too much; give me something to desire.'

The old man was surprized at this new species of affliction, and knew not what to reply, yet was unwilling to be silent. 'Sir, said he, if you had seen the miseries of the world, you would know how to value your present state.' 'Now, said the prince, you have given me something to desire; I shall long to see the miseries of the world, since the sight of them is necessary to happiness.'

CHAP. IV

The prince continues to grieve and muse

At this time the sound of musick proclaimed the hour of repast, and the conversation was concluded. The old man went away sufficiently discontented to find that his reasonings had produced the only conclusion which they were intended to prevent. But in the decline of life shame and grief are of short duration; whether it be that we bear easily what we have born long, or that, finding ourselves in age less regarded, we less regard others; or, that we look with slight regard upon afflictions, to which we know that the hand of death is about to put an end.

The prince, whose views were extended to a wider space, could not speedily quiet his emotions. He had been before terrified at the length of life which nature promised him, because he considered that in a long time much must be endured; he now rejoiced in his youth, because in many years much might be done.

This first beam of hope, that had been ever darted into his mind, rekindled youth in his cheeks, and doubled the lustre of his eyes. He was fired with the desire of doing something, though he knew not yet with distinctness, either end or means.

He was now no longer gloomy and unsocial; but, considering himself as master of a secret stock of happiness, which he could enjoy only by concealing it, he affected to be busy in all schemes of diversion, and endeavoured to make others pleased with the state of which he himself was weary. But pleasures never can be so multiplied or continued, as not to leave much of life unemployed; there were many hours, both of the night and day, which he could spend without suspicion in solitary thought. The load of life was much lightened: he went eagerly into the assemblies, because he supposed the frequency of his presence necessary to the success of his purposes; he retired gladly to privacy, because he had now a subject of thought.

His chief amusement was to picture to himself that world which he had never seen; to place himself in various conditions; to be entangled in imaginary difficulties, and to be engaged in wild adventures: but his benevolence always terminated his projects in the relief of distress, the detection of fraud, the defeat of oppression, and the diffusion of happiness.

Thus passed twenty months of the life of Rasselas. He busied himself so intensely in visionary bustle, that he forgot his real solitude; and, amidst hourly preparations for the various incidents of human affairs, neglected to consider by what means he should mingle with mankind.

One day, as he was sitting on a bank, he feigned to himself an orphan virgin robbed of her little portion by a treacherous lover, and crying after him for restitution and redress. So strongly was the image impressed upon his mind, that he started up in the maid's defence, and run forward to seize the plunderer with all the eagerness of real persuit. Fear naturally quickens the flight of guilt. Rasselas could not catch the fugitive with his utmost efforts; but, resolving to weary, by perseverance, him whom he could not surpass in speed, he pressed on till the foot of the mountain stopped his course.

Here he recollected himself, and smiled at his own useless impetuosity. Then raising his eyes to the mountain, 'This, said he, is the fatal obstacle that hinders at once the enjoyment of pleasure, and the exercise of virtue. How long is it that my hopes and wishes have flown beyond this boundary of my life, which yet I never have attempted to surmount!'

Struck with this reflection, he sat down to muse, and remembered, that since he first resolved to escape from his confinement, the sun had passed twice over him in his annual course. He now felt a degree of regret with which he had never been before acquainted. He considered how much might have been done in the time which had passed, and left nothing real behind it. He compared twenty months with the life of man. 'In life, said he, is not to be counted the ignorance of infancy, or imbecility of age. We are long before we are able to think, and we soon cease from the power of acting.

The true period of human existence may be reasonably esti-
mated as forty years, of which I have mused away the four
and twentieth part. What I have lost was certain, for I have
certainly possessed it; but of twenty months to come who
can assure me?'

The consciousness of his own folly pierced him deeply, and
he was long before he could be reconciled to himself. 'The
rest of my time, said he, has been lost by the crime or folly of
my ancestors, and the absurd institutions of my country; I
remember it with disgust, yet without remorse: but the
months that have passed since new light darted into my soul,
since I formed a scheme of reasonable felicity, have been
squandered by my own fault. I have lost that which can never
be restored: I have seen the sun rise and set for twenty months,
an idle gazer on the light of heaven: In this time the birds
have left the nest of their mother, and committed themselves
to the woods and to the skies: the kid has forsaken the teat,
and learned by degrees to climb the rocks in quest of inde-
pendant sustenance. I only have made no advances, but am
still helpless and ignorant. The moon by more than twenty
changes, admonished me of the flux of life; the stream that
rolled before my feet upbraided my inactivity. I sat feasting
on intellectual luxury, regardless alike of the examples of the
earth, and the instructions of the planets. Twenty months are
past, who shall restore them!'

These sorrowful meditations fastened upon his mind; he
past four months in resolving to lose no more time in idle resolves, and was awakened to more vigorous exertion by
hearing a maid, who had broken a porcelain cup, remark,
that what cannot be repaired is not to be regretted.

This was obvious; and Rasselas reproached himself that he
had not discovered it, having not known, or not considered,
how many useful hints are obtained by chance, and how often

the mind, hurried by her own ardour to distant views, neg-
lects the truths that lie open before her. He, for a few hours,
regretted his regret, and from that time bent his whole mind
upon the means of escaping from the valley of happiness.

CHAP. V

The prince meditates his escape

HE now found that it would be very difficult to effect that
which it was very easy to suppose effected. When he looked
round about him, he saw himself confined by the bars of
nature which had never yet been broken, and by the gate,
through which none that once had passed it were ever able to
return. He was now impatient as an eagle in a grate. He passed
week after week in clambering the mountains, to see if there
was any aperture which the bushes might conceal, but found
all the summits inaccessible by their prominence. The iron
gate he despaired to open; for it was not only secured with
all the power of art, but was always watched by successive
sentinels, and was by its position exposed to the perpetual
observation of all the inhabitants.

He then examined the cavern through which the waters of
the lake were discharged; and, looking down at a time when
the sun shone strongly upon its mouth, he discovered it to be
full of broken rocks, which, though they permitted the stream
to flow through many narrow passages, would stop any body
of solid bulk. He returned discouraged and dejected; but,
having now known the blessing of hope, resolved never to
despair.

In these fruitless searches he spent ten months. The time,
however, passed chearfully away: in the morning he rose
with new hope, in the evening applauded his own diligence,

and in the night slept sound after his fatigue. He met a thousand amusements which beguiled his labour, and diversified his thoughts. He discerned the various instincts of animals, and properties of plants, and found the place replete with wonders, of which he purposed to solace himself with the contemplation, if he should never be able to accomplish his flight; rejoicing that his endeavours, though yet unsucessful, had supplied him with a source of inexhaustible enquiry.

But his original curiosity was not yet abated; he resolved to obtain some knowledge of the ways of men. His wish still continued, but his hope grew less. He ceased to survey any longer the walls of his prison, and spared to search by new toils for interstices which he knew could not be found, yet determined to keep his design always in view, and lay hold on any expedient that time should offer.

CHAP. VI

A dissertation on the art of flying

AMONG the artists that had been allured into the happy valley, to labour for the accommodation and pleasure of its inhabitants, was a man eminent for his knowledge of the mechanick powers, who had contrived many engines both of use and recreation. By a wheel, which the stream turned, he forced the water into a tower, whence it was distributed to all the apartments of the palace. He erected a pavillion in the garden, around which he kept the air always cool by artificial showers. One of the groves, appropriated to the ladies, was ventilated by fans, to which the rivulet that run through it gave a constant motion; and instruments of soft musick were placed at proper distances, of which some played by the impulse of the wind, and some by the power of the stream.

This artist was sometimes visited by Rasselas, who was pleased with every kind of knowledge, imagining that the time would come when all his acquisitions should be of use to him in the open world. He came one day to amuse himself in his usual manner, and found the master busy in building a sailing chariot: he saw that the design was practicable upon a level surface, and with expressions of great esteem solicited its completion. The workman was pleased to find himself so much regarded by the prince, and resolved to gain yet higher honours. 'Sir, said he, you have seen but a small part of what the mechanick sciences can perform. I have been long of opinion, that, instead of the tardy conveyance of ships and chariots, man might use the swifter migration of wings; that the fields of air are open to knowledge, and that only ignorance and idleness need crawl upon the ground.'

This hint rekindled the prince's desire of passing the mountains; having seen what the mechanist had already performed, he was willing to fancy that he could do more; yet resolved to enquire further before he suffered hope to afflict him by disappointment. 'I am afraid, said he to the artist, that your imagination prevails over your skill, and that you now tell me rather what you wish than what you know. Every animal has his element assigned him; the birds have the air, and man and beasts the earth.' 'So, replied the mechanist, fishes have the water, in which yet beasts can swim by nature, and men by art. He that can swim needs not despair to fly: to swim is to fly in a grosser fluid, and to fly is to swim in a subtler. We are only to proportion our power of resistance to the different density of the matter through which we are to pass. You will be necessarily upborn by the air, if you can renew any impulse upon it, faster than the air can recede from the pressure.'

'But the exercise of swimming, said the prince, is very laborious; the strongest limbs are soon wearied; I am afraid the act of flying will be yet more violent, and wings will be of no great use, unless we can fly further than we can swim.'

'The labour of rising from the ground, said the artist, will be great, as we see it in the heavier domestick fowls; but, as we mount higher, the earth's attraction, and the body's gravity, will be gradually diminished, till we shall arrive at a region where the man will float in the air without any tendency to fall: no care will then be necessary, but to move forwards, which the gentlest impulse will effect. You, Sir, whose curiosity is so extensive, will easily conceive with what pleasure a philosopher, furnished with wings, and hovering in the sky, would see the earth, and all it's inhabitants, rolling beneath him, and presenting to him successively, by it's diurnal motion, all the countries within the same parallel. How must it amuse the pendent spectator to see the moving scene of land and ocean, cities and desarts! To survey with equal security the marts of trade, and the fields of battle; mountains infested by barbarians, and fruitful regions gladdened by plenty, and lulled by peace! How easily shall we then trace the Nile through all his passage; pass over to distant regions, and examine the face of nature from one extremity of the earth to the other!'

'All this, said the prince, is much to be desired, but I am afraid that no man will be able to breathe in these regions of speculation and tranquility. I have been told, that respiration is difficult upon lofty mountains, yet from these precipices, though so high as to produce great tenuity of the air, it is very easy to fall: therefore I suspect, that from any height, where life can be supported, there may be danger of too quick descent.'

'Nothing, replied the artist, will ever be attempted, if all possible objections must be first overcome. If you will favour my project I will try the first flight at my own hazard. I have considered the structure of all volant animals, and find the folding continuity of the bat's wings most easily accommodated to the human form. Upon this model I shall begin my task to morrow, and in a year expect to tower into the air beyond the malice or persuit of man. But I will work only on this condition, that the art shall not be divulged, and that you shall not require me to make wings for any but ourselves.'

'Why, said Rasselas, should you envy others so great an advantage? All skill ought to be exerted for universal good; every man has owed much to others, and ought to repay the kindness that he has received.'

'If men were all virtuous, returned the artist, I should with great alacrity teach them all to fly. But what would be the security of the good, if the bad could at pleasure invade them from the sky? Against an army sailing through the clouds neither walls, nor mountains, nor seas, could afford any security. A flight of northern savages might hover in the wind, and light at once with irresistible violence upon the capital of a fruitful region that was rolling under them. Even this valley, the retreat of princes, the abode of happiness, might be violated by the sudden descent of some of the naked nations that swarm on the coast of the southern sea.'

The prince promised secrecy, and waited for the performance, not wholly hopeless of success. He visited the work from time to time, observed its progress, and remarked many ingenious contrivances to facilitate motion, and unite levity with strength. The artist was every day more certain that he should leave vultures and eagles behind him, and the contagion of his confidence seized upon the prince.

In a year the wings were finished, and, on a morning appointed, the maker appeared furnished for flight on a little promontory: he waved his pinions a while to gather air, then leaped from his stand, and in an instant dropped into the lake.

His wings, which were of no use in the air, sustained him in the water, and the prince drew him to land, half dead with terrour and vexation.

CHAP. VII

The prince finds a man of learning

THE prince was not much afflicted by this disaster, having suffered himself to hope for a happier event, only because he had no other means of escape in view. He still persisted in his design to leave the happy valley by the first opportunity.

His imagination was now at a stand; he had no prospect of entering into the world; and, notwithstanding all his endeavours to support himself, discontent by degrees preyed upon him, and he began again to lose his thoughts in sadness, when the rainy season, which in these countries is periodical, made it inconvenient to wander in the woods.

The rain continued longer and with more violence than had been ever known: the clouds broke on the surrounding mountains, and the torrents streamed into the plain on every side, till the cavern was too narrow to discharge the water. The lake overflowed its banks, and all the level of the valley was covered with the inundation. The eminence, on which the palace was built, and some other spots of rising ground, were all that the eye could now discover. The herds and flocks left the pastures, and both the wild beasts and the tame retreated to the mountains.

This inundation confined all the princes to domestick amusements, and the attention of Rasselas was particularly seized by a poem, which Imlac rehearsed upon the various conditions of humanity. He commanded the poet to attend him in his apartment, and recite his verses a second time;

then entering into familiar talk, he thought himself happy in
having found a man who knew the world so well, and could
so skilfully paint the scenes of life. He asked a thousand questions about things, to which, though common to all other
mortals, his confinement from childhood had kept him a
stranger. The poet pitied his ignorance, and loved his curiosity, and entertained him from day to day with novelty and
instruction, so that the prince regretted the necessity of sleep,
and longed till the morning should renew his pleasure.

As they were sitting together, the prince commanded Imlac
to relate his history, and to tell by what accident he was
forced, or by what motive induced, to close his life in the
happy valley. As he was going to begin his narrative,
Rasselas was called to a concert, and obliged to restrain his
curiosity till the evening.

CHAP. VIII

The history of Imlac

THE close of the day is, in the regions of the torrid zone, the
only season of diversion and entertainment, and it was therefore mid-night before the musick ceased, and the princesses
retired. Rasselas then called for his companion and required
him to begin the story of his life.

'Sir, said Imlac, my history will not be long: the life that is
devoted to knowledge passes silently away, and is very little
diversified by events. To talk in publick, to think in solitude,
to read and to hear, to inquire, and answer inquiries, is the
business of a scholar. He wanders about the world without
pomp or terrour, and is neither known nor valued but by
men like himself.

'I was born in the kingdom of Goiama, at no great distance

from the fountain of the Nile. My father was a wealthy merchant, who traded between the inland countries of Africk and the ports of the red sea. He was honest, frugal and diligent, but of mean sentiments, and narrow comprehension: he desired only to be rich, and to conceal his riches, lest he should be spoiled by the governours of the province.'

'Surely, said the prince, my father must be negligent of his charge, if any man in his dominions dares take that which belongs to another. Does he not know that kings are accountable for injustice permitted as well as done? If I were emperour, not the meanest of my subjects should be oppressed with impunity. My blood boils when I am told that a merchant durst not enjoy his honest gains for fear of losing them by the rapacity of power. Name the governour who robbed the people, that I may declare his crimes to the emperour.'

'Sir, said Imlac, your ardour is the natural effect of virtue animated by youth: the time will come when you will acquit your father, and perhaps hear with less impatience of the governour. Oppression is, in the Abissinian dominions, neither frequent nor tolerated; but no form of government has been yet discovered, by which cruelty can be wholly prevented. Subordination supposes power on one part and subjection on the other; and if power be in the hands of men, it will sometimes be abused. The vigilance of the supreme magistrate may do much, but much will still remain undone. He can never know all the crimes that are committed, and can seldom punish all that he knows.'

'This, said the prince, I do not understand, but I had rather hear thee than dispute. Continue thy narration.'

'My father, proceeded Imlac, originally intended that I should have no other education, than such as might qualify me for commerce; and discovering in me great strength of memory, and quickness of apprehension, often declared his

hope that I should be some time the richest man in Abissinia.'

'Why, said the prince, did thy father desire the increase of
his wealth, when it was already greater than he durst discover
or enjoy? I am unwilling to doubt thy veracity, yet inconsistencies cannot both be true.'

'Inconsistencies, answered Imlac, cannot both be right,
but, imputed to man, they may both be true. Yet diversity is
not inconsistency. My father might expect a time of greater
security. However, some desire is necessary to keep life in
motion, and he, whose real wants are supplied, must admit
those of fancy.'

'This, said the prince, I can in some measure conceive. I
repent that I interrupted thee.'

'With this hope, proceeded Imlac, he sent me to school;
but when I had once found the delight of knowledge, and
felt the pleasure of intelligence and the pride of invention, I
began silently to despise riches, and determined to disappoint
the purpose of my father, whose grossness of conception
raised my pity. I was twenty years old before his tenderness
would expose me to the fatigue of travel, in which time I
had been instructed, by successive masters, in all the literature
of my native country. As every hour taught me something
new, I lived in a continual course of gratifications; but, as I
advanced towards manhood, I lost much of the reverence
with which I had been used to look on my instructors; because, when the lesson was ended, I did not find them wiser
or better than common men.

'At length my father resolved to initiate me in commerce,
and, opening one of his subterranean treasuries, counted out
ten thousand pieces of gold. This, young man, said he, is the
stock with which you must negociate. I began with less than
the fifth part, and you see how diligence and parsimony have

increased it. This is your own to waste or to improve. If you squander it by negligence or caprice, you must wait for my death before you will be rich: if, in four years, you double your stock, we will thenceforward let subordination cease, and live together as friends and partners; for he shall always be equal with me, who is equally skilled in the art of growing rich.

'We laid our money upon camels, concealed in bales of cheap goods, and travelled to the shore of the red sea. When I cast my eye on the expanse of waters my heart bounded like that of a prisoner escaped. I felt an unextinguishable curiosity kindle in my mind, and resolved to snatch this opportunity of seeing the manners of other nations, and of learning sciences unknown in Abissinia.

'I remembered that my father had obliged me to the improvement of my stock, not by a promise which I ought not to violate, but by a penalty which I was at liberty to incur; and therefore determined to gratify my predominant desire, and by drinking at the fountains of knowledge, to quench the thirst of curiosity.

'As I was supposed to trade without connexion with my father, it was easy for me to become acquainted with the master of a ship, and procure a passage to some other country. I had no motives of choice to regulate my voyage; it was sufficient for me that, wherever I wandered, I should see a country which I had not seen before. I therefore entered a ship bound for Surat, having left a letter for my father declaring my intention.

CHAP. IX

The history of Imlac continued

'WHEN I first entered upon the world of waters, and lost sight of land, I looked round about me with pleasing terrour, and thinking my soul enlarged by the boundless prospect, imagined that I could gaze round for ever without satiety; but, in a short time, I grew weary of looking on barren uniformity, where I could only see again what I had already seen. I then descended into the ship, and doubted for a while whether all my future pleasures would not end like this in disgust and disappointment. Yet, surely, said I, the ocean and the land are very different; the only variety of water is rest and motion, but the earth has mountains and vallies, desarts and cities: it is inhabited by men of different customs and contrary opinions; and I may hope to find variety in life, though I should miss it in nature.

'With this thought I quieted my mind; and amused myself during the voyage, sometimes by learning from the sailors the art of navigation, which I have never practised, and sometimes by forming schemes for my conduct in different situations, in not one of which I have been ever placed.

'I was almost weary of my naval amusements when we landed safely at Surat. I secured my money, and purchasing some commodities for show, joined myself to a caravan that was passing into the inland country. My companions, for some reason or other, conjecturing that I was rich, and, by my inquiries and admiration, finding that I was ignorant, considered me as a novice whom they had a right to cheat, and who was to learn at the usual expence the art of fraud. They exposed me to the theft of servants, and the exaction of officers, and saw me plundered upon false pretences, without any advantage to themselves, but that of rejoicing in the superiority of their own knowledge.'

'Stop a moment, said the prince. Is there such depravity in man, as that he should injure another without benefit to himself? I can easily conceive that all are pleased with superiority; but your ignorance was merely accidental, which, being neither your crime nor your folly, could afford them no reason to applaud themselves; and the knowledge which they had, and which you wanted, they might as effectually have shewn by warning, as betraying you.'

'Pride, said Imlac, is seldom delicate, it will please itself with very mean advantages; and envy feels not its own happiness, but when it may be compared with the misery of others. They were my enemies because they grieved to think me rich, and my oppressors because they delighted to find me weak.'

'Proceed, said the prince: I doubt not of the facts which you relate, but imagine that you impute them to mistaken motives.'

'In this company, said Imlac, I arrived at Agra, the capital of Indostan, the city in which the great Mogul commonly resides. I applied myself to the language of the country, and in a few months was able to converse with the learned men; some of whom I found morose and reserved, and others easy and communicative; some were unwilling to teach another what they had with difficulty learned themselves; and some shewed that the end of their studies was to gain the dignity of instructing.

'To the tutor of the young princes I recommended myself so much, that I was presented to the emperour as a man of uncommon knowledge. The emperour asked me many questions concerning my country and my travels; and though I cannot now recollect any thing that he uttered above the power of a common man, he dismissed me astonished at his wisdom, and enamoured of his goodness.

'My credit was now so high, that the merchants, with whom I had travelled, applied to me for recommendations to the ladies of the court. I was surprised at their confidence of solicitation, and gently reproached them with their practices on the road. They heard me with cold indifference, and shewed no tokens of shame or sorrow.

'They then urged their request with the offer of a bribe; but what I would not do for kindness I would not do for money; and refused them, not because they had injured me, but because I would not enable them to injure others; for I knew they would have made use of my credit to cheat those who should buy their wares.

'Having resided at Agra till there was no more to be learned, I travelled into Persia, where I saw many remains of ancient magnificence, and observed many new accommodations of life. The Persians are a nation eminently social, and their assemblies afforded me daily opportunities of remarking characters and manners, and of tracing human nature through all its variations.

'From Persia I passed into Arabia, where I saw a nation at once pastoral and warlike; who live without any settled habitation; whose only wealth is their flocks and herds; and who have yet carried on, through all ages, an hereditary war with all mankind, though they neither covet nor envy their possessions.

CHAP. X

Imlac's history continued. A dissertation upon poetry

'WHEREVER I went, I found that Poetry was considered as the highest learning, and regarded with a veneration somewhat approaching to that which man would pay to the Angelick Nature. And it yet fills me with wonder, that, in almost all countries, the most ancient poets are considered as the best: whether it be that every other kind of knowledge is an acquisition gradually attained, and poetry is a gift conferred at once; or that the first poetry of every nation surprised them as a novelty, and retained the credit by consent which it received by accident at first: or whether, as the province of poetry is to describe Nature and Passion, which are always the same, the first writers took possession of the most striking objects for description, and the most probable occurrences for fiction, and left nothing to those that followed them, but transcription of the same events, and new combinations of the same images. Whatever be the reason, it is commonly observed that the early writers are in possession of nature, and their followers of art: that the first excel in strength and invention, and the latter in elegance and refinement.

'I was desirous to add my name to this illustrious fraternity. I read all the poets of Persia and Arabia, and was able to repeat by memory the volumes that are suspended in the mosque of Mecca. But I soon found that no man was ever great by imitation. My desire of excellence impelled me to transfer my attention to nature and to life. Nature was to be my subject, and men to be my auditors: I could never describe what I had not seen: I could not hope to move those with delight or terrour, whose interests and opinions I did not understand.

'Being now resolved to be a poet, I saw every thing with a new purpose; my sphere of attention was suddenly magnified: no kind of knowledge was to be overlooked. I ranged mountains and deserts for images and resemblances, and pictured upon my mind every tree of the forest and flower of the valley. I observed with equal care the crags of the rock and the pinnacles of the palace. Sometimes I wandered along the mazes of the rivulet, and sometimes watched the changes of the summer clouds. To a poet nothing can be useless. Whatever is beautiful, and whatever is dreadful, must be familiar to his imagination: he must be conversant with all that is awfully vast or elegantly little. The plants of the garden, the animals of the wood, the minerals of the earth, and meteors of the sky, must all concur to store his mind with inexhaustible variety: for every idea is useful for the inforcement or decoration of moral or religious truth; and he, who knows most, will have most power of diversifying his scenes, and of gratifying his reader with remote allusions and unexpected instruction.

'All the appearances of nature I was therefore careful to study, and every country which I have surveyed has contributed something to my poetical powers.'

'In so wide a survey, said the prince, you must surely have left much unobserved. I have lived, till now, within the circuit of these mountains, and yet cannot walk abroad without the sight of something which I had never beheld before, or never heeded.'

'The business of a poet, said Imlac, is to examine, not the individual, but the species; to remark general properties and large appearances: he does not number the streaks of the tulip, or describe the different shades in the verdure of the forest. He is to exhibit in his portraits of nature such prominent and striking features, as recal the original to every mind; and must neglect the minuter discriminations, which one may have remarked, and another have neglected, for those characteristicks which are alike obvious to vigilance and carelessness.

'But the knowledge of nature is only half the task of a poet; he must be acquainted likewise with all the modes of life. His character requires that he estimate the happiness and misery of every condition; observe the power of all the passions in all their combinations, and trace the changes of the human mind as they are modified by various institutions and accidental influences of climate or custom, from the spriteliness of infancy to the despondence of decrepitude. He must divest himself of the prejudices of his age or country; he must consider right and wrong in their abstracted and invariable state; he must disregard present laws and opinions, and rise to general and transcendental truths, which will always be the same: he must therefore content himself with the slow progress of his name; contemn the applause of his own time, and commit his claims to the justice of posterity. He must write as the interpreter of nature, and the legislator of mankind, and consider himself as presiding over the thoughts and manners of future generations; as a being superiour to time and place.

'His labour is not yet at an end: he must know many languages and many sciences; and, that his stile may be worthy of his thoughts, must, by incessant practice, familiarize to himself every delicacy of speech and grace of harmony.'

CHAP. XI

Imlac's narrative continued. A hint on pilgrimage

IMLAC now felt the enthusiastic fit, and was proceeding to aggrandize his own profession, when the prince cried out, 'Enough! Thou hast convinced me, that no human being can ever be a poet. Proceed with thy narration.'

'To be a poet, said Imlac, is indeed very difficult.' 'So difficult, returned the prince, that I will at present hear no more of his labours. Tell me whither you went when you had seen Persia.'

'From Persia, said the poet, I travelled through Syria, and for three years resided in Palestine, where I conversed with great numbers of the northern and western nations of Europe; the nations which are now in possession of all power and all knowledge; whose armies are irresistible, and whose fleets command the remotest parts of the globe. When I compared these men with the natives of our own kingdom, and those that surround us, they appeared almost another order of beings. In their countries it is difficult to wish for any thing that may not be obtained: a thousand arts, of which we never heard, are continually labouring for their convenience and pleasure; and whatever their own climate has denied them is supplied by their commerce.'

'By what means, said the prince, are the Europeans thus powerful? or why, since they can so easily visit Asia and Africa for trade or conquest, cannot the Asiaticks and Africans invade their coasts, plant colonies in their ports, and give laws to their natural princes? The same wind that carries them back would bring us thither.'

'They are more powerful, Sir, than we, answered Imlac,

because they are wiser; knowledge will always predominate over ignorance, as man governs the other animals. But why their knowledge is more than ours, I know not what reason can be given, but the unsearchable will of the Supreme Being.'

'When, said the prince with a sigh, shall I be able to visit Palestine, and mingle with this mighty confluence of nations? Till that happy moment shall arrive, let me fill up the time with such representations as thou canst give me. I am not ignorant of the motive that assembles such numbers in that place, and cannot but consider it as the center of wisdom and piety, to which the best and wisest men of every land must be continually resorting.'

'There are some nations, said Imlac, that send few visitants to Palestine; for many numerous and learned sects in Europe, concur to censure pilgrimage as superstitious, or deride it as ridiculous.'

'You know, said the prince, how little my life has made me acquainted with diversity of opinions: it will be too long to hear the arguments on both sides; you, that have considered them, tell me the result.'

'Pilgrimage, said Imlac, like many other acts of piety, may be reasonable or superstitious, according to the principles upon which it is performed. Long journies in search of truth are not commanded. Truth, such as is necessary to the regulation of life, is always found where it is honestly sought. Change of place is no natural cause of the increase of piety, for it inevitably produces dissipation of mind. Yet, since men go every day to view the fields where great actions have been performed, and return with stronger impressions of the event, curiosity of the same kind may naturally dispose us to view that country whence our religion had its beginning; and I believe no man surveys those awful scenes without some confirmation of holy resolutions. That the Supreme Being may be more easily propitiated in one place than in another, is the dream of idle superstition; but that some places may operate upon our own minds in an uncommon manner, is an opinion which hourly experience will justify. He who supposes that his vices may be more successfully combated in Palestine, will, perhaps, find himself mistaken, yet he may go thither without folly: he who thinks they will be more freely pardoned, dishonours at once his reason and religion.'

'These, said the prince, are European distinctions. I will consider them another time. What have you found to be the effect of knowledge? Are those nations happier than we?'

'There is so much infelicity, said the poet, in the world, that scarce any man has leisure from his own distresses to estimate the comparative happiness of others. Knowledge is certainly one of the means of pleasure, as is confessed by the natural desire which every mind feels of increasing its ideas. Ignorance is mere privation, by which nothing can be produced: it is a vacuity in which the soul sits motionless and torpid for want of attraction; and, without knowing why, we always rejoice when we learn, and grieve when we forget. I am therefore inclined to conclude, that, if nothing counteracts the natural consequence of learning, we grow more happy as our minds take a wider range.

'In enumerating the particular comforts of life we shall find many advantages on the side of the Europeans. They cure wounds and diseases with which we languish and perish. We suffer inclemencies of weather which they can obviate. They have engines for the despatch of many laborious works, which we must perform by manual industry. There is such communication between distant places, that one friend can hardly be said to be absent from another. Their policy removes all publick inconveniencies: they have roads cut through their mountains, and bridges laid upon their rivers. And, if we descend to the privacies of life, their habitations are more commodious, and their possessions are more secure.'

'They are surely happy, said the prince, who have all these conveniencies, of which I envy none so much as the facility with which separated friends interchange their thoughts.'

'The Europeans, answered Imlac, are less unhappy than we, but they are not happy. Human life is every where a state in which much is to be endured, and little to be enjoyed.'

CHAP. XII

The story of Imlac continued

'I AM not yet willing, said the prince, to suppose that happiness is so parsimoniously distributed to mortals; nor can believe but that, if I had the choice of life, I should be able to fill every day with pleasure. I would injure no man, and should provoke no resentment: I would relieve every distress, and should enjoy the benedictions of gratitude. I would choose my friends among the wise, and my wife among the virtuous; and therefore should be in no danger from treachery, or unkindness. My children should, by my care, be learned and pious, and would repay to my age what their childhood had received. What would dare to molest him who might call on every side to thousands enriched by his bounty, or assisted by his power? And why should not life glide quietly away in the soft reciprocation of protection and reverence? All this may be done without the help of European refinements, which appear by their effects to be rather specious than useful. Let us leave them and persue our journey.'

'From Palestine, said Imlac, I passed through many regions of Asia; in the more civilized kingdoms as a trader, and among the Barbarians of the mountains as a pilgrim. At last I began to long for my native country, that I might repose after my travels, and fatigues, in the places where I had spent my earliest years, and gladden my old companions with the recital of my adventures. Often did I figure to myself those, with whom I had sported away the gay hours of dawning life, sitting round me in its evening, wondering at my tales, and listening to my counsels.

'When this thought had taken possession of my mind, I considered every moment as wasted which did not bring me nearer to Abissinia. I hastened into Egypt, and, notwithstanding my impatience, was detained ten months in the contemplation of its ancient magnificence, and in enquiries after the remains of its ancient learning. I found in Cairo a mixture of all nations; some brought thither by the love of knowledge, some by the hope of gain, and many by the desire of living after their own manner without observation, and of lying hid in the obscurity of multitudes: for, in a city, populous as Cairo, it is possible to obtain at the same time the gratifications of society, and the secrecy of solitude.

'From Cairo I travelled to Suez, and embarked on the Red sea, passing along the coast till I arrived at the port from which I had departed twenty years before. Here I joined myself to a caravan and re-entered my native country.

'I now expected the caresses of my kinsmen, and the congratulations of my friends, and was not without hope that my father, whatever value he had set upon riches, would own with gladness and pride a son who was able to add to the felicity and honour of the nation. But I was soon convinced that my thoughts were vain. My father had been dead fourteen years, having divided his wealth among my brothers, who were removed to some other provinces. Of my companions the greater part was in the grave, of the rest some could with difficulty remember me, and some considered me as one corrupted by foreign manners.

'A man used to vicissitudes is not easily dejected. I forgot, after a time, my disappointment, and endeavoured to recommend myself to the nobles of the kingdom: they admitted me to their tables, heard my story, and dismissed me. I opened a school, and was prohibited to teach. I then resolved to sit down in the quiet of domestick life, and addressed a lady that was fond of my conversation, but rejected my suit, because my father was a merchant.

'Wearied at last with solicitation and repulses, I resolved to hide myself for ever from the world, and depend no longer on the opinion or caprice of others. I waited for the time when the gate of the *happy valley* should open, that I might bid farewell to hope and fear: the day came; my performance was distinguished with favour, and I resigned myself with joy to perpetual confinement.'

'Hast thou here found happiness at last? said Rasselas. Tell me without reserve; art thou content with thy condition? or, dost thou wish to be again wandering and inquiring? All the inhabitants of this valley celebrate their lot, and, at the annual visit of the emperour, invite others to partake of their felicity.'

'Great prince, said Imlac, I shall speak the truth: I know not one of all your attendants who does not lament the hour when he entered this retreat. I am less unhappy than the rest, because I have a mind replete with images, which I can vary and combine at pleasure. I can amuse my solitude by the renovation of the knowledge which begins to fade from my memory, and by recollection of the accidents of my past life. Yet all this ends in the sorrowful consideration, that my acquirements are now useless, and that none of my pleasures can be again enjoyed. The rest, whose minds have no impression but of the present moment, are either corroded by malignant passions, or sit stupid in the gloom of perpetual vacancy.'

'What passions can infest those, said the prince, who have no rivals? We are in a place where impotence precludes malice, and where all envy is repressed by community of enjoyments.'

'There may be community, said Imlac, of material possessions, but there can never be community of love or of esteem. It must happen that one will please more than another; he that knows himself despised will always be envious; and still more envious and malevolent, if he is condemned to live in the presence of those who despise him. The invitations, by which they allure others to a state which they feel to be wretched, proceed from the natural malignity of hopeless misery. They are weary of themselves, and of each other, and expect to find relief in new companions. They envy the liberty which their folly has forfeited, and would gladly see all mankind imprisoned like themselves.

'From this crime, however, I am wholly free. No man can say that he is wretched by my persuasion. I look with pity on the crowds who are annually soliciting admission to captivity, and wish that it were lawful for me to warn them of their danger.'

'My dear Imlac, said the prince, I will open to thee my whole heart. I have long meditated an escape from the happy valley. I have examined the mountains on every side, but find myself insuperably barred: teach me the way to break my prison; thou shalt be the companion of my flight, the guide of my rambles, the partner of my fortune, and my sole director in the *choice of life*.'

'Sir, answered the poet, your escape will be difficult, and, perhaps, you may soon repent your curiosity. The world, which you figure to yourself smooth and quiet as the lake in the valley, you will find a sea foaming with tempests, and boiling with whirlpools: you will be sometimes overwhelmed by the waves of violence, and sometimes dashed against the rocks of treachery. Amidst wrongs and frauds, competitions and anxieties, you will wish a thousand times for these seats of quiet, and willingly quit hope to be free from fear.'

'Do not seek to deter me from my purpose, said the prince: I am impatient to see what thou hast seen; and, since thou art thyself weary of the valley, it is evident, that thy former state was better than this. Whatever be the consequence of my experiment, I am resolved to judge with my own eyes of the various conditions of men, and then to make deliberately my *choice of life.*'

'I am afraid, said Imlac, you are hindered by stronger restraints than my persuasions; yet, if your determination is fixed, I do not counsel you to despair. Few things are impossible to diligence and skill.'

CHAP. XIII

Rasselas discovers the means of escape

THE prince now dismissed his favourite to rest, but the narrative of wonders and novelties filled his mind with perturbation. He revolved all that he had heard, and prepared innumerable questions for the morning.

Much of his uneasiness was now removed. He had a friend to whom he could impart his thoughts, and whose experience could assist him in his designs. His heart was no longer condemned to swell with silent vexation. He thought that even the *happy valley* might be endured with such a companion, and that, if they could range the world together, he should have nothing further to desire.

In a few days the water was discharged, and the ground dried. The prince and Imlac then walked out together to converse without the notice of the rest. The prince, whose thoughts were always on the wing, as he passed by the gate, said, with a countenance of sorrow, 'Why art thou so strong, and why is man so weak?'

'Man is not weak, answered his companion; knowledge is more than equivalent to force. The master of mechanicks laughs at strength. I can burst the gate, but cannot do it secretly. Some other expedient must be tried.'

As they were walking on the side of the mountain, they observed that the conies, which the rain had driven from their burrows, had taken shelter among the bushes, and formed holes behind them, tending upwards in an oblique line. 'It has been the opinion of antiquity, said Imlac, that human reason borrowed many arts from the instinct of animals; let us, therefore, not think ourselves degraded by learning from the coney. We may escape by piercing the mountain in the same direction. We will begin where the summit hangs over the middle part, and labour upward till we shall issue out beyond the prominence.'

The eyes of the prince, when he heard this proposal, sparkled with joy. The execution was easy, and the success certain.

No time was now lost. They hastened early in the morning to chuse a place proper for their mine. They clambered with great fatigue among crags and brambles, and returned without having discovered any part that favoured their design. The second and the third day were spent in the same manner, and with the same frustration. But, on the fourth, they found a small cavern, concealed by a thicket, where they resolved to make their experiment.

Imlac procured instruments proper to hew stone and remove earth, and they fell to their work on the next day with more eagerness than vigour. They were presently exhausted by their efforts, and sat down to pant upon the grass. The prince, for a moment, appeared to be discouraged. 'Sir, said his companion, practice will enable us to continue our labour for a longer time; mark, however, how far we have advanced, and you will find that our toil will some time have an end. Great works are performed, not by strength, but perseverance: yonder palace was raised by single stones, yet you see its height and spaciousness. He that shall walk with vigour three hours a day will pass in seven years a space equal to the circumference of the globe.'

They returned to their work day after day, and, in a short time, found a fissure in the rock, which enabled them to pass far with very little obstruction. This Rasselas considered as a good omen. 'Do not disturb your mind, said Imlac, with other hopes or fears than reason may suggest: if you are pleased with prognosticks of good, you will be terrified likewise with tokens of evil, and your whole life will be a prey to superstition. Whatever facilitates our work is more than an omen, it is a cause of success. This is one of those pleasing surprises which often happen to active resolution. Many things difficult to design prove easy to performance.'

CHAP. XIV

Rasselas and Imlac receive an unexpected visit

THEY had now wrought their way to the middle, and solaced their toil with the approach of liberty, when the prince, coming down to refresh himself with air, found his sister Nekayah standing before the mouth of the cavity. He started and stood confused, afraid to tell his design, and yet hopeless to conceal it. A few moments determined him to repose on her fidelity, and secure her secrecy by a declaration without reserve.

'Do not imagine, said the princess, that I came hither as a spy: I had long observed from my window, that you and Imlac directed your walk every day towards the same point, but I did not suppose you had any better reason for the preference than a cooler shade, or more fragrant bank; nor followed you with any other design than to partake of your conversation. Since then not suspicion but fondness has detected you, let me not lose the advantage of my discovery. I am equally weary of confinement with yourself, and not less desirous of knowing what is done or suffered in the world. Permit me to fly with you from this tasteless tranquility, which will yet grow more loathsome when you have left me. You may deny me to accompany you, but cannot hinder me from following.'

The prince, who loved Nekayah above his other sisters, had no inclination to refuse her request, and grieved that he had lost an opportunity of shewing his confidence by a voluntary communication. It was therefore agreed that she should leave the valley with them; and that, in the mean time, she should watch, lest any other straggler should, by chance or curiosity, follow them to the mountain.

At length their labour was at an end; they saw light beyond the prominence, and, issuing to the top of the mountain, beheld the Nile, yet a narrow current, wandering beneath them.

The prince looked round with rapture, anticipated all the pleasures of travel, and in thought was already transported beyond his father's dominions. Imlac, though very joyful at his escape, had less expectation of pleasure in the world, which he had before tried, and of which he had been weary.

Rasselas was so much delighted with a wider horizon, that he could not soon be persuaded to return into the valley. He informed his sister that the way was open, and that nothing now remained but to prepare for their departure.

CHAP. XV

The prince and princess leave the valley, and see many wonders

THE prince and princess had jewels sufficient to make them rich whenever they came into a place of commerce, which, by Imlac's direction, they hid in their cloaths, and, on the night of the next full moon, all left the valley. The princess was followed only by a single favourite, who did not know whither she was going.

They clambered through the cavity, and began to go down on the other side. The princess and her maid turned their eyes towards every part, and, seeing nothing to bound their prospect, considered themselves as in danger of being lost in a dreary vacuity. They stopped and trembled. 'I am almost afraid, said the princess, to begin a journey of which I cannot

perceive an end, and to venture into this immense plain where
I may be approached on every side by men whom I never
saw.' The prince felt nearly the same emotions, though he
thought it more manly to conceal them.

Imlac smiled at their terrours, and encouraged them to
proceed; but the princess continued irresolute till she had
been imperceptibly drawn forward too far to return.

In the morning they found some shepherds in the field,
who set milk and fruits before them. The princess wondered
that she did not see a palace ready for her reception, and a
table spread with delicacies; but, being faint and hungry, she
drank the milk and eat the fruits, and thought them of a
higher flavour than the products of the valley.

They travelled forward by easy journeys, being all unaccustomed to toil or difficulty, and knowing, that though they
might be missed, they could not be persued. In a few days
they came into a more populous region, where Imlac was
diverted with the admiration which his companions expressed at the diversity of manners, stations and employments.

Their dress was such as might not bring upon them the
suspicion of having any thing to conceal, yet the prince,
wherever he came, expected to be obeyed, and the princess
was frighted, because those that came into her presence
did not prostrate themselves before her. Imlac was forced to
observe them with great vigilance, lest they should betray
their rank by their unusual behaviour, and detained them
several weeks in the first village to accustom them to the
sight of common mortals.

By degrees the royal wanderers were taught to understand
that they had for a time laid aside their dignity, and were to
expect only such regard as liberality and courtesy could procure. And Imlac, having, by many admonitions, prepared
them to endure the tumults of a port, and the ruggedness of

the commercial race, brought them down to the sea-coast.

The prince and his sister, to whom every thing was new, were gratified equally at all places, and therefore remained for some months at the port without any inclination to pass further. Imlac was content with their stay, because he did not think it safe to expose them, unpractised in the world, to the hazards of a foreign country.

At last he began to fear lest they should be discovered, and proposed to fix a day for their departure. They had no pretensions to judge for themselves, and referred the whole scheme to his direction. He therefore took passage in a ship to Suez; and, when the time came, with great difficulty prevailed on the princess to enter the vessel. They had a quick and prosperous voyage, and from Suez travelled by land to Cairo.

CHAP. XVI

They enter Cairo, and find every man happy

As they approached the city, which filled the strangers with astonishment, 'This, said Imlac to the prince, is the place where travellers and merchants assemble from all the corners of the earth. You will here find men of every character, and every occupation. Commerce is here honourable: I will act as a merchant, and you shall live as strangers, who have no other end of travel than curiosity; it will soon be observed that we are rich; our reputation will procure us access to all whom we shall desire to know; you will see all the conditions of humanity, and enable yourself at leisure to make your *choice of life*.'

They now entered the town, stunned by the noise, and offended by the crowds. Instruction had not yet so prevailed over habit, but that they wondered to see themselves pass undistinguished along the street, and met by the lowest of the people without reverence or notice. The princess could not at first bear the thought of being levelled with the vulgar, and, for some days, continued in her chamber, where she was served by her favourite Pekuah as in the palace of the valley.

Imlac, who understood traffick, sold part of the jewels the next day, and hired a house, which he adorned with such magnificence, that he was immediately considered as a merchant of great wealth. His politeness attracted many acquaintance, and his generosity made him courted by many dependants. His table was crowded by men of every nation, who all admired his knowledge, and solicited his favour. His companions, not being able to mix in the conversation, could make no discovery of their ignorance or surprise, and were gradually initiated in the world as they gained knowledge of the language.

The prince had, by frequent lectures, been taught the use and nature of money; but the ladies could not, for a long time, comprehend what the merchants did with small pieces of gold and silver, or why things of so little use should be received as equivalent to the necessaries of life.

They studied the language two years, while Imlac was preparing to set before them the various ranks and conditions of mankind. He grew acquainted with all who had any thing uncommon in their fortune or conduct. He frequented the voluptuous and the frugal, the idle and the busy, the merchants and the men of learning.

The prince, being now able to converse with fluency, and having learned the caution necessary to be observed in his intercourse with strangers, began to accompany Imlac to places of resort, and to enter into all assemblies, that he might make his *choice of life*.

For some time he thought choice needless, because all appeared to him equally happy. Wherever he went he met gayety and kindness, and heard the song of joy, or the laugh of carelessness. He began to believe that the world over-flowed with universal plenty, and that nothing was withheld either from want or merit; that every hand showered liberal-ity, and every heart melted with benevolence: 'and who then, says he, will be suffered to be wretched?'

Imlac permitted the pleasing delusion, and was unwilling to crush the hope of inexperience; till one day, having sat a while silent, 'I know not, said the prince, what can be the reason that I am more unhappy than any of our friends. I see them perpetually and unalterably chearful, but feel my own mind restless and uneasy. I am unsatisfied with those pleasures which I seem most to court; I live in the crowds of jollity, not so much to enjoy company as to shun myself, and am only loud and merry to conceal my sadness.'

'Every man, said Imlac, may, by examining his own mind, guess what passes in the minds of others: when you feel that your own gaiety is counterfeit, it may justly lead you to suspect that of your companions not to be sincere. Envy is commonly reciprocal. We are long before we are convinced that happiness is never to be found, and each believes it pos-sessed by others, to keep alive the hope of obtaining it for himself. In the assembly, where you passed the last night, there appeared such spriteliness of air, and volatility of fancy, as might have suited beings of an higher order, formed to inhabit serener regions inaccessible to care or sorrow: yet, believe me, prince, there was not one who did not dread the moment when solitude should deliver him to the tyranny of reflection.'

'This, said the prince, may be true of others, since it is true of me; yet, whatever be the general infelicity of man, one condition is more happy than another, and wisdom surely directs us to take the least evil in the *choice of life*.'

'The causes of good and evil, answered Imlac, are so various and uncertain, so often entangled with each other, so diversified by various relations, and so much subject to accidents which cannot be foreseen, that he who would fix his condition upon incontestable reasons of preference, must live and die inquiring and deliberating.'

'But surely, said Rasselas, the wise men, to whom we listen with reverence and wonder, chose that mode of life for themselves which they thought most likely to make them happy.'

'Very few, said the poet, live by choice. Every man is placed in his present condition by causes which acted without his foresight, and with which he did not always willingly co-operate; and therefore you will rarely meet one who does not think the lot of his neighbour better than his own.'

'I am pleased to think, said the prince, that my birth has given me at least one advantage over others, by enabling me to determine for myself. I have here the world before me; I will review it at leisure: surely happiness is somewhere to be found.'

CHAP. XVII

The prince associates with young men of spirit and gaiety

RASSELAS rose next day, and resolved to begin his experiments upon life. 'Youth, cried he, is the time of gladness: I will join myself to the young men, whose only business is to gratify their desires, and whose time is all spent in a succession of enjoyments.'

To such societies he was readily admitted, but a few days brought him back weary and disgusted. Their mirth was without images, their laughter without motive; their pleasures were gross and sensual, in which the mind had no part; their conduct was at once wild and mean; they laughed at order and at law, but the frown of power dejected, and the eye of wisdom abashed them.

The prince soon concluded, that he should never be happy in a course of life of which he was ashamed. He thought it unsuitable to a reasonable being to act without a plan, and to be sad or chearful only by chance. 'Happiness, said he, must be something solid and permanent, without fear and without uncertainty.'

But his young companions had gained so much of his regard by their frankness and courtesy, that he could not leave them without warning and remonstrance. 'My friends, said he, I have seriously considered our manners and our prospects, and find that we have mistaken our own interest. The first years of man must make provision for the last. He that never thinks never can be wise. Perpetual levity must end in ignorance; and intemperance, though it may fire the spirits for an hour, will make life short or miserable. Let us consider that youth is of no long duration, and that in maturer age, when the enchantments of fancy shall cease, and phantoms of delight dance no more about us, we shall have no comforts but the esteem of wise men, and the means of doing good. Let us, therefore, stop, while to stop is in our power: let us live as men who are sometime to grow old, and to whom it will be the most dreadful of all evils not to count their past years but by follies, and to be reminded of their former luxuriance of health only by the maladies which riot has produced.'

They stared a while in silence one upon another, and, at

last, drove him away by a general chorus of continued laughter.

The consciousness that his sentiments were just, and his intentions kind, was scarcely sufficient to support him against the horrour of derision. But he recovered his tranquility, and persued his search.

CHAP. XVIII

The prince finds a wise and happy man

As he was one day walking in the street, he saw a spacious building which all were, by the open doors, invited to enter: he followed the stream of people, and found it a hall or school of declamation, in which professors read lectures to their auditory. He fixed his eye upon a sage raised above the rest, who discoursed with great energy on the government of the passions. His look was venerable, his action graceful, his pronunciation clear, and his diction elegant. He shewed, with great strength of sentiment, and variety of illustration, that human nature is degraded and debased, when the lower faculties predominate over the higher; that when fancy, the parent of passion, usurps the dominion of the mind, nothing ensues but the natural effect of unlawful government, perturbation and confusion; that she betrays the fortresses of the intellect to rebels, and excites her children to sedition against reason their lawful sovereign. He compared reason to the sun, of which the light is constant, uniform, and lasting; and fancy to a meteor, of bright but transitory lustre, irregular in its motion, and delusive in its direction.

He then communicated the various precepts given from time to time for the conquest of passion, and displayed the happiness of those who had obtained the important victory, after which man is no longer the slave of fear, nor the fool of hope; is no more emaciated by envy, inflamed by anger, emasculated by tenderness, or depressed by grief; but walks on calmly through the tumults or the privacies of life, as the sun persues alike his course through the calm or the stormy sky.

He enumerated many examples of heroes immovable by pain or pleasure, who looked with indifference on those modes or accidents to which the vulgar give the names of good and evil. He exhorted his hearers to lay aside their prejudices, and arm themselves against the shafts of malice or misfortune, by invulnerable patience; concluding, that this state only was happiness, and that this happiness was in every one's power.

Rasselas listened to him with the veneration due to the instructions of a superior being, and, waiting for him at the door, humbly implored the liberty of visiting so great a master of true wisdom. The lecturer hesitated a moment, when Rasselas put a purse of gold into his hand, which he received with a mixture of joy and wonder.

'I have found, said the prince, at his return to Imlac, a man who can teach all that is necessary to be known, who, from the unshaken throne of rational fortitude, looks down on the scenes of life changing beneath him. He speaks, and attention watches his lips. He reasons, and conviction closes his periods. This man shall be my future guide: I will learn his doctrines, and imitate his life.'

'Be not too hasty, said Imlac, to trust, or to admire, the teachers of morality: they discourse like angels, but they live like men.'

Rasselas, who could not conceive how any man could reason so forcibly without feeling the cogency of his own arguments, paid his visit in a few days, and was denied ad-

mission. He had now learned the power of money, and made
his way by a piece of gold to the inner apartment, where he
found the philosopher in a room half darkened, with his eyes
misty, and his face pale. 'Sir, said he, you are come at a time
when all human friendship is useless; what I suffer cannot be
remedied, what I have lost cannot be supplied. My daughter,
my only daughter, from whose tenderness I expected all the
comforts of my age, died last night of a fever. My views, my
purposes, my hopes are at an end: I am now a lonely being
disunited from society.'

   'Sir, said the prince, mortality is an event by which a wise
man can never be surprised: we know that death is always
near, and it should therefore always be expected.' 'Young
man, answered the philosopher, you speak like one that has
never felt the pangs of separation.' 'Have you then forgot
the precepts, said Rasselas, which you so powerfully enforced? Has wisdom no strength to arm the heart against
calamity? Consider, that external things are naturally vari-
able, but truth and reason are always the same.' 'What comfort, said the mourner, can truth and reason afford me? of
what effect are they now, but to tell me, that my daughter
will not be restored?'

   The prince, whose humanity would not suffer him to insult
misery with reproof, went away convinced of the emptiness
of rhetorical sound, and the inefficacy of polished periods and
studied sentences.

CHAP. XIX

A Glimpse of pastoral life

HE was still eager upon the same enquiry; and, having heard of a hermit, that lived near the lowest cataract of the Nile, and filled the whole country with the fame of his sanctity, resolved to visit his retreat, and enquire whether that felicity, which publick life could not afford, was to be found in solitude; and whether a man, whose age and virtue made him venerable, could teach any peculiar art of shunning evils, or enduring them.

Imlac and the princess agreed to accompany him, and, after the necessary preparations, they began their journey. Their way lay through fields, where shepherds tended their flocks, and the lambs were playing upon the pasture. 'This, said the poet, is the life which has been often celebrated for its innocence and quiet: let us pass the heat of the day among the shepherds tents, and know whether all our searches are not to terminate in pastoral simplicity.'

The proposal pleased them, and they induced the shepherds, by small presents and familiar questions, to tell their opinion of their own state: they were so rude and ignorant, so little able to compare the good with the evil of the occupation, and so indistinct in their narratives and descriptions, that very little could be learned from them. But it was evident that their hearts were cankered with discontent; that they considered themselves as condemned to labour for the luxury of the rich, and looked up with stupid malevolence toward those that were placed above them.

The princess pronounced with vehemence, that she would never suffer these envious savages to be her companions, and that she should not soon be desirous of seeing any more

specimens of rustick happiness; but could not believe that all
the accounts of primeval pleasures were fabulous, and was
yet in doubt whether life had any thing that could be justly
preferred to the placid gratifications of fields and woods. She
hoped that the time would come, when with a few virtuous
and elegant companions, she should gather flowers planted
by her own hand, fondle the lambs of her own ewe, and
listen, without care, among brooks and breezes, to one of her
maidens reading in the shade.

CHAP. XX

The danger of prosperity

ON the next day they continued their journey, till the heat
compelled them to look round for shelter. At a small distance
they saw a thick wood, which they no sooner entered than
they perceived that they were approaching the habitations of
men. The shrubs were diligently cut away to open walks
where the shades were darkest; the boughs of opposite trees
were artificially interwoven; seats of flowery turf were raised
in vacant spaces, and a rivulet, that wantoned along the side
of a winding path, had its banks sometimes opened into small
basons, and its stream sometimes obstructed by little mounds
of stone heaped together to increase its murmurs.

They passed slowly through the wood, delighted with
such unexpected accommodations, and entertained each
other with conjecturing what, or who, he could be, that, in
those rude and unfrequented regions, had leisure and art for
such harmless luxury.

As they advanced, they heard the sound of musick, and
saw youths and virgins dancing in the grove; and, going still
further, beheld a stately palace built upon a hill surrounded

with woods. The laws of eastern hospitality allowed them to enter, and the master welcomed them like a man liberal and wealthy.

He was skilful enough in appearances soon to discern that they were no common guests, and spread his table with magnificence. The eloquence of Imlac caught his attention, and the lofty courtesy of the princess excited his respect. When they offered to depart he entreated their stay, and was the next day still more unwilling to dismiss them than before. They were easily persuaded to stop, and civility grew up in time to freedom and confidence.

The prince now saw all the domesticks chearful, and all the face of nature smiling round the place, and could not forbear to hope that he should find here what he was seeking; but when he was congratulating the master upon his possessions, he answered with a sigh, 'My condition has indeed the appearance of happiness, but appearances are delusive. My prosperity puts my life in danger; the Bassa of Egypt is my enemy, incensed only by my wealth and popularity. I have been hitherto protected against him by the princes of the country; but, as the favour of the great is uncertain, I know not how soon my defenders may be persuaded to share the plunder with the Bassa. I have sent my treasures into a distant country, and, upon the first alarm, am prepared to follow them. Then will my enemies riot in my mansion, and enjoy the gardens which I have planted.'

They all joined in lamenting his danger, and deprecating his exile; and the princess was so much disturbed with the tumult of grief and indignation, that she retired to her apartment. They continued with their kind inviter a few days longer, and then went forward to find the hermit.

CHAP. XXI

The happiness of solitude. The hermit's history

THEY came on the third day, by the direction of the peasants, to the hermit's cell: it was a cavern in the side of a mountain, over-shadowed with palm-trees; at such a distance from the cataract, that nothing more was heard than a gentle uniform murmur, such as composed the mind to pensive meditation, especially when it was assisted by the wind whistling among the branches. The first rude essay of nature had been so much improved by human labour, that the cave contained several apartments, appropriated to different uses, and often afforded lodging to travellers, whom darkness or tempests happened to overtake.

The hermit sat on a bench at the door, to enjoy the coolness of the evening. On one side lay a book with pens and papers, on the other mechanical instruments of various kinds. As they approached him unregarded, the princess observed that he had not the countenance of a man that had found, or could teach, the way to happiness.

They saluted him with great respect, which he repaid like a man not unaccustomed to the forms of courts. 'My children, said he, if you have lost your way, you shall be willingly supplied with such conveniencies for the night as this cavern will afford. I have all that nature requires, and you will not expect delicacies in a hermit's cell.'

They thanked him, and, entering, were pleased with the neatness and regularity of the place. The hermit set flesh and wine before them, though he fed only upon fruits and water. His discourse was chearful without levity, and pious without enthusiasm. He soon gained the esteem of his guests, and the princess repented of her hasty censure.

At last Imlac began thus: 'I do not now wonder that your reputation is so far extended; we have heard at Cairo of your wisdom, and came hither to implore your direction for this young man and maiden in the *choice of life*.'

'To him that lives well, answered the hermit, every form of life is good; nor can I give any other rule for choice, than to remove from all apparent evil.'

'He will remove most certainly from evil, said the prince, who shall devote himself to that solitude which you have recommended by your example.'

'I have indeed lived fifteen years in solitude, said the hermit, but have no desire that my example should gain any imitators. In my youth I professed arms, and was raised by degrees to the highest military rank. I have traversed wide countries at the head of my troops, and seen many battles and sieges. At last, being disgusted by the preferment of a younger officer, and feeling that my vigour was beginning to decay, I resolved to close my life in peace, having found the world full of snares, discord, and misery. I had once escaped from the persuit of the enemy by the shelter of this cavern, and therefore chose it for my final residence. I employed artificers to form it into chambers, and stored it with all that I was likely to want.

'For some time after my retreat, I rejoiced like a tempest-beaten sailor at his entrance into the harbour, being delighted with the sudden change of the noise and hurry of war, to stillness and repose. When the pleasure of novelty went away, I employed my hours in examining the plants which grow in the valley, and the minerals which I collected from the rocks. But that enquiry is now grown tasteless and irksome. I have been for some time unsettled and distracted: my mind is disturbed with a thousand perplexities of doubt, and vanities of imagination, which hourly prevail upon me, because I have no opportunities of relaxation or diversion. I am sometimes ashamed to think that I could not secure myself from vice, but by retiring from the exercise of virtue, and begin to suspect that I was rather impelled by resentment, than led by devotion, into solitude. My fancy riots in scenes of folly, and I lament that I have lost so much, and have gained so little. In solitude, if I escape the example of bad men, I want likewise the counsel and conversation of the good. I have been long comparing the evils with the advantages of society, and resolve to return into the world to morrow. The life of a solitary man will be certainly miserable, but not certainly devout.'

They heard his resolution with surprise, but, after a short pause, offered to conduct him to Cairo. He dug up a considerable treasure which he had hid among the rocks, and accompanied them to the city, on which, as he approached it, he gazed with rapture.

CHAP. XXII

The happiness of a life led according to nature

RASSELAS went often to an assembly of learned men, who met at stated times to unbend their minds, and compare their opinions. Their manners were somewhat coarse, but their conversation was instructive, and their disputations acute, though sometimes too violent, and often continued till neither controvertist remembered upon what question they began. Some faults were almost general among them: every one was desirous to dictate to the rest, and every one was pleased to hear the genius or knowledge of another depreciated.

In this assembly Rasselas was relating his interview with the hermit, and the wonder with which he heard him censure a course of life which he had so deliberately chosen, and so laudably followed. The sentiments of the hearers were various. Some were of opinion, that the folly of his choice had been justly punished by condemnation to perpetual perseverance. One of the youngest among them, with great vehemence, pronounced him an hypocrite. Some talked of the right of society to the labour of individuals, and considered retirement as a desertion of duty. Others readily allowed, that there was a time when the claims of the publick were satisfied, and when a man might properly sequester himself, to review his life, and purify his heart.

One, who appeared more affected with the narrative than the rest, thought it likely, that the hermit would, in a few years, go back to his retreat, and, perhaps, if shame did not restrain, or death intercept him, return once more from his retreat into the world: 'For the hope of happiness, said he, is so strongly impressed, that the longest experience is not able to efface it. Of the present state, whatever it be, we feel, and are forced to confess, the misery, yet, when the same state is again at a distance, imagination paints it as desirable. But the time will surely come, when desire will be no longer our torment, and no man shall be wretched but by his own fault.'

'This, said a philosopher, who had heard him with tokens of great impatience, is the present condition of a wise man. The time is already come, when none are wretched but by their own fault. Nothing is more idle, than to inquire after happiness, which nature has kindly placed within our reach. The way to be happy is to live according to nature, in obedience to that universal and unalterable law with which

every heart is originally impressed; which is not written on
it by precept, but engraven by destiny, not instilled by education, but infused at our nativity. He that lives according to
nature will suffer nothing from the delusions of hope, or
importunities of desire: he will receive and reject with
equability of temper; and act or suffer as the reason of things
shall alternately prescribe. Other men may amuse themselves
with subtle definitions, or intricate raciocination. Let them
learn to be wise by easier means: let them observe the hind of
the forest, and the linnet of the grove: let them consider the
life of animals, whose motions are regulated by instinct; they
obey their guide and are happy. Let us therefore, at length,
cease to dispute, and learn to live; throw away the incum-
brance of precepts, which they who utter them with so much
pride and pomp do not understand, and carry with us this
simple and intelligible maxim, That deviation from nature is
deviation from happiness.'

When he had spoken, he looked round him with a placid
air, and enjoyed the consciousness of his own beneficence.
'Sir, said the prince, with great modesty, as I, like all the rest
of mankind, am desirous of felicity, my closest attention has
been fixed upon your discourse: I doubt not the truth of a
position which a man so learned has so confidently advanced.
Let me only know what it is to live according to nature.'

'When I find young men so humble and so docile, said the
philosopher, I can deny them no information which my
studies have enabled me to afford. To live according to nature,
is to act always with due regard to the fitness arising from
the relations and qualities of causes and effects; to concur
with the great and unchangeable scheme of universal felicity;
to co-operate with the general disposition and tendency of
the present system of things.'

The prince soon found that this was one of the sages whom

he should understand less as he heard him longer. He therefore bowed and was silent, and the philosopher, supposing him satisfied, and the rest vanquished, rose up and departed with the air of a man that had co-operated with the present system.

CHAP. XXIII

The prince and his sister divide between them the work of observation

RASSELAS returned home full of reflexions, doubtful how to direct his future steps. Of the way to happiness he found the learned and simple equally ignorant; but, as he was yet young, he flattered himself that he had time remaining for more experiments, and further enquiries. He communicated to Imlac his observations and his doubts, but was answered by him with new doubts, and remarks that gave him no comfort. He therefore discoursed more frequently and freely with his sister, who had yet the same hope with himself, and always assisted him to give some reason why, though he had been hitherto frustrated, he might succeed at last.

'We have hitherto, said she, known but little of the world: we have never yet been either great or mean. In our own country, though we had royalty, we had no power, and in this we have not yet seen the private recesses of domestick peace. Imlac favours not our search, lest we should in time find him mistaken. We will divide the task between us: you shall try what is to be found in the splendour of courts, and I will range the shades of humbler life. Perhaps command and authority may be the supreme blessings, as they afford most opportunities of doing good: or, perhaps, what this world can give may be found in the modest habitations of middle fortune; too low for great designs, and too high for penury and distress.'

CHAP. XXIV

The prince examines the happiness of high stations

RASSELAS applauded the design, and appeared next day with a splendid retinue at the court of the Bassa. He was soon distinguished for his magnificence, and admitted, as a prince whose curiosity had brought him from distant countries, to an intimacy with the great officers, and frequent conversation with the Bassa himself.

He was at first inclined to believe, that the man must be pleased with his own condition, whom all approached with reverence, and heard with obedience, and who had the power to extend his edicts to a whole kingdom. 'There can be no pleasure, said he, equal to that of feeling at once the joy of thousands all made happy by wise administration. Yet, since, by the law of subordination, this sublime delight can be in one nation but the lot of one, it is surely reasonable to think that there is some satisfaction more popular and accessible, and that millions can hardly be subjected to the will of a single man, only to fill his particular breast with incommunicable content.'

These thoughts were often in his mind, and he found no solution of the difficulty. But as presents and civilities gained him more familiarity, he found that almost every man who stood high in employment hated all the rest, and was hated by them, and that their lives were a continual succession of plots and detections, stratagems and escapes, faction and treachery. Many of those, who surrounded the Bassa, were sent only to watch and report his conduct; every tongue was muttering censure and every eye was searching for a fault.

At last the letters of revocation arrived, the Bassa was carried in chains to Constantinople, and his name was mentioned no more.

'What are we now to think of the prerogatives of power, said Rasselas to his sister; is it without any efficacy to good? or, is the subordinate degree only dangerous, and the supreme safe and glorious? Is the Sultan the only happy man in his dominions? or, is the Sultan himself subject to the torments of suspicion, and the dread of enemies?'

In a short time the second Bassa was deposed. The Sultan, that had advanced him, was murdered by the Janisaries, and his successor had other views and different favourites.

CHAP. XXV

The princess persues her enquiry with more diligence than success

THE princess, in the mean time, insinuated herself into many families; for there are few doors, through which liberality, joined with good humour, cannot find its way. The daughters of many houses were airy and chearful, but Nekayah had been too long accustomed to the conversation of Imlac and her brother to be much pleased with childish levity and prattle which had no meaning. She found their thoughts narrow, their wishes low, and their merriment often artificial. Their pleasures, poor as they were, could not be preserved pure, but were embittered by petty competitions and worthless emulation. They were always jealous of the beauty of each other; of a quality to which solicitude can add nothing, and from which detraction can take nothing away. Many

were in love with triflers like themselves, and many fancied
that they were in love when in truth they were only idle.
Their affection was seldom fixed on sense or virtue, and
therefore seldom ended but in vexation. Their grief, however, like their joy, was transient; every thing floated in their
mind unconnected with the past or future, so that one desire
easily gave way to another, as a second stone cast into the
water effaces and confounds the circles of the first.

With these girls she played as with inoffensive animals, and
found them proud of her countenance, and weary of her
company.

But her purpose was to examine more deeply, and her
affability easily persuaded the hearts that were swelling with
sorrow to discharge their secrets in her ear: and those whom
hope flattered, or prosperity delighted, often courted her to
partake their pleasures.

The princess and her brother commonly met in the evening
in a private summer-house on the bank of the Nile, and related to each other the occurrences of the day. As they were
sitting together, the princess cast her eyes upon the river that
flowed before her. 'Answer, said she, great father of waters,
thou that rollest thy floods through eighty nations, to the
invocations of the daughter of thy native king. Tell me if
thou waterest, through all thy course, a single habitation
from which thou dost not hear the murmurs of complaint?'

'You are then, said Rasselas, not more successful in private
houses than I have been in courts.' 'I have, since the last parti-
tion of our provinces, said the princess, enabled myself to
enter familiarly into many families, where there was the
fairest show of prosperity and peace, and know not one house
that is not haunted by some fury that destroys its quiet.

'I did not seek ease among the poor, because I concluded
that there it could not be found. But I saw many poor whom

I had supposed to live in affluence. Poverty has, in large cities, very different appearances: it is often concealed in splendour, and often in extravagance. It is the care of a very great part of mankind to conceal their indigence from the rest: they support themselves by temporary expedients, and every day is lost in contriving for the morrow.

'This, however, was an evil, which, though frequent, I saw with less pain, because I could relieve it. Yet some have refused my bounties; more offended with my quickness to detect their wants, than pleased with my readiness to succour them: and others, whose exigencies compelled them to admit my kindness, have never been able to forgive their bene-factress. Many, however, have been sincerely grateful with-out the ostentation of gratitude, or the hope of other favours.'

CHAP. XXVI

The princess continues her remarks upon private life

NEKAYAH perceiving her brother's attention fixed, proceeded in her narrative.

'In families, where there is or is not poverty, there is commonly discord: if a kingdom be, as Imlac tells us, a great family, a family likewise is a little kingdom, torn with factions and exposed to revolutions. An unpractised observer expects the love of parents and children to be constant and equal; but this kindness seldom continues beyond the years of infancy: in a short time the children become rivals to their parents. Benefits are allayed by reproaches, and gratitude debased by envy.

'Parents and children seldom act in concert: each child

endeavours to appropriate the esteem or fondness of the
parents, and the parents, with yet less temptation, betray
each other to their children; thus some place their confidence
in the father, and some in the mother, and, by degrees, the
house is filled with artifices and feuds.

'The opinions of children and parents, of the young and
the old, are naturally opposite, by the contrary effects of hope
and despondence, of expectation and experience, without
crime or folly on either side. The colours of life in youth and
age appear different, as the face of nature in spring and winter.
And how can children credit the assertions of parents, which
their own eyes show them to be false?

'Few parents act in such a manner as much to enforce their
maxims by the credit of their lives. The old man trusts
wholly to slow contrivance and gradual progression: the
youth expects to force his way by genius, vigour, and pre-
cipitance. The old man pays regard to riches, and the youth
reverences virtue. The old man deifies prudence: the youth
commits himself to magnanimity and chance. The young
man, who intends no ill, believes that none is intended, and
therefore acts with openness and candour: but his father,
having suffered the injuries of fraud, is impelled to suspect,
and too often allured to practice it. Age looks with anger on
the temerity of youth, and youth with contempt on the
scrupulosity of age. Thus parents and children, for the greatest part, live on to love less and less: and, if those whom
nature has thus closely united are the torments of each other,
where shall we look for tenderness and consolation?'

'Surely, said the prince, you must have been unfortunate
in your choice of acquaintance: I am unwilling to believe,
that the most tender of all relations is thus impeded in its
effects by natural necessity.'

'Domestick discord, answered she, is not inevitably and

fatally necessary; but yet is not easily avoided. We seldom see that a whole family is virtuous: the good and evil cannot well agree; and the evil can yet less agree with one another: even the virtuous fall sometimes to variance, when their virtues are of different kinds, and tending to extremes. In general, those parents have most reverence who most deserve it: for he that lives well cannot be despised.

'Many other evils infest private life. Some are the slaves of servants whom they have trusted with their affairs. Some are kept in continual anxiety to the caprice of rich relations, whom they cannot please, and dare not offend. Some husbands are imperious, and some wives perverse: and, as it is always more easy to do evil than good, though the wisdom or virtue of one can very rarely make many happy, the folly or vice of one may often make many miserable.'

'If such be the general effect of marriage, said the prince, I shall, for the future, think it dangerous to connect my interest with that of another, lest I should be unhappy by my partner's fault.'

'I have met, said the princess, with many who live single for that reason; but I never found that their prudence ought to raise envy. They dream away their time without friendship, without fondness, and are driven to rid themselves of the day, for which they have no use, by childish amusements, or vicious delights. They act as beings under the constant sense of some known inferiority, that fills their minds with rancour, and their tongues with censure. They are peevish at home, and malevolent abroad; and, as the out-laws of human nature, make it their business and their pleasure to disturb that society which debars them from its privileges. To live without feeling or exciting sympathy, to be fortunate without adding to the felicity of others, or afflicted without tasting the balm of pity, is a state more gloomy than solitude:

it is not retreat but exclusion from mankind. Marriage has many pains, but celibacy has no pleasures.'

'What then is to be done? said Rasselas; the more we enquire, the less we can resolve. Surely he is most likely to please himself that has no other inclination to regard.'

CHAP. XXVII

Disquisition upon greatness

THE conversation had a short pause. The prince having considered his sister's observations, told her, that she had surveyed life with prejudice, and supposed misery where she did not find it. 'Your narrative, says he, throws yet a darker gloom upon the prospects of futurity: the predictions of Imlac were but faint sketches of the evils painted by Nekayah. I have been lately convinced that quiet is not the daughter of grandeur, or of power: that her presence is not to be bought by wealth, nor enforced by conquest. It is evident, that as any man acts in a wider compass, he must be more exposed to opposition from enmity or miscarriage from chance; whoever has many to please or to govern, must use the ministry of many agents, some of whom will be wicked, and some ignorant; by some he will be misled, and by others betrayed. If he gratifies one he will offend another: those that are not favoured will think themselves injured; and, since favours can be conferred but upon few, the greater number will be always discontented.'

'The discontent, said the princess, which is thus unreasonable, I hope that I shall always have spirit to despise, and you, power to repress.'

'Discontent, answered Rasselas, will not always be without reason under the most just or vigilant administration of publick affairs. None, however attentive, can always discover that merit which indigence or faction may happen to obscure; and none, however powerful, can always reward it. Yet, he that sees inferiour desert advanced above him, will naturally impute that preference to partiality or caprice; and, indeed, it can scarcely be hoped that any man, however magnanimous by nature, or exalted by condition, will be able to persist for ever in fixed and inexorable justice of distribution: he will sometimes indulge his own affections, and sometimes those of his favourites; he will permit some to please him who can never serve him; he will discover in those whom he loves qualities which in reality they do not possess; and to those, from whom he receives pleasure, he will in his turn endeavour to give it. Thus will recommendations sometimes prevail which were purchased by money, or by the more destructive bribery of flattery and servility.

'He that has much to do will do something wrong, and of that wrong must suffer the consequences; and, if it were possible that he should always act rightly, yet when such numbers are to judge of his conduct, the bad will censure and obstruct him by malevolence, and the good sometimes by mistake.

'The highest stations cannot therefore hope to be the abodes of happiness, which I would willingly believe to have fled from thrones and palaces to seats of humble privacy and placid obscurity. For what can hinder the satisfaction, or intercept the expectations, of him whose abilities are adequate to his employments, who sees with his own eyes the whole circuit of his influence, who chooses by his own knowledge all whom he trusts, and whom none are tempted to deceive by hope or fear? Surely he has nothing to do but to love and to be loved, to be virtuous and to be happy.'

'Whether perfect happiness would be procured by perfect

goodness, said Nekayah, this world will never afford an opportunity of deciding. But this, at least, may be maintained, that we do not always find visible happiness in proportion to visible virtue. All natural and almost all political evils, are incident alike to the bad and good: they are confounded in the misery of a famine, and not much distinguished in the fury of a faction; they sink together in a tempest, and are driven together from their country by invaders. All that virtue can afford is quietness of conscience, a steady prospect of a happier state; this may enable us to endure calamity with patience; but remember that patience must suppose pain.'

CHAP. XXVIII

Rasselas and Nekayah continue their conversation

'DEAR princess, said Rasselas, you fall into the common errours of exaggeratory declamation, by producing, in a familiar disquisition, examples of national calamities, and scenes of extensive misery, which are found in books rather than in the world, and which, as they are horrid, are ordained to be rare. Let us not imagine evils which we do not feel, nor injure life by misrepresentations. I cannot bear that querelous eloquence which threatens every city with a siege like that of Jerusalem, that makes famine attend on every flight of locusts, and suspends pestilence on the wing of every blast that issues from the south.

'On necessary and inevitable evils, which overwhelm kingdoms at once, all disputation is vain: when they happen they must be endured. But it is evident, that these bursts of universal distress are more dreaded than felt: thousands and ten thousands flourish in youth, and wither in age, without the knowledge of any other than domestick evils, and share the same pleasures and vexations whether their kings are mild or cruel, whether the armies of their country persue their enemies, or retreat before them. While courts are disturbed with intestine competitions, and ambassadours are negotiating in foreign countries, the smith still plies his anvil, and the husbandman drives his plow forward; the necessaries of life are required and obtained, and the successive business of the seasons continues to make its wonted revolutions.

'Let us cease to consider what, perhaps, may never happen, and what, when it shall happen, will laugh at human speculation. We will not endeavour to modify the motions of the elements, or to fix the destiny of kingdoms. It is our business to consider what beings like us may perform; each labouring for his own happiness, by promoting within his circle, however narrow, the happiness of others.

'Marriage is evidently the dictate of nature; men and women were made to be companions of each other, and therefore I cannot be persuaded but that marriage is one of the means of happiness.'

'I know not, said the princess, whether marriage be more than one of the innumerable modes of human misery. When I see and reckon the various forms of connubial infelicity, the unexpected causes of lasting discord, the diversities of temper, the oppositions of opinion, the rude collisions of contrary desire where both are urged by violent impulses, the obstinate contests of disagreeing virtues, where both are supported by consciousness of good intention, I am sometimes disposed to think with the severer casuists of most nations, that marriage is rather permitted than approved, and that none, but by the instigation of a passion too much indulged, entangle themselves with indissoluble compacts.'

'You seem to forget, replied Rasselas, that you have, even

now, represented celibacy as less happy than marriage. Both
conditions may be bad, but they cannot both be worst.
Thus it happens when wrong opinions are entertained, that
they mutually destroy each other, and leave the mind open
to truth.'

'I did not expect, answered the princess, to hear that imputed to falshood which is the consequence only of frailty.
To the mind, as to the eye, it is difficult to compare with
exactness objects vast in their extent, and various in their
parts. Where we see or conceive the whole at once we
readily note the discriminations and decide the preference:
but of two systems, of which neither can be surveyed by any
human being in its full compass of magnitude and multiplicity of complication, where is the wonder, that judging of
the whole by parts, I am alternately affected by one and the
other as either presses on my memory or fancy? We differ
from ourselves just as we differ from each other, when we
see only part of the question, as in the multifarious relations
of politicks and morality: but when we perceive the whole
at once, as in numerical computations, all agree in one
judgment, and none ever varies his opinion.'

'Let us not add, said the prince, to the other evils of life,
the bitterness of controversy, nor endeavour to vie with
each other in subtilties of argument. We are employed in a
search, of which both are equally to enjoy the success, or
suffer by the miscarriage. It is therefore fit that we assist each
other. You surely conclude too hastily from the infelicity of
marriage against its institution; will not the misery of life
prove equally that life cannot be the gift of heaven? The
world must be peopled by marriage, or peopled without it.'

'How the world is to be peopled, returned Nekayah, is not
my care, and needs not be yours. I see no danger that the
present generation should omit to leave successors behind

them: we are not now enquiring for the world, but for ourselves.'

CHAP. XXIX

The debate on marriage continued

'THE good of the whole, says Rasselas, is the same with the good of all its parts. If marriage be best for mankind it must be evidently best for individuals, or a permanent and necessary duty must be the cause of evil, and some must be inevitably sacrificed to the convenience of others. In the estimate which you have made of the two states, it appears that the incommodities of a single life are, in a great measure, necessary and certain, but those of the conjugal state accidental and avoidable.

'I cannot forbear to flatter myself that prudence and benevolence will make marriage happy. The general folly of mankind is the cause of general complaint. What can be expected but disappointment and repentance from a choice made in the immaturity of youth, in the ardour of desire, without judgment, without foresight, without enquiry after conformity of opinions, similarity of manners, rectitude of judgment, or purity of sentiment.

'Such is the common process of marriage. A youth and maiden meeting by chance, or brought together by artifice, exchange glances, reciprocate civilities, go home, and dream of one another. Having little to divert attention, or diversify thought, they find themselves uneasy when they are apart, and therefore conclude that they shall be happy together. They marry, and discover what nothing but voluntary blindness had before concealed; they wear out life in altercations, and charge nature with cruelty.

'From those early marriages proceeds likewise the rivalry

of parents and children: the son is eager to enjoy the world
before the father is willing to forsake it, and there is hardly
room at once for two generations. The daughter begins to
bloom before the mother can be content to fade, and neither
can forbear to wish for the absence of the other.

'Surely all these evils may be avoided by that deliberation
and delay which prudence prescribes to irrevocable choice.
In the variety and jollity of youthful pleasures life may be
well enough supported without the help of a partner. Longer
time will increase experience, and wider views will allow
better opportunities of enquiry and selection: one advantage,
at least, will be certain; the parents will be visibly older than
their children.'

'What reason cannot collect, said Nekayah, and what
experiment has not yet taught, can be known only from the
report of others. I have been told that late marriages are not
eminently happy. This is a question too important to be
neglected, and I have often proposed it to those, whose
accuracy of remark, and comprehensiveness of knowledge,
made their suffrages worthy of regard. They have generally
determined, that it is dangerous for a man and woman to
suspend their fate upon each other, at a time when opinions
are fixed, and habits are established; when friendships have
been contracted on both sides, when life has been planned
into method, and the mind has long enjoyed the contemplation of its own prospects.

'It is scarcely possible that two travelling through the
world under the conduct of chance, should have been both
directed to the same path, and it will not often happen that
either will quit the track which custom has made pleasing.
When the desultory levity of youth has settled into regularity, it is soon succeeded by pride ashamed to yield, or
obstinacy delighting to contend. And even though mutual

esteem produces mutual desire to please, time itself, as it
modifies unchangeably the external mien, determines likewise the direction of the passions, and gives an inflexible
rigidity to the manners. Long customs are not easily broken:
he that attempts to change the course of his own life, very
often labours in vain; and how shall we do that for others
which we are seldom able to do for ourselves?'

'But surely, interposed the prince, you suppose the chief
motive of choice forgotten or neglected. Whenever I shall
seek a wife, it shall be my first question, whether she be
willing to be led by reason?'

'Thus it is, said Nekayah, that philosophers are deceived.
There are a thousand familiar disputes which reason never
can decide; questions that elude investigation, and make
logick ridiculous; cases where something must be done, and
where little can be said. Consider the state of mankind, and
enquire how few can be supposed to act upon any occasions,
whether small or great, with all the reasons of action present
to their minds. Wretched would be the pair above all names
of wretchedness, who should be doomed to adjust by reason
every morning all the minute detail of a domestick day.

'Those who marry at an advanced age, will probably
escape the encroachments of their children; but, in diminution of this advantage, they will be likely to leave them,
ignorant and helpless, to a guardian's mercy: or, if that
should not happen, they must at least go out of the world
before they see those whom they love best either wise or
great.

'From their children, if they have less to fear, they have
less also to hope, and they lose, without equivalent, the joys
of early love, and the convenience of uniting with manners
pliant, and minds susceptible of new impressions, which
might wear away their dissimilitudes by long cohabitation,

as soft bodies, by continual attrition, conform their surfaces
to each other.

'I believe it will be found that those who marry late are
best pleased with their children, and those who marry early
with their partners.'

'The union of these two affections, said Rasselas, would
produce all that could be wished. Perhaps there is a time
when marriage might unite them, a time neither too early
for the father, nor too late for the husband.'

'Every hour, answered the princess, confirms my prejudice
in favour of the position so often uttered by the mouth of
Imlac, "That nature sets her gifts on the right hand and on
the left." Those conditions, which flatter hope and attract
desire, are so constituted, that, as we approach one, we recede
from another. There are goods so opposed that we cannot
seize both, but, by too much prudence, may pass between
them at too great a distance to reach either. This is often the
fate of long consideration; he does nothing who endeavours
to do more than is allowed to humanity. Flatter not yourself
with contrarieties of pleasure. Of the blessings set before you
make your choice, and be content. No man can taste the
fruits of autumn while he is delighting his scent with the
flowers of the spring: no man can, at the same time, fill his
cup from the source and from the mouth of the Nile.'

CHAP. XXX

Imlac enters, and changes the conversation

HERE Imlac entered, and interrupted them. 'Imlac, said
Rasselas, I have been taking from the princess the dismal
history of private life, and am almost discouraged from
further search.'

'It seems to me, said Imlac, that while you are making the choice of life, you neglect to live. You wander about a single city, which, however large and diversified, can now afford few novelties, and forget that you are in a country, famous among the earliest monarchies for the power and wisdom of its inhabitants; a country where the sciences first dawned that illuminate the world, and beyond which the arts cannot be traced of civil society or domestick life.

'The old Egyptians have left behind them monuments of industry and power before which all European magnificence is confessed to fade away. The ruins of their architecture are the schools of modern builders, and from the wonders which time has spared we may conjecture, though uncertainly, what it has destroyed.'

'My curiosity, said Rasselas, does not very strongly lead me to survey piles of stone, or mounds of earth; my business is with man. I came hither not to measure fragments of temples, or trace choaked aqueducts, but to look upon the various scenes of the present world.'

'The things that are now before us, said the princess, require attention, and deserve it. What have I to do with the heroes or the monuments of ancient times? with times which never can return, and heroes, whose form of life was different from all that the present condition of mankind requires or allows.'

'To know any thing, returned the poet, we must know its effects; to see men we must see their works, that we may learn what reason has dictated, or passion has incited, and find what are the most powerful motives of action. To judge rightly of the present we must oppose it to the past; for all judgment is comparative, and of the future nothing can be known. The truth is, that no mind is much employed upon the present: recollection and anticipation fill up almost all our moments. Our passions are joy and grief, love and hatred, hope and fear. Of joy and grief the past is the object, and the future of hope and fear; even love and hatred respect the past, for the cause must have been before the effect.

'The present state of things is the consequence of the former, and it is natural to inquire what were the sources of the good that we enjoy, or of the evil that we suffer. If we act only for ourselves, to neglect the study of history is not prudent: if we are entrusted with the care of others, it is not just. Ignorance, when it is voluntary, is criminal; and he may properly be charged with evil who refused to learn how he might prevent it.

'There is no part of history so generally useful as that which relates the progress of the human mind, the gradual improvement of reason, the successive advances of science, the vicissitudes of learning and ignorance, which are the light and darkness of thinking beings, the extinction and resuscitation of arts, and all the revolutions of the intellectual world. If accounts of battles and invasions are peculiarly the business of princes, the useful or elegant arts are not to be neglected; those who have kingdoms to govern, have understandings to cultivate.

'Example is always more efficacious than precept. A soldier is formed in war, and a painter must copy pictures. In this, contemplative life has the advantage: great actions are seldom seen, but the labours of art are always at hand for those who desire to know what art has been able to perform.

'When the eye or the imagination is struck with any uncommon work the next transition of an active mind is to the means by which it was performed. Here begins the true use of such contemplation; we enlarge our comprehension by new ideas, and perhaps recover some art lost to mankind, or learn what is less perfectly known in our own country. At least we compare our own with former times, and either rejoice at our improvements, or, what is the first motion towards good, discover our defects.'

'I am willing, said the prince, to see all that can deserve my search.' 'And I, said the princess, shall rejoice to learn something of the manners of antiquity.'

'The most pompous monument of Egyptian greatness, and one of the most bulky works of manual industry, said Imlac, are the pyramids; fabricks raised before the time of history, and of which the earliest narratives afford us only uncertain traditions. Of these the greatest is still standing, very little injured by time.'

'Let us visit them to morrow, said Nekayah. I have often heard of the Pyramids, and shall not rest, till I have seen them within and without with my own eyes.'

CHAP. XXXI

They visit the Pyramids

THE resolution being thus taken, they set out the next day. They laid tents upon their camels, being resolved to stay among the pyramids till their curiosity was fully satisfied. They travelled gently, turned aside to every thing remarkable, stopped from time to time and conversed with the inhabitants, and observed the various appearances of towns ruined and inhabited, of wild and cultivated nature.

When they came to the great pyramid they were astonished at the extent of the base, and the height of the top. Imlac explained to them the principles upon which the pyramidal form was chosen for a fabrick intended to co-extend its duration with that of the world: he showed that its gradual diminution gave it such stability, as defeated all the common attacks of the elements, and could scarcely be overthrown by earthquakes themselves, the least resistible of natural violence. A concussion that should shatter the pyramid would threaten the dissolution of the continent.

They measured all its dimensions, and pitched their tents at its foot. Next day they prepared to enter its interiour apartments, and having hired the common guides climbed up to the first passage, when the favourite of the princess, looking into the cavity, stepped back and trembled. 'Pekuah, said the princess, of what art thou afraid?' 'Of the narrow entrance, answered the lady, and of the dreadful gloom. I dare not enter a place which must surely be inhabited by unquiet souls. The original possessors of these dreadful vaults will start up before us, and, perhaps, shut us in for ever.' She spoke, and threw her arms round the neck of her mistress.

'If all your fear be of apparitions, said the prince, I will promise you safety: there is no danger from the dead; he that is once buried will be seen no more.'

'That the dead are seen no more, said Imlac, I will not undertake to maintain against the concurrent and unvaried testimony of all ages, and of all nations. There is no people, rude or learned, among whom apparitions of the dead are not related and believed. This opinion, which, perhaps, prevails as far as human nature is diffused, could become universal only by its truth: those, that never heard of one another, would not have agreed in a tale which nothing but experience can make credible. That it is doubted by single cavillers can very little weaken the general evidence, and some who deny it with their tongues confess it by their fears.

'Yet I do not mean to add new terrours to those which have already seized upon Pekuah. There can be no reason why spectres should haunt the pyramid more than other places, or why they should have power or will to hurt innocence and purity. Our entrance is no violation of their priviledges; we can take nothing from them, how then can we offend them?'

'My dear Pekuah, said the princess, I will always go before you, and Imlac shall follow you. Remember that you are the companion of the princess of Abissinia.'

'If the princess is pleased that her servant should die, returned the lady, let her command some death less dreadful than enclosure in this horrid cavern. You know I dare not disobey you: I must go if you command me; but, if I once enter, I never shall come back.'

The princess saw that her fear was too strong for expostulation or reproof, and embracing her, told her that she should stay in the tent till their return. Pekuah was yet not satisfied, but entreated the princess not to persue so dreadful a purpose as that of entering the recesses of the pyramid. 'Though I cannot teach courage, said Nekayah, I must not learn cowardise; nor leave at last undone what I came hither only to do.'

CHAP. XXXII

They enter the Pyramid

PEKUAH descended to the tents, and the rest entered the pyramid: they passed through the galleries, surveyed the vaults of marble, and examined the chest in which the body of the founder is supposed to have been reposited. They then sat down in one of the most spacious chambers to rest a while before they attempted to return.

'We have now, said Imlac, gratified our minds with an exact view of the greatest work of man, except the wall of China.

'Of the wall it is very easy to assign the motives. It secured a wealthy and timorous nation from the incursions of Barbarians, whose unskilfulness in arts made it easier for them to supply their wants by rapine than by industry, and who from time to time poured in upon the habitations of peaceful commerce, as vultures descend upon domestick fowl. Their celerity and fierceness made the wall necessary, and their ignorance made it efficacious.

'But for the pyramids no reason has ever been given adequate to the cost and labour of the work. The narrowness of the chambers proves that it could afford no retreat from enemies, and treasures might have been reposited at far less expence with equal security. It seems to have been erected only in compliance with that hunger of imagination which preys incessantly upon life, and must be always appeased by some employment. Those who have already all that they can enjoy, must enlarge their desires. He that has built for use, till use is supplied, must begin to build for vanity, and extend his plan to the utmost power of human performance, that he may not be soon reduced to form another wish.

'I consider this mighty structure as a monument of the insufficiency of human enjoyments. A king, whose power is unlimited, and whose treasures surmount all real and imaginary wants, is compelled to solace, by the erection of a pyramid, the satiety of dominion and tastelesness of pleasures, and to amuse the tediousness of declining life, by seeing thousands labouring without end, and one stone, for no purpose, laid upon another. Whoever thou art, that, not content with a moderate condition, imaginest happiness in royal magnificence, and dreamest that command or riches can feed the appetite of novelty with perpetual gratifications, survey the pyramids, and confess thy folly!'

CHAP. XXXIII

The princess meets with an unexpected misfortune

THEY rose up, and returned through the cavity at which they had entered, and the princess prepared for her favourite a long narrative of dark labyrinths, and costly rooms, and of the different impressions which the varieties of the way had made upon her. But, when they came to their train, they found every one silent and dejected: the men discovered shame and fear in their countenances, and the women were weeping in the tents.

What had happened they did not try to conjecture, but immediately enquired. 'You had scarcely entered into the pyramid, said one of the attendants, when a troop of Arabs rushed upon us: we were too few to resist them, and too slow to escape. They were about to search the tents, set us on our camels, and drive us along before them, when the approach of some Turkish horsemen put them to flight; but they seized the lady Pekuah with her two maids, and carried them away: the Turks are now persuing them by our instigation, but I fear they will not be able to overtake them.'

The princess was overpowered with surprise and grief. Rasselas, in the first heat of his resentment, ordered his servants to follow him, and prepared to persue the robbers with his sabre in his hand. 'Sir, said Imlac, what can you hope from violence or valour? the Arabs are mounted on horses trained to battle and retreat; we have only beasts of burden. By leaving our present station we may lose the princess, but cannot hope to regain Pekuah.'

In a short time the Turks returned, having not been able to

reach the enemy. The princess burst out into new lamentations, and Rasselas could scarcely forbear to reproach them with cowardice; but Imlac was of opinion, that the escape of the Arabs was no addition to their misfortune, for, perhaps, they would have killed their captives rather than have resigned them.

CHAP. XXXIV

They return to Cairo without Pekuah

THERE was nothing to be hoped from longer stay. They returned to Cairo repenting of their curiosity, censuring the negligence of the government, lamenting their own rashness which had neglected to procure a guard, imagining many expedients by which the loss of Pekuah might have been prevented, and resolving to do something for her recovery, though none could find any thing proper to be done.

Nekayah retired to her chamber, where her women attempted to comfort her, by telling her that all had their troubles, and that lady Pekuah had enjoyed much happiness in the world for a long time, and might reasonably expect a change of fortune. They hoped that some good would befal her wheresoever she was, and that their mistress would find another friend who might supply her place.

The princess made them no answer, and they continued the form of condolence, not much grieved in their hearts that the favourite was lost.

Next day the prince presented to the Bassa a memorial of the wrong which he had suffered, and a petition for redress. The Bassa threatened to punish the robbers, but did not attempt to catch them, nor, indeed, could any account or description be given by which he might direct the persuit.

It soon appeared that nothing would be done by authority.

Governors, being accustomed to hear of more crimes than they can punish, and more wrongs than they can redress, set themselves at ease by indiscriminate negligence, and presently forget the request when they lose sight of the petitioner.

Imlac then endeavoured to gain some intelligence by private agents. He found many who pretended to an exact knowledge of all the haunts of the Arabs, and to regular correspondence with their chiefs, and who readily undertook the recovery of Pekuah. Of these, some were furnished with money for their journey, and came back no more; some were liberally paid for accounts which a few days discovered to be false. But the princess would not suffer any means, however improbable, to be left untried. While she was doing something she kept her hope alive. As one expedient failed, another was suggested; when one messenger returned unsuccessful, another was despatched to a different quarter.

Two months had now passed, and of Pekuah nothing had been heard; the hopes which they had endeavoured to raise in each other grew more languid, and the princess, when she saw nothing more to be tried, sunk down inconsolable in hopeless dejection. A thousand times she reproached herself with the easy compliance by which she permitted her favourite to stay behind her. 'Had not my fondness, said she, lessened my authority, Pekuah had not dared to talk of her terrours. She ought to have feared me more than spectres. A severe look would have overpowered her; a peremptory command would have compelled obedience. Why did foolish indulgence prevail upon me? Why did I not speak and refuse to hear?'

'Great princess, said Imlac, do not reproach yourself for your virtue, or consider that as blameable by which evil has accidentally been caused. Your tenderness for the timidity of Pekuah was generous and kind. When we act according to our duty, we commit the event to him by whose laws our actions are governed, and who will suffer none to be finally punished for obedience. When, in prospect of some good, whether natural or moral, we break the rules prescribed us, we withdraw from the direction of superiour wisdom, and take all consequences upon ourselves. Man cannot so far know the connexion of causes and events, as that he may venture to do wrong in order to do right. When we persue our end by lawful means, we may always console our miscarriage by the hope of future recompense. When we consult only our own policy, and attempt to find a nearer way to good, by overleaping the settled boundaries of right and wrong, we cannot be happy even by success, because we cannot escape the consciousness of our fault; but, if we miscarry, the disappointment is irremediably embittered. How comfortless is the sorrow of him, who feels at once the pangs of guilt, and the vexation of calamity which guilt has brought upon him?

'Consider, princess, what would have been your condition, if the lady Pekuah had entreated to accompany you, and, being compelled to stay in the tents, had been carried away; or how would you have born the thought, if you had forced her into the pyramid, and she had died before you in agonies of terrour.'

'Had either happened, said Nekayah, I could not have endured life till now: I should have been tortured to madness by the remembrance of such cruelty, or must have pined away in abhorrence of myself.'

'This at least, said Imlac, is the present reward of virtuous conduct, that no unlucky consequence can oblige us to repent it.'

CHAP. XXXV

The princess languishes for want of Pekuah

NEKAYAH, being thus reconciled to herself, found that no evil is insupportable but that which is accompanied with consciousness of wrong. She was, from that time, delivered from the violence of tempestuous sorrow, and sunk into silent pensiveness and gloomy tranquillity. She sat from morning to evening recollecting all that had been done or said by her Pekuah, treasured up with care every trifle on which Pekuah had set an accidental value, and which might recal to mind any little incident or careless conversation. The sentiments of her, whom she now expected to see no more, were treasured in her memory as rules of life, and she deliberated to no other end than to conjecture on any occasion what would have been the opinion and counsel of Pekuah.

The women, by whom she was attended, knew nothing of her real condition, and therefore she could not talk to them but with caution and reserve. She began to remit her curiosity, having no great care to collect notions which she had no convenience of uttering. Rasselas endeavoured first to comfort and afterwards to divert her; he hired musicians, to whom she seemed to listen, but did not hear them, and procured masters to instruct her in various arts, whose lectures, when they visited her again, were again to be repeated. She had lost her taste of pleasure and her ambition of excellence. And her mind, though forced into short excursions, always recurred to the image of her friend.

Imlac was every morning earnestly enjoined to renew his enquiries, and was asked every night whether he had yet heard of Pekuah, till not being able to return the princess the answer that she desired, he was less and less willing to come into her presence. She observed his backwardness, and commanded him to attend her. 'You are not, said she, to confound impatience with resentment, or to suppose that I charge you with negligence, because I repine at your unsuccessfulness. I do not much wonder at your absence; I know that the unhappy are never pleasing, and that all naturally avoid the contagion of misery. To hear complaints is wearisome alike to the wretched and the happy; for who would cloud by adventitious grief the short gleams of gaiety which life allows us? or who, that is struggling under his own evils, will add to them the miseries of another?

'The time is at hand, when none shall be disturbed any longer by the sighs of Nekayah: my search after happiness is now at an end. I am resolved to retire from the world with all its flatteries and deceits, and will hide myself in solitude, without any other care than to compose my thoughts, and regulate my hours by a constant succession of innocent occupations, till, with a mind purified from all earthly desires, I shall enter into that state, to which all are hastening, and in which I hope again to enjoy the friendship of Pekuah.'

'Do not entangle your mind, said Imlac, by irrevocable determinations, nor increase the burthen of life by a voluntary accumulation of misery: the weariness of retirement will continue or increase when the loss of Pekuah is forgotten. That you have been deprived of one pleasure is no very good reason for rejection of the rest.'

'Since Pekuah was taken from me, said the princess, I have no pleasure to reject or to retain. She that has no one to love or trust has little to hope. She wants the radical principle of happiness. We may, perhaps, allow that what satisfaction this world can afford, must arise from the conjunction of wealth, knowledge and goodness: wealth is nothing but as it is bestowed, and knowledge nothing but as it is communicated: they must therefore be imparted to others, and to whom could I now delight to impart them? Goodness affords the only comfort which can be enjoyed without a partner, and goodness may be practised in retirement.'

'How far solitude may admit goodness, or advance it, I shall not, replied Imlac, dispute at present. Remember the confession of the pious hermit. You will wish to return into the world, when the image of your companion has left your thoughts.' 'That time, said Nekayah, will never come. The generous frankness, the modest obsequiousness, and the faithful secrecy of my dear Pekuah, will always be more missed, as I shall live longer to see vice and folly.'

'The state of a mind oppressed with a sudden calamity, said Imlac, is like that of the fabulous inhabitants of the new created earth, who, when the first night came upon them, supposed that day never would return. When the clouds of sorrow gather over us, we see nothing beyond them, nor can imagine how they will be dispelled: yet a new day succeeded to the night, and sorrow is never long without a dawn of ease. But they who restrain themselves from receiving comfort, do as the savages would have done, had they put out their eyes when it was dark. Our minds, like our bodies, are in continual flux; something is hourly lost, and something acquired. To lose much at once is inconvenient to either, but while the vital powers remain uninjured, nature will find the means of reparation. Distance has the same effect on the mind as on the eye, and while we glide along the stream of time, whatever we leave behind us is always lessening, and that which we approach increasing in magnitude. Do not suffer life to stagnate; it will grow muddy for want of motion: commit yourself again to the current of the world; Pekuah will vanish by degrees; you will meet in your way some other favourite, or learn to diffuse yourself in general conversation.'

'At least, said the prince, do not despair before all remedies have been tried: the enquiry after the unfortunate lady is still continued, and shall be carried on with yet greater diligence, on condition that you will promise to wait a year for the event, without any unalterable resolution.'

Nekayah thought this a reasonable demand, and made the promise to her brother, who had been advised by Imlac to require it. Imlac had, indeed, no great hope of regaining Pekuah, but he supposed, that if he could secure the interval of a year, the princess would be then in no danger of a cloister.

CHAP. XXXVI

Pekuah is still remembered. The progress of sorrow

NEKAYAH, seeing that nothing was omitted for the recovery of her favourite, and having, by her promise, set her intention of retirement at a distance, began imperceptibly to return to common cares and common pleasures. She rejoiced without her own consent at the suspension of her sorrows, and sometimes caught herself with indignation in the act of turning away her mind from the remembrance of her, whom yet she resolved never to forget.

She then appointed a certain hour of the day for meditation on the merits and fondness of Pekuah, and for some weeks retired constantly at the time fixed, and returned with her eyes swollen and her countenance clouded. By degrees she grew less scrupulous, and suffered any important and pressing avocation to delay the tribute of daily tears. She then yielded to less occasions; sometimes forgot what she was indeed afraid to remember, and, at last, wholly released herself from the duty of periodical affliction.

Her real love of Pekuah was yet not diminished. A thousand occurrences brought her back to memory, and a thousand wants, which nothing but the confidence of friendship can supply, made her frequently regretted. She, therefore, solicited Imlac never to desist from enquiry, and to leave no art of intelligence untried, that, at least, she might have the comfort of knowing that she did not suffer by negligence or sluggishness. 'Yet what, said she, is to be expected from our persuit of happiness, when we find the state of life to be such, that happiness itself is the cause of misery? Why should we endeavour to attain that, of which the possession cannot be secured? I shall henceforward fear to yield my heart to excellence, however bright, or to fondness, however tender, lest I should lose again what I have lost in Pekuah.'

CHAP. XXXVII

The princess hears news of Pekuah

IN seven months, one of the messengers, who had been sent away upon the day when the promise was drawn from the princess, returned, after many unsuccessful rambles, from the borders of Nubia, with an account that Pekuah was in the hands of an Arab chief, who possessed a castle or fortress on the extremity of Egypt. The Arab, whose revenue was plunder, was willing to restore her, with her two attendants, for two hundred ounces of gold.

The price was no subject of debate. The princess was in extasies when she heard that her favourite was alive, and might so cheaply be ransomed. She could not think of delaying for a moment Pekuah's happiness or her own, but entreated her brother to send back the messenger with the sum required. Imlac, being consulted, was not very confident of the veracity of the relator, and was still more doubtful of the Arab's faith, who might, if he were too liberally trusted, detain at once the money and the captives. He thought it dangerous to put themselves in the power of the Arab, by going into his district, and could not expect that the Rover would so much expose himself as to come into the lower country, where he might be seized by the forces of the Bassa.

It is difficult to negotiate where neither will trust. But Imlac, after some deliberation, directed the messenger to propose that Pekuah should be conducted by ten horsemen to the monastry of St. Anthony, which is situated in the deserts of Upper-Egypt, where she should be met by the same number, and her ransome should be paid.

That no time might be lost, as they expected that the proposal would not be refused, they immediately began their journey to the monastry; and, when they arrived, Imlac went forward with the former messenger to the Arab's fortress. Rasselas was desirous to go with them, but neither his sister nor Imlac would consent. The Arab, according to the custom of his nation, observed the laws of hospitality with great exactness to those who put themselves into his power, and, in a few days, brought Pekuah with her maids, by easy journeys, to their place appointed, where receiving the stipulated price, he restored her with great respect to liberty and her friends, and undertook to conduct them back towards Cairo beyond all danger of robbery or violence.

The princess and her favourite embraced each other with transport too violent to be expressed, and went out together to pour the tears of tenderness in secret, and exchange professions of kindness and gratitude. After a few hours they returned into the refectory of the convent, where, in the presence of the prior and his brethren, the prince required of Pekuah the history of her adventures.

CHAP. XXXVIII

The adventures of the lady Pekuah

'AT what time, and in what manner, I was forced away, said Pekuah, your servants have told you. The suddenness of the event struck me with surprise, and I was at first rather stupified than agitated with any passion of either fear or sorrow. My confusion was encreased by the speed and tumult of our flight while we were followed by the Turks, who, as it seemed, soon despaired to overtake us, or were afraid of those whom they made a shew of menacing.

'When the Arabs saw themselves out of danger they slackened their course, and, as I was less harassed by external violence, I began to feel more uneasiness in my mind. After some time we stopped near a spring shaded with trees in a pleasant meadow, where we were set upon the ground, and offered such refreshments as our masters were partaking. I was suffered to sit with my maids apart from the rest, and none attempted to comfort or insult us. Here I first began to feel the full weight of my misery. The girls sat weeping in silence, and from time to time looked on me for succour. I knew not to what condition we were doomed, nor could conjecture where would be the place of our captivity, or whence to draw any hope of deliverance. I was in the hands of robbers and savages, and had no reason to suppose that their pity was more than their justice, or that they would forbear the gratification of any ardour of desire, or caprice of cruelty. I, however, kissed my maids, and endeavoured to pacify them by remarking, that we were yet treated with decency, and that, since we were now carried beyond persuit, there was no danger of violence to our lives.

'When we were to be set again on horseback, my maids clung round me, and refused to be parted, but I commanded them not to irritate those who had us in their power. We travelled the remaining part of the day through an unfrequented and pathless country, and came by moonlight to the side of a hill, where the rest of the troop was stationed. Their tents were pitched, and their fires kindled, and our chief was welcomed as a man much beloved by his dependants.

'We were received into a large tent, where we found women who had attended their husbands in the expedition. They set before us the supper which they had provided, and I eat it rather to encourage my maids than to comply with any appetite of my own. When the meat was taken away they spread the carpets for repose. I was weary, and hoped to find in sleep that remission of distress which nature seldom denies. Ordering myself therefore to be undrest, I observed that the women looked very earnestly upon me, not expecting, I suppose, to see me so submissively attended. When my upper vest was taken off, they were apparently struck with the splendour of my cloaths, and one of them timorously laid her hand upon the embroidery. She then went out, and, in a short time, came back with another woman, who seemed to be of higher rank, and greater authority. She did, at her entrance, the usual act of reverence, and, taking me by the hand, placed me in a smaller tent, spread with finer carpets, where I spent the night quietly with my maids.

'In the morning, as I was sitting on the grass, the chief of the troop came towards me. I rose up to receive him, and he bowed with great respect. 'Illustrious lady, said he, my fortune is better than I had presumed to hope; I am told by my women, that I have a princess in my camp.' Sir, answered I, your women have deceived themselves and you; I am not a princess, but an unhappy stranger who intended soon to have left this country, in which I am now to be imprisoned for ever. 'Whoever, or whencesoever, you are, returned the Arab, your dress, and that of your servants, show your rank to be high, and your wealth to be great. Why should you, who can so easily procure your ransome, think yourself in danger of perpetual captivity? The purpose of my incursions is to encrease my riches, or more properly to gather tribute. The sons of Ishmael are the natural and hereditary lords of this part of the continent, which is usurped by late invaders, and low-born tyrants, from whom we are compelled to take by the sword what is denied to justice. The violence of war admits no distinction; the lance that is lifted at guilt and power will sometimes fall on innocence and gentleness.'

'How little, said I, did I expect that yesterday it should have fallen upon me.'

'Misfortunes, answered the Arab, should always be expected. If the eye of hostility could learn reverence or pity, excellence like yours had been exempt from injury. But the angels of affliction spread their toils alike for the virtuous and the wicked, for the mighty and the mean. Do not be disconsolate; I am not one of the lawless and cruel rovers of the desart; I know the rules of civil life: I will fix your ransome, give a pasport to your messenger, and perform my stipulation with nice punctuality.'

'You will easily believe that I was pleased with his courtesy; and finding that his predominant passion was desire of money, I began now to think my danger less, for I knew that no sum would be thought too great for the release of Pekuah. I told him that he should have no reason to charge

me with ingratitude, if I was used with kindness, and that
any ransome, which could be expected for a maid of common rank, would be paid, but that he must not persist to rate
me as a princess. He said, he would consider what he should
demand, and then, smiling, bowed and retired.

'Soon after the women came about me, each contending
to be more officious than the other, and my maids themselves
were served with reverence. We travelled onward by short
journeys. On the fourth day the chief told me, that my
ransome must be two hundred ounces of gold, which I not
only promised him, but told him, that I would add fifty
more, if I and my maids were honourably treated.

'I never knew the power of gold before. From that time I
was the leader of the troop. The march of every day was
longer or shorter as I commanded, and the tents were pitched
where I chose to rest. We now had camels and other conveniencies for travel, my own women were always at my
side, and I amused myself with observing the manners of the
vagrant nations, and with viewing remains of ancient edifices
with which these deserted countries appear to have been, in
some distant age, lavishly embellished.

'The chief of the band was a man far from illiterate: he
was able to travel by the stars or the compass, and had
marked in his erratick expeditions such places as are most
worthy the notice of a passenger. He observed to me, that
buildings are always best preserved in places little frequented,
and difficult of access: for, when once a country declines
from its primitive splendour, the more inhabitants are left,
the quicker ruin will be made. Walls supply stones more
easily than quarries, and palaces and temples will be demolished to make stables of granate, and cottages of
porphyry.

CHAP. XXXIX

The adventures of Pekuah continued

'WE wandered about in this manner for some weeks, whether, as our chief pretended, for my gratification, or, as I rather suspected, for some convenience of his own. I endeavoured to appear contented where sullenness and resentment would have been of no use, and that endeavour conduced much to the calmness of my mind; but my heart was always with Nekayah, and the troubles of the night much overbalanced the amusements of the day. My women, who threw all their cares upon their mistress, set their minds at ease from the time when they saw me treated with respect, and gave themselves up to the incidental alleviations of our fatigue without solicitude or sorrow. I was pleased with their pleasure, and animated with their confidence. My condition had lost much of its terrour, since I found that the Arab ranged the country merely to get riches. Avarice is an uniform and tractable vice: other intellectual distempers are different in different constitutions of mind; that which sooths the pride of one will offend the pride of another; but to the favour of the covetous there is a ready way, bring money and nothing is denied.

'At last we came to the dwelling of our chief, a strong and spacious house built with stone in an island of the Nile, which lies, as I was told, under the tropick. 'Lady, said the Arab, you shall rest after your journey a few weeks in this place, where you are to consider yourself as sovereign. My occupation is war: I have therefore chosen this obscure residence, from which I can issue unexpected, and to which I can retire unpersued. You may now repose in security: here are few pleasures, but here is no danger.' He then led me into the inner apartments, and seating me on the richest couch, bowed to the ground. His women, who considered me as a rival, looked on me with malignity; but being soon informed that I was a great lady detained only for my ransome, they began to vie with each other in obsequiousness and reverence.

'Being again comforted with new assurances of speedy liberty, I was for some days diverted from impatience by the novelty of the place. The turrets overlooked the country to a great distance, and afforded a view of many windings of the stream. In the day I wandered from one place to another as the course of the sun varied the splendour of the prospect, and saw many things which I had never seen before. The crocodiles and river-horses are common in this unpeopled region, and I often looked upon them with terrour, though I knew that they could not hurt me. For some time I expected to see mermaids and tritons, which, as Imlac has told me, the European travellers have stationed in the Nile, but no such beings ever appeared, and the Arab, when I enquired after them, laughed at my credulity.

'At night the Arab always attended me to a tower set apart for celestial observations, where he endeavoured to teach me the names and courses of the stars. I had no great inclination to this study, but an appearance of attention was necessary to please my instructor, who valued himself for his skill, and, in a little while, I found some employment requisite to beguile the tediousness of time, which was to be passed always amidst the same objects. I was weary of looking in the morning on things from which I had turned away weary in the evening: I therefore was at last willing to observe the stars rather than do nothing, but could not always compose my thoughts, and was very often thinking on Nekayah when others imagined me contemplating the sky. Soon after the

Arab went upon another expedition, and then my only pleasure was to talk with my maids about the accident by which we were carried away, and the happiness that we should all enjoy at the end of our captivity.'

'There were women in your Arab's fortress, said the princess, why did you not make them your companions, enjoy their conversation, and partake their diversions? In a place where they found business or amusement, why should you alone sit corroded with idle melancholy? or why could not you bear for a few months that condition to which they were condemned for life?'

'The diversions of the women, answered Pekuah, were only childish play, by which the mind accustomed to stronger operations could not be kept busy. I could do all which they delighted in doing by powers merely sensitive, while my intellectual faculties were flown to Cairo. They ran from room to room as a bird hops from wire to wire in his cage. They danced for the sake of motion, as lambs frisk in a meadow. One sometimes pretended to be hurt that the rest might be alarmed, or hid herself that another might seek her. Part of their time passed in watching the progress of light bodies that floated on the river, and part in marking the various forms into which clouds broke in the sky.

'Their business was only needlework, in which I and my maids sometimes helped them; but you know that the mind will easily straggle from the fingers, nor will you suspect that captivity and absence from Nekayah could receive solace from silken flowers.

'Nor was much satisfaction to be hoped from their conversation: for of what could they be expected to talk? They had seen nothing; for they had lived from early youth in that narrow spot: of what they had not seen they could have no knowledge, for they could not read. They had no ideas but of the few things that were within their view, and had hardly names for any thing but their cloaths and their food. As I bore a superiour character, I was often called to terminate their quarrels, which I decided as equitably as I could. If it could have amused me to hear the complaints of each against the rest, I might have been often detained by long stories, but the motives of their animosity were so small that I could not listen without intercepting the tale.'

'How, said Rasselas, can the Arab, whom you represented as a man of more than common accomplishments, take any pleasure in his seraglio, when it is filled only with women like these. Are they exquisitely beautiful?'

'They do not, said Pekuah, want that unaffecting and ignoble beauty which may subsist without spriteliness or sublimity, without energy of thought or dignity of virtue. But to a man like the Arab such beauty was only a flower casually plucked and carelessly thrown away. Whatever pleasures he might find among them, they were not those of friendship or society. When they were playing about him he looked on them with inattentive superiority: when they vied for his regard he sometimes turned away disgusted. As they had no knowledge, their talk could take nothing from the tediousness of life: as they had no choice, their fondness, or appearance of fondness, excited in him neither pride nor gratitude; he was not exalted in his own esteem by the smiles of a woman who saw no other man, nor was much obliged by that regard, of which he could never know the sincerity, and which he might often perceive to be exerted not so much to delight him as to pain a rival. That which he gave, and they received, as love, was only a careless distribution of superfluous time, such love as man can bestow upon that which he despises, such as has neither hope nor fear, neither joy nor sorrow.'

'You have reason, lady, to think yourself happy, said Imlac, that you have been thus easily dismissed. How could a mind, hungry for knowledge, be willing, in an intellectual famine, to lose such a banquet as Pekuah's conversation?'

'I am inclined to believe, answered Pekuah, that he was for some time in suspense; for, notwithstanding his promise, whenever I proposed to dispatch a messenger to Cairo, he found some excuse for delay. While I was detained in his house he made many incursions into the neighbouring countries, and, perhaps, he would have refused to discharge me, had his plunder been equal to his wishes. He returned always courteous, related his adventures, delighted to hear my observations, and endeavoured to advance my acquaintance with the stars. When I importuned him to send away my letters, he soothed me with professions of honour and sincerity; and, when I could be no longer decently denied, put his troop again in motion, and left me to govern in his absence. I was much afflicted by this studied procrastination, and was sometimes afraid that I should be forgotten; that you would leave Cairo, and I must end my days in an island of the Nile.

'I grew at last hopeless and dejected, and cared so little to entertain him, that he for a while more frequently talked with my maids. That he should fall in love with them, or with me, might have been equally fatal, and I was not much pleased with the growing friendship. My anxiety was not long; for, as I recovered some degree of chearfulness, he returned to me, and I could not forbear to despise my former uneasiness.

'He still delayed to send for my ransome, and would, perhaps, never have determined, had not your agent found his way to him. The gold, which he would not fetch, he could not reject when it was offered. He hastened to prepare for our journey hither, like a man delivered from the pain of an intestine conflict. I took leave of my companions in the house, who dismissed me with cold indifference.'

Nekayah, having heard her favourite's relation, rose and embraced her, and Rasselas gave her an hundred ounces of gold, which she presented to the Arab for the fifty that were promised.

CHAP. XL

The history of a man of learning

THEY returned to Cairo, and were so well pleased at finding themselves together, that none of them went much abroad. The prince began to love learning, and one day declared to Imlac, that he intended to devote himself to science, and pass the rest of his days in literary solitude.

'Before you make your final choice, answered Imlac, you ought to examine its hazards, and converse with some of those who are grown old in the company of themselves. I have just left the observatory of one of the most learned astronomers in the world, who has spent forty years in unwearied attention to the motions and appearances of the celestial bodies, and has drawn out his soul in endless calculations. He admits a few friends once a month to hear his deductions and enjoy his discoveries. I was introduced as a man of knowledge worthy of his notice. Men of various ideas and fluent conversation are commonly welcome to those whose thoughts have been long fixed upon a single point, and who find the images of other things stealing away. I delighted him with my remarks, he smiled at the narrative of my travels, and was glad to forget the constellations, and descend for a moment into the lower world.

'On the next day of vacation I renewed my visit, and was

so fortunate as to please him again. He relaxed from that time
the severity of his rule, and permitted me to enter at my own
choice. I found him always busy, and always glad to be relieved. As each knew much which the other was desirous of
learning, we exchanged our notions with great delight. I
perceived that I had every day more of his confidence, and
always found new cause of admiration in the profundity of
his mind. His comprehension is vast, his memory capacious
and retentive, his discourse is methodical, and his expression
clear.

'His integrity and benevolence are equal to his learning.
His deepest researches and most favourite studies are willingly interrupted for any opportunity of doing good by his
counsel or his riches. To his closest retreat, at his most busy
moments, all are admitted that want his assistance: 'For
though I exclude idleness and pleasure, I will never, says he,
bar my doors against charity. To man is permitted the
contemplation of the skies, but the practice of virtue is
commanded.'

'Surely, said the princess, this man is happy.'

'I visited him, said Imlac, with more and more frequency,
and was every time more enamoured of his conversation: he
was sublime without haughtiness, courteous without for-
mality, and communicative without ostentation. I was at
first, great princess, of your opinion, thought him the happiest of mankind, and often congratulated him on the blessing
that he enjoyed. He seemed to hear nothing with indifference
but the praises of his condition, to which he always returned
a general answer, and diverted the conversation to some
other topick.

'Amidst this willingness to be pleased, and labour to please,
I had quickly reason to imagine that some painful sentiment
pressed upon his mind. He often looked up earnestly towards

the sun, and let his voice fall in the midst of his discourse. He would sometimes, when we were alone, gaze upon me in silence with the air of a man who longed to speak what he was yet resolved to suppress. He would often send for me with vehement injunctions of haste, though, when I came to him, he had nothing extraordinary to say. And sometimes, when I was leaving him, would call me back, pause a few moments and then dismiss me.

CHAP. XLI

The astronomer discovers the cause of his uneasiness

'AT last the time came when the secret burst his reserve. We were sitting together last night in the turret of his house, watching the emersion of a satellite of Jupiter. A sudden tempest clouded the sky, and disappointed our observation. We sat a while silent in the dark, and then he addressed himself to me in these words: 'Imlac, I have long considered thy friendship as the greatest blessing of my life. Integrity without knowledge is weak and useless, and knowledge without integrity is dangerous and dreadful. I have found in thee all the qualities requisite for trust, benevolence, experience, and fortitude. I have long discharged an office which I must soon quit at the call of nature, and shall rejoice in the hour of imbecility and pain to devolve it upon thee.'

'I thought myself honoured by this testimony, and protested that whatever could conduce to his happiness would add likewise to mine.'

'Hear, Imlac, what thou wilt not without difficulty credit. I have possessed for five years the regulation of weather, and the distribution of the seasons: the sun has listened to my dictates, and passed from tropick to tropick by my direction; the clouds, at my call, have poured their waters, and the Nile has overflowed at my command; I have restrained the rage of the dog-star, and mitigated the fervours of the crab. The winds alone, of all the elemental powers, have hitherto refused my authority, and multitudes have perished by equinoctial tempests which I found myself unable to prohibit or restrain. I have administered this great office with exact justice, and made to the different nations of the earth an impartial dividend of rain and sunshine. What must have been the misery of half the globe, if I had limited the clouds to particular regions, or confined the sun to either side of the equator?'

CHAP. XLII

The opinion of the astronomer is explained and justified

'I suppose he discovered in me, through the obscurity of the room, some tokens of amazement and doubt, for, after a short pause, he proceeded thus:

'Not to be easily credited will neither surprise nor offend me; for I am, probably, the first of human beings to whom this trust has been imparted. Nor do I know whether to deem this distinction a reward or punishment; since I have possessed it I have been far less happy than before, and nothing but the consciousness of good intention could have enabled me to support the weariness of unremitted vigilance.'

'How long, Sir, said I, has this great office been in your hands?'

'About ten years ago, said he, my daily observations of the changes of the sky led me to consider, whether, if I had the power of the seasons, I could confer greater plenty upon the inhabitants of the earth. This contemplation fastened on my mind, and I sat days and nights in imaginary dominion, pouring upon this country and that the showers of fertility, and seconding every fall of rain with a due proportion of sunshine. I had yet only the will to do good, and did not imagine that I should ever have the power.

'One day as I was looking on the fields withering with heat, I felt in my mind a sudden wish that I could send rain on the southern mountains, and raise the Nile to an inundation. In the hurry of my imagination I commanded rain to fall, and, by comparing the time of my command, with that of the inundation, I found that the clouds had listened to my lips.'

'Might not some other cause, said I, produce this concurrence? the Nile does not always rise on the same day.'

'Do not believe, said he with impatience, that such objections could escape me: I reasoned long against my own conviction, and laboured against truth with the utmost obstinacy. I sometimes suspected myself of madness, and should not have dared to impart this secret but to a man like you, capable of distinguishing the wonderful from the impossible, and the incredible from the false.'

'Why, Sir, said I, do you call that incredible, which you know, or think you know, to be true?'

'Because, said he, I cannot prove it by any external evidence; and I know too well the laws of demonstration to think that my conviction ought to influence another, who cannot, like me, be conscious of its force. I, therefore, shall not attempt to gain credit by disputation. It is sufficient that I feel this power, that I have long possessed, and every day exerted it. But the life of man is short, the infirmities of age increase upon me, and the time will soon come when the regulator of the year must mingle with the dust. The care of appointing a successor has long disturbed me; the night and the day have been spent in comparisons of all the characters which have come to my knowledge, and I have yet found none so worthy as thyself.

CHAP. XLIII

The astronomer leaves Imlac his directions

'HEAR therefore, what I shall impart, with attention, such as the welfare of a world requires. If the task of a king be considered as difficult, who has the care only of a few millions, to whom he cannot do much good or harm, what must be the anxiety of him, on whom depend the action of the elements, and the great gifts of light and heat!—Hear me therefore with attention.

'I have diligently considered the position of the earth and sun, and formed innumerable schemes in which I changed their situation. I have sometimes turned aside the axis of the earth, and sometimes varied the ecliptick of the sun: but I have found it impossible to make a disposition by which the world may be advantaged; what one region gains, another loses by any imaginable alteration, even without considering the distant parts of the solar system with which we are unacquainted. Do not, therefore, in thy administration of the year, indulge thy pride by innovation; do not please thyself with thinking that thou canst make thyself renowned to all future ages, by disordering the seasons. The memory of mischief is no desirable fame. Much less will it become thee to let kindness or interest prevail. Never rob other countries of rain to pour it on thine own. For us the Nile is sufficient.'

'I promised that when I possessed the power, I would use it with inflexible integrity, and he dismissed me, pressing my hand.' 'My heart, said he, will be now at rest, and my benevolence will no more destroy my quiet: I have found a man of wisdom and virtue, to whom I can chearfully bequeath the inheritance of the sun.'

The prince heard this narration with very serious regard, but the princess smiled, and Pekuah convulsed herself with laughter. 'Ladies, said Imlac, to mock the heaviest of human afflictions is neither charitable nor wise. Few can attain this man's knowledge, and few practise his virtues; but all may suffer his calamity. Of the uncertainties of our present state, the most dreadful and alarming is the uncertain continuance of reason.'

The princess was recollected, and the favourite was abashed. Rasselas, more deeply affected, enquired of Imlac, whether he thought such maladies of the mind frequent, and how they were contracted.

CHAP. XLIV

The dangerous prevalence of imagination

'Disorders of intellect, answered Imlac, happen much more often than superficial observers will easily believe. Perhaps, if we speak with rigorous exactness, no human mind is in its right state. There is no man whose imagination does not sometimes predominate over his reason, who can regulate his attention wholly by his will, and whose ideas will come and go at his command. No man will be found in whose mind airy notions do not sometimes tyrannise, and force him to hope or fear beyond the limits of sober probability. All power of fancy over reason is a degree of insanity; but while this power is such as we can controul and repress, it is not visible to others, nor considered as any depravation of the mental faculties: it is not pronounced madness but when it comes ungovernable, and apparently influences speech or action.

'To indulge the power of fiction, and send imagination out upon the wing, is often the sport of those who delight too much in silent speculation. When we are alone we are not always busy; the labour of excogitation is too violent to last long; the ardour of enquiry will sometimes give way to idleness or satiety. He who has nothing external that can divert him, must find pleasure in his own thoughts, and must conceive himself what he is not; for who is pleased with what he is? He then expatiates in boundless futurity, and culls from all imaginable conditions that which for the present moment he should most desire, amuses his desires with impossible enjoyments, and confers upon his pride unattainable dominion. The mind dances from scene to scene, unites all pleasures in all combinations, and riots in delights which nature and fortune, with all their bounty, cannot bestow.

'In time some particular train of ideas fixes the attention, all other intellectual gratifications are rejected, the mind, in weariness or leisure, recurs constantly to the favourite conception, and feasts on the luscious falsehood whenever she is offended with the bitterness of truth. By degrees the reign of fancy is confirmed; she grows first imperious, and in time despotick. Then fictions begin to operate as realities, false opinions fasten upon the mind, and life passes in dreams of rapture or of anguish.

'This, Sir, is one of the dangers of solitude, which the hermit has confessed not always to promote goodness, and the astronomer's misery has proved to be not always propitious to wisdom.'

'I will no more, said the favourite, imagine myself the

queen of Abissinia. I have often spent the hours, which the princess gave to my own disposal, in adjusting ceremonies and regulating the court; I have repressed the pride of the powerful, and granted the petitions of the poor; I have built new palaces in more happy situations, planted groves upon the tops of mountains, and have exulted in the beneficence of royalty, till, when the princess entered, I had almost forgotten to bow down before her.'

'And I, said the princess, will not allow myself any more to play the shepherdess in my waking dreams. I have often soothed my thoughts with the quiet and innocence of pastoral employments, till I have in my chamber heard the winds whistle, and the sheep bleat; sometimes freed the lamb entangled in the thicket, and sometimes with my crook encountered the wolf. I have a dress like that of the village maids, which I put on to help my imagination, and a pipe on which I play softly, and suppose myself followed by my flocks.'

'I will confess, said the prince, an indulgence of fantastick delight more dangerous than yours. I have frequently endeavoured to image the possibility of a perfect government, by which all wrong should be restrained, all vice reformed, and all the subjects preserved in tranquility and innocence. This thought produced innumerable schemes of reformation, and dictated many useful regulations and salutary edicts. This has been the sport and sometimes the labour of my solitude; and I start, when I think with how little anguish I once supposed the death of my father and my brothers.'

'Such, says Imlac, are the effects of visionary schemes: when we first form them we know them to be absurd, but familiarise them by degrees, and in time lose sight of their folly.'

CHAP. XLV

They discourse with an old man

THE evening was now far past, and they rose to return home. As they walked along the bank of the Nile, delighted with the beams of the moon quivering on the water, they saw at a small distance an old man, whom the prince had often heard in the assembly of the sages. 'Yonder, said he, is one whose years have calmed his passions, but not clouded his reason: let us close the disquisitions of the night, by enquiring what are his sentiments of his own state, that we may know whether youth alone is to struggle with vexation, and whether any better hope remains for the latter part of life.'

Here the sage approached and saluted them. They invited him to join their walk, and prattled a while as acquaintance that had unexpectedly met one another. The old man was chearful and talkative, and the way seemed short in his company. He was pleased to find himself not disregarded, accompanied them to their house, and, at the prince's request, entered with them. They placed him in the seat of honour, and set wine and conserves before him.

'Sir, said the princess, an evening walk must give to a man of learning, like you, pleasures which ignorance and youth can hardly conceive. You know the qualities and the causes of all that you behold, the laws by which the river flows, the periods in which the planets perform their revolutions. Every thing must supply you with contemplation, and renew the consciousness of your own dignity.'

'Lady, answered he, let the gay and the vigorous expect pleasure in their excursions, it is enough that age can obtain ease. To me the world has lost its novelty: I look round, and see what I remember to have seen in happier days. I rest against a tree, and consider, that in the same shade I once disputed upon the annual overflow of the Nile with a friend who is now silent in the grave. I cast my eyes upwards, fix them on the changing moon, and think with pain on the vicissitudes of life. I have ceased to take much delight in physical truth; for what have I to do with those things which I am soon to leave?'

'You may at least recreate yourself, said Imlac, with the recollection of an honourable and useful life, and enjoy the praise which all agree to give you.'

'Praise, said the sage, with a sigh, is to an old man an empty sound. I have neither mother to be delighted with the reputation of her son, nor wife to partake the honours of her husband. I have outlived my friends and my rivals. Nothing is now of much importance; for I cannot extend my interest beyond myself. Youth is delighted with applause, because it is considered as the earnest of some future good, and because the prospect of life is far extended: but to me, who am now declining to decrepitude, there is little to be feared from the malevolence of men, and yet less to be hoped from their affection or esteem. Something they may yet take away, but they can give me nothing. Riches would now be useless, and high employment would be pain. My retrospect of life recalls to my view many opportunities of good neglected, much time squandered upon trifles, and more lost in idleness and vacancy. I leave many great designs unattempted, and many great attempts unfinished. My mind is burthened with no heavy crime, and therefore I compose myself to tranquility; endeavour to abstract my thoughts from hopes and cares, which, though reason knows them to be vain, still try to keep their old possession of the heart; expect, with serene humility, that hour which nature cannot long delay; and hope to possess in a better state that happiness which here I could not find, and that virtue which here I have not attained.'

He rose and went away, leaving his audience not much elated with the hope of long life. The prince consoled himself with remarking, that it was not reasonable to be disappointed by this account; for age had never been considered as the season of felicity, and, if it was possible to be easy in decline and weakness, it was likely that the days of vigour and alacrity might be happy: that the moon of life might be bright, if the evening could be calm.

The princess suspected that age was querulous and malignant, and delighted to repress the expectations of those who had newly entered the world. She had seen the possessors of estates look with envy on their heirs, and known many who enjoy pleasure no longer than they can confine it to themselves.

Pekuah conjectured, that the man was older than he appeared, and was willing to impute his complaints to delirious dejection; or else supposed that he had been unfortunate, and was therefore discontented: 'For nothing, said she, is more common than to call our own condition, the condition of life.'

Imlac, who had no desire to see them depressed, smiled at the comforts which they could so readily procure to themselves, and remembered, that at the same age, he was equally confident of unmingled prosperity, and equally fertile of consolatory expedients. He forbore to force upon them unwelcome knowledge, which time itself would too soon impress. The princess and her lady retired; the madness of the astronomer hung upon their minds, and they desired Imlac to enter upon his office, and delay next morning the rising of the sun.

CHAP. XLVI

The princess and Pekuah visit the astronomer

THE princess and Pekuah having talked in private of Imlac's astronomer, thought his character at once so amiable and so strange, that they could not be satisfied without a nearer knowledge, and Imlac was requested to find the means of bringing them together.

This was somewhat difficult; the philosopher had never received any visits from women, though he lived in a city that had in it many Europeans who followed the manners of their own countries, and many from other parts of the world that lived there with European liberty. The ladies would not be refused, and several schemes were proposed for the accomplishment of their design. It was proposed to introduce them as strangers in distress, to whom the sage was always accessible; but, after some deliberation, it appeared, that by this artifice, no acquaintance could be formed, for their conversation would be short, and they could not decently importune him often. 'This, said Rasselas, is true; but I have yet a stronger objection against the misrepresentation of your state. I have always considered it as treason against the great republick of human nature, to make any man's virtues the means of deceiving him, whether on great or little occasions. All imposture weakens confidence and chills benevolence. When the sage finds that you are not what you seemed, he will feel the resentment natural to a man who, conscious of great abilities, discovers that he has been tricked by understandings meaner than his own, and, perhaps, the distrust, which he can never afterwards wholly lay aside, may stop the voice of counsel, and close the hand of charity;

and where will you find the power of restoring his benefactions to mankind, or his peace to himself?'

To this no reply was attempted, and Imlac began to hope that their curiosity would subside; but, next day, Pekuah told him, she had now found an honest pretence for a visit to the astronomer, for she would solicit permission to continue under him the studies in which she had been initiated by the Arab, and the princess might go with her either as a fellow-student, or because a woman could not decently come alone. 'I am afraid, said Imlac, that he will be soon weary of your company: men advanced far in knowledge do not love to repeat the elements of their art, and I am not certain that even of the elements, as he will deliver them connected with inferences, and mingled with reflections, you are a very capable auditress.' 'That, said Pekuah, must be my care: I ask of you only to take me thither. My knowledge is, perhaps, more than you imagine it, and by concurring always with his opinions I shall make him think it greater than it is.'

The astronomer, in pursuance of this resolution, was told, that a foreign lady, travelling in search of knowledge, had heard of his reputation, and was desirous to become his scholar. The uncommonness of the proposal raised at once his surprize and curiosity, and when, after a short deliberation, he consented to admit her, he could not stay without impatience till the next day.

The ladies dressed themselves magnificently, and were attended by Imlac to the astronomer, who was pleased to see himself approached with respect by persons of so splendid an appearance. In the exchange of the first civilities he was timorous and bashful; but when the talk became regular, he recollected his powers, and justified the character which Imlac had given. Enquiring of Pekuah what could have turned her inclination towards astronomy, he received from her a history of her adventure at the pyramid, and of the time passed in the Arab's island. She told her tale with ease and elegance, and her conversation took possession of his heart. The discourse was then turned to astronomy: Pekuah displayed what she knew: he looked upon her as a prodigy of genius, and intreated her not to desist from a study which she had so happily begun.

They came again and again, and were every time more welcome than before. The sage endeavoured to amuse them, that they might prolong their visits, for he found his thoughts grow brighter in their company; the clouds of solicitude vanished by degrees, as he forced himself to entertain them, and he grieved when he was left at their departure to his old employment of regulating the seasons.

The princess and her favourite had now watched his lips for several months, and could not catch a single word from which they could judge whether he continued, or not, in the opinion of his preternatural commission. They often contrived to bring him to an open declaration, but he easily eluded all their attacks, and on which side soever they pressed him escaped from them to some other topick.

As their familiarity increased they invited him often to the house of Imlac, where they distinguished him by extraordinary respect. He began gradually to delight in sublunary pleasures. He came early and departed late; laboured to recommend himself by assiduity and compliance; excited their curiosity after new arts, that they might still want his assistance; and when they made any excursion of pleasure or enquiry, entreated to attend them.

By long experience of his integrity and wisdom, the prince and his sister were convinced that he might be trusted without danger; and lest he should draw any false hopes from the civilities which he received, discovered to him their condition, with the motives of their journey, and required his opinion on the choice of life.

'Of the various conditions which the world spreads before you, which you shall prefer, said the sage, I am not able to instruct you. I can only tell that I have chosen wrong. I have passed my time in study without experience; in the attainment of sciences which can, for the most part, be but remotely useful to mankind. I have purchased knowledge at the expence of all the common comforts of life: I have missed the endearing elegance of female friendship, and the happy commerce of domestick tenderness. If I have obtained any prerogatives above other students, they have been accompanied with fear, disquiet, and scrupulosity; but even of these prerogatives, whatever they were, I have, since my thoughts have been diversified by more intercourse with the world, begun to question the reality. When I have been for a few days lost in pleasing dissipation, I am always tempted to think that my enquiries have ended in errour, and that I have suffered much, and suffered it in vain.'

Imlac was delighted to find that the sage's understanding was breaking through its mists, and resolved to detain him from the planets till he should forget his task of ruling them, and reason should recover its original influence.

From this time the astronomer was received into familiar friendship, and partook of all their projects and pleasures: his respect kept him attentive, and the activity of Rasselas did not leave much time unengaged. Something was always to be done; the day was spent in making observations which furnished talk for the evening, and the evening was closed with a scheme for the morrow.

The sage confessed to Imlac, that since he had mingled in the gay tumults of life, and divided his hours by a succession of amusements, he found the conviction of his authority over

the skies fade gradually from his mind, and began to trust
less to an opinion which he never could prove to others, and
which he now found subject to variation from causes in
which reason had no part. 'If I am accidentally left alone for
a few hours, said he, my inveterate persuasion rushes upon
my soul, and my thoughts are chained down by some irresistible violence, but they are soon disentangled by the prince's
conversation, and instantaneously released at the entrance of
Pekuah. I am like a man habitually afraid of spectres, who is
set at ease by a lamp, and wonders at the dread which harras-
sed him in the dark, yet, if his lamp be extinguished, feels
again the terrours which he knows that when it is light he
shall feel no more. But I am sometimes afraid lest I indulge
my quiet by criminal negligence, and voluntarily forget the
great charge with which I am intrusted. If I favour myself in
a known errour, or am determined by my own ease in a
doubtful question of this importance, how dreadful is my
crime!'

'No disease of the imagination, answered Imlac, is so difficult of cure, as that which is complicated with the dread of
guilt: fancy and conscience then act interchangeably upon
us, and so often shift their places, that the illusions of one are
not distinguished from the dictates of the other. If fancy presents images not moral or religious, the mind drives them
away when they give it pain, but when melancholick notions take the form of duty, they lay hold on the faculties
without opposition, because we are afraid to exclude or
banish them. For this reason the superstitious are often
melancholy, and the melancholy almost always superstitious.

'But do not let the suggestions of timidity overpower
your better reason: the danger of neglect can be but as the
probability of the obligation, which when you consider it
with freedom, you find very little, and that little growing

every day less. Open your heart to the influence of the light, which, from time to time, breaks in upon you: when scruples importune you, which you in your lucid moments know to be vain, do not stand to parley, but fly to business or to Pekuah, and keep this thought always prevalent, that you are only one atom of the mass of humanity, and have neither such virtue nor vice, as that you should be singled out for supernatural favours or afflictions.'

CHAP. XLVII
The prince enters and brings a new topick

'ALL this, said the astronomer, I have often thought, but my reason has been so long subjugated by an uncontrolable and overwhelming idea, that it durst not confide in its own decisions. I now see how fatally I betrayed my quiet, by suffering chimeras to prey upon me in secret; but melancholy shrinks from communication, and I never found a man before, to whom I could impart my troubles, though I had been certain of relief. I rejoice to find my own sentiments confirmed by yours, who are not easily deceived, and can have no motive or purpose to deceive. I hope that time and variety will dissipate the gloom that has so long surrounded me, and the latter part of my days will be spent in peace.'

'Your learning and virtue, said Imlac, may justly give you hopes.'

Rasselas then entered with the princess and Pekuah, and enquired whether they had contrived any new diversion for the next day. 'Such, said Nekayah, is the state of life, that none are happy but by the anticipation of change: the change itself is nothing; when we have made it, the next wish is to change again. The world is not yet exhausted; let me see something to morrow which I never saw before.'

'Variety, said Rasselas, is so necessary to content, that even the happy valley disgusted me by the recurrence of its luxuries; yet I could not forbear to reproach myself with impatience, when I saw the monks of St. Anthony support without complaint, a life, not of uniform delight, but uniform hardship.'

'Those men, answered Imlac, are less wretched in their silent convent than the Abissinian princes in their prison of pleasure. Whatever is done by the monks is incited by an adequate and reasonable motive. Their labour supplies them with necessaries; it therefore cannot be omitted, and is certainly rewarded. Their devotion prepares them for another state, and reminds them of its approach, while it fits them for it. Their time is regularly distributed; one duty succeeds another, so that they are not left open to the distraction of unguided choice, nor lost in the shades of listless inactivity. There is a certain task to be performed at an appropriated hour; and their toils are cheerful, because they consider them as acts of piety, by which they are always advancing towards endless felicity.'

'Do you think, said Nekayah, that the monastick rule is a more holy and less imperfect state than any other? May not he equally hope for future happiness who converses openly with mankind, who succours the distressed by his charity, instructs the ignorant by his learning, and contributes by his industry to the general system of life; even though he should omit some of the mortifications which are practised in the cloister, and allow himself such harmless delights as his condition may place within his reach?'

'This, said Imlac, is a question which has long divided the wise, and perplexed the good. I am afraid to decide on either part. He that lives well in the world is better than he that lives well in a monastery. But, perhaps, every one is not able to stem the temptations of publick life; and, if he cannot conquer, he may properly retreat. Some have little power to do good, and have likewise little strength to resist evil. Many are weary of their conflicts with adversity, and are willing to eject those passions which have long busied them in vain. And many are dismissed by age and diseases from the more laborious duties of society. In monasteries the weak and timorous may be happily sheltered, the weary may repose, and the penitent may meditate. Those retreats of prayer and contemplation have something so congenial to the mind of man, that, perhaps, there is scarcely one that does not purpose to close his life in pious abstraction with a few associates serious as himself.'

'Such, said Pekuah, has often been my wish, and I have heard the princess declare, that she should not willingly die in a croud.'

'The liberty of using harmless pleasures, proceeded Imlac, will not be disputed; but it is still to be examined what pleasures are harmless. The evil of any pleasure that Nekayah can image is not in the act itself, but in its consequences. Pleasure, in itself harmless, may become mischievous, by endearing to us a state which we know to be transient and probatory, and withdrawing our thoughts from that, of which every hour brings us nearer to the beginning, and of which no length of time will bring us to the end. Mortification is not virtuous in itself, nor has any other use, but that it disengages us from the allurements of sense. In the state of future perfection, to which we all aspire, there will be pleasure without danger, and security without restraint.'

The princess was silent, and Rasselas, turning to the astronomer, asked him, whether he could not delay her

retreat, by shewing her something which she had not seen
before.

'Your curiosity, said the sage, has been so general, and
your pursuit of knowledge so vigorous, that novelties are
not now very easily to be found: but what you can no longer
procure from the living may be given by the dead. Among
the wonders of this country are the catacombs, or the ancient
repositories, in which the bodies of the earliest generations
were lodged, and where, by the virtue of the gums which
embalmed them, they yet remain without corruption.'

'I know not, said Rasselas, what pleasure the sight of the
catacombs can afford; but, since nothing else is offered, I am
resolved to view them, and shall place this with many other
things which I have done, because I would do something.'

They hired a guard of horsemen, and the next day visited
the catacombs. When they were about to descend into the
sepulchral caves, 'Pekuah, said the princess, we are now again
invading the habitations of the dead; I know that you will
stay behind; let me find you safe when I return.' 'No, I will
not be left, answered Pekuah; I will go down between you
and the prince.'

They then all descended, and roved with wonder through
the labyrinth of subterraneous passages, where the bodies
were laid in rows on either side.

CHAP. XLVIII

Imlac discourses on the nature of the soul

'WHAT reason, said the prince, can be given, why the Egyptians should thus expensively preserve those carcasses which
some nations consume with fire, others lay to mingle with

the earth, and all agree to remove from their sight, as soon as decent rites can be performed?'

'The original of ancient customs, said Imlac, is commonly unknown; for the practice often continues when the cause has ceased; and concerning superstitious ceremonies it is vain to conjecture; for what reason did not dictate reason cannot explain. I have long believed that the practice of embalming arose only from tenderness to the remains of relations or friends, and to this opinion I am more inclined, because it seems impossible that this care should have been general: had all the dead been embalmed, their repositories must in time have been more spacious than the dwellings of the living. I suppose only the rich or honourable were secured from corruption, and the rest left to the course of nature.

'But it is commonly supposed that the Egyptians believed the soul to live as long as the body continued undissolved, and therefore tried this method of eluding death.'

'Could the wise Egyptians, said Nekayah, think so grosly of the soul? If the soul could once survive its separation, what could it afterwards receive or suffer from the body?'

'The Egyptians would doubtless think erroneously, said the astronomer, in the darkness of heathenism, and the first dawn of philosophy. The nature of the soul is still disputed amidst all our opportunities of clearer knowledge: some yet say, that it may be material, who, nevertheless, believe it to be immortal.'

'Some, answered Imlac, have indeed said that the soul is material, but I can scarcely believe that any man has thought it, who knew how to think; for all the conclusions of reason enforce the immateriality of mind, and all the notices of sense and investigations of science concur to prove the unconsciousness of matter.

'It was never supposed that cogitation is inherent in matter, or that every particle is a thinking being. Yet, if any part of matter be devoid of thought, what part can we suppose to think? Matter can differ from matter only in form, density, bulk, motion, and direction of motion: to which of these, however varied or combined, can consciousness be annexed? To be round or square, to be solid or fluid, to be great or little, to be moved slowly or swiftly one way or another, are modes of material existence, all equally alien from the nature of cogitation. If matter be once without thought, it can only be made to think by some new modification, but all the modifications which it can admit are equally unconnected with cogitative powers.'

'But the materialists, said the astronomer, urge that matter may have qualities with which we are unacquainted.'

'He who will determine, returned Imlac, against that which he knows, because there may be something which he knows not; he that can set hypothetical possibility against acknowledged certainty, is not to be admitted among reasonable beings. All that we know of matter is, that matter is inert, senseless and lifeless; and if this conviction cannot be opposed but by referring us to something that we know not, we have all the evidence that human intellect can admit. If that which is known may be over-ruled by that which is unknown, no being, not omniscient, can arrive at certainty.'

'Yet let us not, said the astronomer, too arrogantly limit the Creator's power.'

'It is no limitation of omnipotence, replied the poet, to suppose that one thing is not consistent with another, that the same proposition cannot be at once true and false, that the same number cannot be even and odd, that cogitation cannot be conferred on that which is created incapable of cogitation.'

'I know not, said Nekayah, any great use of this question.

Does that immateriality, which, in my opinion, you have sufficiently proved, necessarily include eternal duration?'

'Of immateriality, said Imlac, our ideas are negative, and therefore obscure. Immateriality seems to imply a natural power of perpetual duration as a consequence of exemption from all causes of decay: whatever perishes, is destroyed by the solution of its contexture, and separation of its parts; nor can we conceive how that which has no parts, and therefore admits no solution, can be naturally corrupted or impaired.'

'I know not, said Rasselas, how to conceive any thing without extension: what is extended must have parts, and you allow, that whatever has parts may be destroyed.'

'Consider your own conceptions, replied Imlac, and the difficulty will be less. You will find substance without extension. An ideal form is no less real than material bulk: yet an ideal form has no extension. It is no less certain, when you think on a pyramid, that your mind possesses the idea of a pyramid, than that the pyramid itself is standing. What space does the idea of a pyramid occupy more than the idea of a grain of corn? or how can either idea suffer laceration? As is the effect such is the cause; as thought is, such is the power that thinks; a power impassive and indiscerptible.'

'But the Being, said Nekayah, whom I fear to name, the Being which made the soul, can destroy it.'

'He, surely, can destroy it, answered Imlac, since, however unperishable, it receives from a superiour nature its power of duration. That it will not perish by any inherent cause of decay, or principle of corruption, may be shown by philosophy; but philosophy can tell no more. That it will not be annihilated by him that made it, we must humbly learn from higher authority.'

The whole assembly stood a while silent and collected. 'Let us return, said Rasselas, from this scene of mortality.

How gloomy would be these mansions of the dead to him who did not know that he shall never die; that what now acts shall continue its agency, and what now thinks shall think on for ever. Those that lie here stretched before us, the wise and the powerful of antient times, warn us to remember the shortness of our present state; they were, perhaps, snatched away while they were busy, like us, in the choice of life.'

'To me, said the princess, the choice of life is become less important; I hope hereafter to think only on the choice of eternity.'

They then hastened out of the caverns, and, under the protection of their guard, returned to Cairo.

CHAP. XLIX

The conclusion, in which nothing is concluded

It was now the time of the inundation of the Nile: a few days after their visit to the catacombs, the river began to rise.

They were confined to their house. The whole region being under water gave them no invitation to any excursions, and, being well supplied with materials for talk, they diverted themselves with comparisons of the different forms of life which they had observed, and with various schemes of happiness which each of them had formed.

Pekuah was never so much charmed with any place as the convent of St. Anthony, where the Arab restored her to the princess, and wished only to fill it with pious maidens, and to be made prioress of the order: she was weary of expectation and disgust, and would gladly be fixed in some unvariable state.

The princess thought, that of all sublunary things, knowledge was the best: She desired first to learn all sciences, and then purposed to found a college of learned women, in which she would preside, that, by conversing with the old, and educating the young, she might divide her time between the acquisition and communication of wisdom, and raise up for the next age models of prudence, and patterns of piety.

The prince desired a little kingdom, in which he might administer justice in his own person, and see all the parts of government with his own eyes; but he could never fix the limits of his dominion, and was always adding to the number of his subjects.

Imlac and the astronomer were contented to be driven along the stream of life without directing their course to any particular port.

Of these wishes that they had formed they well knew that none could be obtained. They deliberated a while what was to be done, and resolved, when the inundation should cease, to return to Abissinia.

NOTES

p. 1, l. 4. *Rasselas.* Since Johnson owned a copy of what was almost certainly the English version of Job Ludolf's *Historia Aethiopica* (1681), D. M. Lockhart plausibly suggests that he adapted *Rasselas* from *Rasselach*, used to translate *Rasselaxum* (the accusative form of *Ras-Seelaxos*) which had been mistakenly written as one word in Ludolf's genealogical table (*PMLA*, lxxviii, 1963, 517–18). The same name appears in its uncontracted form in Johnson's translation of Lobo, where reference is made to '*Rassela Christos* Lieutenant General to *Sultan Segued*' (p. 102). Another passage gives the meaning of *Ras* as 'chief' (p. 262). According to Ludolf, *Sela Christos* means 'image of Christ'. Abyssinian names were often constructed from Christian names like Christ and Mary (v. Emerson, p. 143).

p. 1, l. 8. *Ye who . . .* This opening sentence is addressed to all men, and not, as has sometimes been suggested, merely to the adherents of contemporary optimistic philosophies. Cf. Johnson's elegy on Robert Levet, ll. 1–2:

> Condemn'd to hope's delusive mine,
> As on we toil from day to day . . . (Yale, vi. 314);

Rambler 2: 'The natural flights of the human mind are not from pleasure to pleasure, but from hope to hope'; *Rambler* 67: 'There is no temper so generally indulged as hope: other passions operate by starts on particular occasions, or in certain parts of life; but hope begins with our first power of comparing our actual with our possible state, and attends us through every stage and period, always urging us forward to new acquisitions, and holding out some distant blessing to our view, promising us either relief from pain, or increase of happiness'; *Rambler* 165: 'He that indulges hope will always be disappointed.'

p. 1, l. 13. *the fourth son.* Lockhart points out that Ludolf's genealogical table lists a fourth child of the emperor as having 'Escap'd from the Rock of *Amhara*' (*op. cit.* p. 518). C. J. Rawson suggests the propriety of Johnson's hero being the fourth son 'so that his philosophic quest for happiness might be uncomplicated by the prospect of immediate succession to the throne' (*Bicentenary*

Essays, p. 92). Johnson refers in his next paragraph to 'the order of succession', even though the following sentence occurs in Lobo: 'The reigning Prince has the Power of choosing out of the Royal Family whom he pleases for a Successor' (p. 259).

p. 1, l. 13. *emperour.* 'The Kings of *Abyssinia* having formerly had several Princes Tributary to them, still retain the Title of Emperor' (Lobo, p. 260).

p. 1, l. 14. *the Father of waters.* 'The *Nile,* which the Natives call *Abavi,* that is, the Father of Waters, rises first in *Sacala* a Province of the Kingdom of *Goiama,* which is one of the most fruitful and agreeable of all the *Abyssinian* Dominion's . . . . In the Eastern part of this Kingdom on the declivity of a Mountain . . . is [the] Source of the *Nile*' (Lobo, pp. 97–98).

p. 1, l. 24. *valley.* Lockhart states that the only writer before Johnson to locate the Abyssinian princes' place of confinement in a valley (instead of on a mountain) was Francisco Alvares, whose work, published in Lisbon, 1540, became available in an English version in 1625 (*op. cit.* p. 520). Cf. J. R. Moore, '*Rasselas* and the Early Travellers to Abyssinia', *MLQ,* xv (1954), 40; G. J. Kolb, 'The "Paradise" in Abyssinia and the "Happy Valley" in *Rasselas*', *MP,* lvi (1958–9), 14, n.23.

Amhara, surrounded . . . Lockhart conjectures that Johnson's description of the mountains whose 'summits overhang the middle part' may have resulted from a conflation of Alvares's 'valley' with the Dominican Father Luis de Urreta's description of the oddly shaped mountain where the Abyssinian princes were confined. At its summit, according to Urreta, 'the stones and rocks protrude, jutting out beyond the wall for a space of more than a thousand paces' (*op. cit.* pp. 520–21, esp. n.19). Emerson quotes from the English version of the same passage, which occurs in *Purchas his Pilgrimage,* both in his summary of the literature dealing with the Abyssinian paradise (p. xxv), and in his Notes (pp. 144, 146). Cf. *Paradise Lost,* iv. 280–84:

> Nor where *Abassin* Kings thir issue Guard,
> Mount *Amara,* though this by som suppos'd
> True Paradise under the *Ethiop* Line
> By *Nilus* head, enclosd with shining Rock,
> A whole days journy high.

p. 2, l. 8. *massy:* 'weighty, ponderous, bulky' (*Dict.*), now archaic. Cf. p. 3, l. 22.

p. 2, l. 9. *engines:* mechanical contrivances.

p. 2, l. 14. *superfluities.* This word is here used in its literal sense 'overflowings' (cf. Latin *superfluere*).

p. 2, l. 18. *The sides* . . . Emerson, Kolb, and Lockhart all suggest similarities between Johnson's description of the Happy Valley and previous accounts of Abyssinia, especially that of Urreta. Cf. also Milton's description of Eden, *Paradise Lost*, iv. 246–56:

> . . . Thus was this place,
> A happy rural seat of various view;
> Groves whose rich Trees wept odorous Gumms and Balme,
> Others whose fruit burnisht with Golden Rinde
> Hung amiable, *Hesperian* Fables true,
> If true, here only, and of delicious taste:
> Betwixt them Lawns, or Level Downs, and Flocks
> Grasing the tender herb, were interpos'd,
> Or palmie hilloc, or the flourie lap
> Of som irriguous Valley spred her store,
> Flours of all hue . . .

p. 2, l. 20. *every month.* 'They sow and reap here [i.e. in a province of "the Kingdom of Damot"] in every Season, the Ground is always producing, and the Fruits ripen throughout the Year' (Lobo, p. 109).

p. 2, l. 21. *bite:* 'to go on nipping (portions of food), to nibble; to eat' (*OED*), a sense that is now obsolete. Cf. p. 5, l. 16.

p. 2, l. 27. *subtle:* 'clever; dexterous; crafty, wily' (*OED*); 'sly, artful, cunning' (*Dict.*). Lobo refers to 'the Monkies, creatures so cunning, that they would not stir if a Man came unarmed, but would run immediately when they saw a Gun' (p. 41).

solemn. However appropriately this epithet may describe an elephant 'reposing in the shade', it probably also carries overtones of its meaning 'awe-inspiring' (*OED*), 'awful' (*Dict.*). According to Augustin Calmet's *Dictionary of the Bible* (from the English translation of which Johnson quoted in *Dict.*), the elephant 'is naturally very gentle; but when enraged, no creature is more terrible'.

p. 2, l. 33. *the annual visit.* Emerson points out (pp. xxvi–xxvii) that an annual visit by the emperor is mentioned in the Italian Giacomo Baratti's narrative of his travels, an English version of which appeared in 1670. The relevant passage is quoted by Kolb, *op. cit.* p. 13.

p. 3, l. 4. *seclusion.* This word is not given in *Dict.*, though *to seclude* is there defined in its now obsolete sense 'to shut up apart'.

p. 3, l. 12. *security:* 'freedom from care, protection' (*Dict.*).

p. 3, l. 18. *paces.* In this sense a *pace* is 'a measure of five feet' (*Dict.*), the distance 'between successive stationary positions of the same foot' (*OED*). Cf. note to p. 1, l. 24.

p. 3, l. 25. *reparation:* 'the act of repairing, supply of what is wasted' (*Dict.*). (The other meaning given by Johnson—'recompense for any injury'—is now the usual one.)

p. 4, l. 1. *reposited:* 'laid up, lodged as in a place of safety' (*Dict.*). *treasures.* Emerson notes that some previous accounts of Amara mention it as a repository of the emperor's treasure (pp. xxvii, xxx).

p. 4, l. 9. *Abissinia:* the emperor of Abyssinia.

p. 4, l. 16. *publick life:* life in the world.

p. 5, l. 6. *luxury:* 'delicious fare' (*Dict.*), sumptuous and exquisite food.

p. 5, l. 10. *officiousness:* 'forwardness of civility, or respect, or endeavour (commonly in an ill sense)' (*Dict.*). (This word is no longer used in a favourable sense.)

p. 5, l. 14. *anon:* 'sometimes, now and then, at other times' (*Dict.*).

p. 6, l. 1. *I long again* . . . When bad weather on Skye had confined them indoors, Boswell expressed feelings that may well have been shared by his fellow-traveller Johnson: 'Corrichatachin [i.e. Coirechatachan], which was last night a hospital house, was, in my mind, changed to-day into a prison . . . . I was happy when tea came. Such, I take it, is the state of those who live in the country. Meals are wished for from the cravings of vacuity of mind, as well as from the desire of eating' (*Life*, v. 159).

p. 6, l. 9. *its proper pleasure:* its peculiar pleasure, the pleasure that belongs to it.

p. 6, l. 18. *it is not* . . . When a 'learned gentleman' cited, with obvious approval, the 'reflection' of an officer who had claimed to enjoy the height of human happiness in the wilds of America, Johnson replied: 'Do not allow yourself, Sir, to be imposed upon by such gross absurdity. It is sad stuff; it is brutish. If a bull could speak, he might as well exclaim—Here am I with this cow and this grass; what being can enjoy greater felicity' (*Life*, ii. 228).

p. 6, l. 26. *discovered:* 'showed, disclosed' (*Dict.*), a sense that is now rare.

p. 6, l. 27. *some solace of* . . . Emerson notes that 'Johnson had little sympathy with the sentimentalist who thinks he is unhappy when he is not really so' (p. 147). On Bennet Langton's authority, Boswell reports Johnson as saying: 'Depend upon it, that if a man *talks* of his misfortunes, there is something in them that is not disagreeable to him; for where there is nothing but pure misery, there never is any recourse to the mention of it' (*Life*, iv. 31). Johnson wrote to Boswell: 'You are always complaining of melancholy, and I conclude from those complaints that you are fond of it. No man talks of that which he is desirous to conceal' (*ib.* iii. 421).

p. 7, l. 3. *his old instructor* . . . Hill compares this with the situation existing between Polonius and the Prince in *Hamlet* (p. 163). It is interesting to note that when he wrote *Rasselas* Johnson was currently preparing an edition of Shakespeare's plays.

p. 7, l. 7. *intellects:* 'intellectual powers, mental faculties, "wits"' (*OED*), a usage common in the seventeenth and eighteenth centuries, but now archaic. Cf. *Rambler* 164: 'No man, however enslaved to his appetites, or hurried by his passions, can, while he preserves his intellects unimpaired, please himself with promoting the corruption of others'; also *Rambler* 167; *Idler* 19 (Yale, ii. 243).

p. 7, l. 21. *loneliness:* 'solitude, want of company, disposition to avoid company' (*Dict.*). Cf. l. 22, *lonely.*

p. 8, l. 6. *and sleep will* . . . Johnson once alluded to the 'effect of sleep in weakening the power of reflection (*Life*, iv. 6). On another occasion, when Boswell suggested that a man should try to combat melancholy and 'distressing' thoughts, Johnson replied: 'No, Sir. . . . He should have a lamp constantly burning in his bed-chamber during the night, and if wakefully disturbed, take a book, and read, and compose himself to rest' (*ib.* ii. 440).

p. 8, l. 18. *Sir, said he* . . . Hill cites *Cymbeline*, III. iii (p. 163), where compare Belarius's reply to the two young princes.

p. 9, l. 1. *we less regard others.* Cf. *Rambler* 78: 'Custom so far regulates the sentiments, at least of common minds, that I believe men may be generally observed to grow less tender as they advance in age.'

p. 10, l. 12. *run.* Johnson gives this form for both 'the preterite imperfect and participle passive' in 'A Grammar of the English Tongue', prefixed to *Dict.*, adding that of this and similar verbs the preterite forms in *a* are mostly obsolete. In the body of his work he gives only *ran.* Cf. p. 13, l. 27.

p. 10, l. 28. *He considered* . . . Johnson often took himself to task for his misuse of time. On his fifty-fifth birthday, for example, he wrote in his diary: 'I have now spent fifty five years in resolving, having from the earliest time almost that I can remember been forming schemes of a better life. I have done nothing; the need of doing therefore is pressing, since the time of doing is short' (Yale, i. 81). Almost nine years later he doubts 'whether I have not lived resolving, till the possibility of performance is past' (*ib.* i. 159).

p. 11, l. 23. *intellectual luxury:* imaginary delights.

p. 11, l. 27. *idle resolves.* Cf. *Idler* 27: 'I believe most men may review all the lives that have passed within their observation, without remembring one efficacious resolution' (Yale, ii. 85); note to p. 10, l. 28.

p. 12, l. 12. *grate:* 'a barred place of confinement for animals, also, a prison or cage for human beings' (*OED*), a sense that is now obsolete.

p. 12, l. 13. *clambering.* With this transitive use cf. Johnson's *Journey*: 'The inhabitants of *Sky*, and of the other Islands, which I have seen, are commonly of the middle stature. . . . Their strength is proportionate to their size, but they are accustomed to run upon rough ground, and therefore can with great agility skip over the bog, or clamber the mountain' (pp. 190, 191).

p. 12, l. 15. *prominence:* projecting part, overhang. Cf. p. 2, ll. 1–2.

p. 12, l. 26. *the blessing of hope.* Cf. *Rambler* 67: 'Hope is necessary in every condition . . . Nor does it appear that the happiest lot of terrestrial existence can set us above the want of this general blessing'; *Idler* 58: 'It is necessary to hope, tho' hope should always be deluded, for hope itself is happiness, and its frustrations, however frequent, are yet less dreadful than its extinction' (Yale, ii. 182).

p. 13, l. 2. *amusements.* Johnson often used *amuse* in the sense 'fill with thoughts that engage the mind' (*Dict.*). For example, he described *Coriolanus* as 'one of the most amusing' of Shakespeare's plays (Raleigh, p. 179). Cf. p. 22, l. 22.

p. 13, l. 3. *he discerned* . . . Cf. *Rambler* 5: 'A man that has formed [the] habit of turning every new object to his entertainment, finds in the productions of nature an inexhaustible stock of materials upon which he can employ himself.'

p. 13, l. 17. *A dissertation* . . . G. J. Kolb points out that this chapter is indebted to John Wilkins's *Mathematical Magick* (1648), ii. esp. chaps. 1, 2, 6–8 ('Johnson's "Dissertation on Flying" and John Wilkins's "Mathematical Magick"', *MP*, xlvii, 1949, 24–31; reprinted in *New Light on Dr. Johnson*, 1959). R. G. Lawrence suggests that this episode may also have been inspired by the fatal 'flight' (which Johnson could have witnessed) of Robert Cadman from the spire of St. Mary's Church, Shrewsbury, 2 Feb. 1740 (*NQ*, ccii, 1957, 348–51). In *Rambler* 199 'Hermeticus' says: 'I have twice dislocated my limbs, and once fractured my skull, in essaying to fly.'

p. 13, l. 18. *artists:* 'professors of an art, generally of an art manual' (*Dict.*).

p. 13, l. 19. *accommodation:* 'the supplying with what is suitable or requisite' (*OED*). Cf. *Rambler* 145: 'The meanest artizan or manufacturer contributes more to the accommodation of life, than the profound scholar and argumentative theorist.'

p. 13, l. 22. *By a wheel* . . . 'Johnson was perhaps thinking of the great waterwheels at Marly, constructed in 1685, by which Versailles and St. Cloud were supplied with water' (Hill, p. 164).

p. 14, l. 6. *a sailing chariot:* a vehicle that travels by means of sails. The title of Wilkins's *Mathematical Magick*, ii. chap. 2, reads: 'Of a Sailing Chariot, that may without Horses be driven on the Land by the Wind, as Ships are on the Sea.'

p. 14, l. 27. *subtler*. Johnson defines *subtile* in this sense as 'thin, not dense, not gross' (*Dict.*).

p. 15, l. 20. *trace the Nile* ... The would-be aviator is proposing the possibility of an aerial view of the whole course of the Nile. Johnson's contemporary reader might also have recalled that the actual source of the Nile had long been a subject of speculation. Herodotus says (ii. 28) that he has met no one able to give him certain knowledge of the source of the Nile. The pursuit of such knowledge (along with speculations on the stars and the causes of the tides) was traditionally associated with the evils of *curiositas* or improper 'curiosity', with 'star-knowledge' as opposed to the more important 'self-knowledge' (v. Howard Schultz, *Milton and Forbidden Knowledge*, 1955, pp. 12–13, 62). Cf. Raphael's warning to Adam in *Paradise Lost*, viii; Swift's satire on the Laputians in *Gulliver's Travels*, pt. iii, esp. chap. 2.

p. 15, l. 31 *Nothing* ... Cf. Johnson's observation 'that so many objections might be made to every thing, that nothing could overcome them but the necessity of doing something' (*Life*, ii. 128).

p. 16, l. 1. *volant*: 'flying, passing through the air' (*Dict.*), a sense Johnson illustrated by a quotation from Wilkins's *Mathematical Magick*.

p. 16, l. 10. *every man has* ... Cf. *Rambler* 44 (written by Mrs. Elizabeth Carter): 'Society is the true sphere of human virtue'; *Rambler* 56: 'The great end of society is mutual beneficence.'

p. 16, l. 26. *levity*: 'lightness, not heaviness' (*Dict.*).

p. 17, l. 2. *half dead*. 'Johnson is content with giving the artist a ducking. Voltaire would have crippled him for life at the very least; most likely would have killed him on the spot' (Hill, p. 165).

p. 17, l. 12. *support*: keep from giving way to weakness or despair.

p. 17, l. 14. *the rainy season*. 'The Winter begins here in *May*, and its greatest rigour is from the middle of *June*, to the middle of *September*. The Rains that are almost continually falling in this Season make it impossible to go far from Home' (Lobo, p. 63).

p. 17, l. 28. *imlac*. On Bennet Langton's authority, Boswell reports Johnson as saying: 'Imlac in "Rasselas", I spelt with a *c* at the end, because it is less like English, which should always have the Saxon *k* added to the *c*' (*Life*, iv. 31). Kolb (following Emerson,

p. 150) points out that the name 'Icon-Imlac' occurs in Ludolf's *History* (*MP*, lvi, 1958–9, 11). Lockhart adds that in the form used by Johnson it occurs only there, and that, curiously enough, reference to this emperor is made 'in connection with the establishment of the custom of enforced exile for the princes' (*PMLA*, lxxviii, 518–19).

p. 17, l. 28. *rehearsed:* recited aloud.

the various conditions of humanity. Emerson notes that this was 'such a subject as Johnson chose over and over again in his Essays' (p. 150).

p. 18, l. 6. *loved his curiosity.* Cf. Johnson's Dedication to Lobo: 'A generous and elevated Mind is distinguish'd by nothing more Certainly than an eminent Degree of Curiosity, nor is that Curiosity ever more agreeably or usefully employ'd, than in examining the Laws and Customs of foreign Nations' (sig. A2ᵛ); *Rambler* 103: 'Curiosity is, in great and generous minds, the first passion and the last; and perhaps always predominates in proportion to the strength of the contemplative faculties'; *Rambler* 150: 'Curiosity is one of the permanent and certain characteristics of a vigorous intellect.' For an account of Johnson's attitude to 'curiosity' v. my article in *Johnson, Boswell*, pp. 122–36.

p. 18, l. 25. *To talk in publick*... Dr. William Maxwell considered Johnson himself 'as a kind of publick oracle, whom every body thought they had a right to visit and consult' (*Life*, ii. 118–19). Cf. *Adventurer* 85: 'To read, write, and converse in due proportions, is, therefore, the business of a man of letters' (Yale, ii. 416). C. G. Osgood suggests that Johnson's sentence may owe something to Macrobius, *Saturnalia*, I. ii. 4: 'neque enim recte institutus animus requiescere aut utilius aut honestius usquam potest, quam in aliqua opportunitate docte ac liberaliter colloquendi, interrogandique et respondendi comitate' (*MLN*, lxix, 1954, 246).

p. 18, l. 30. *Goiama:* one of the five kingdoms belonging to the empire of Abyssinia (Lobo, p. 46). Cf. note to p. 1, l. 14.

p. 19, l. 1. *the fountain of the Nile:* the source of the Nile, for a description of which cf. Lobo: 'This Spring, or rather these two Springs, are two Holes each about two Feet Diameter, a Stones cast Distant from each other... 'Tis believed here, that these Springs are the Vents of a great Subterraneous Lake' (p. 98).

p. 19, l. 2. *Africk.* 'Johnson, in his translation of Lobo, writes *Africa* or *Africk* indifferently' (Hill, p. 166).

p. 19, l. 6. *spoiled:* despoiled.

governours. 'The Governors purchase their Commissions, or to speak properly their privilege of pillaging the Provinces' (Lobo, p. 263). But cf. also Imlac's next speech.

p. 19, l. 22. *Subordination* . . . Johnson remarked to Boswell: 'Sir, I am a friend to subordination, as most conducive to the happiness of society' (*Life*, i. 408). It was his considered view that 'order cannot be had but by subordination' (*ib.* iii. 383).

p. 19, l. 24. *the supreme magistrate:* the ruler or principal officer of government.

p. 20, l. 10. *some desire is* . . . Boswell writes: 'When I, in a low-spirited fit, was talking to him [i.e. Johnson] with indifference of the pursuits which generally engage us in a course of action, and inquiring a *reason* for taking so much trouble; "Sir (said he, in an animated tone) it is driving on the system of life"' (*Life*, iv. 112).

p. 20, l. 23. *As every hour* . . . Cf. *Rambler* 121: 'That power of giving pleasure which novelty supplies'; *Rambler* 135: 'Novelty is itself a source of gratification'; *Life of Prior:* 'Novelty is the great source of pleasure' (*Lives*, ii. 206). According to William Maxwell, Johnson observed that 'the mind, like the body . . . delighted in change and novelty' (*Life*, ii. 123). Cf. also *Spectator* 626, which Johnson described as 'one of the finest pieces in the English language' (*ib.* iii. 33): 'Novelty is . . . the source of admiration, which lessens in proportion to our familiarity with objects, and upon a thorough acquaintance is utterly extinguished. . . . It is with knowledge as with wealth, the pleasure of which lies more in making endless additions, than in taking a review of our old store.'

p. 20, l. 27. *I did not* . . . Cf. Johnson's remarks about his own tutor at Pembroke College, Oxford: 'He was a very worthy man, but a heavy man, and I did not profit much by his instructions' (*Life*, i. 59).

p. 20, l. 32. *negociate:* 'do business or trade, traffic' (*OED*), a sense that is now obsolete. Cf. p. 88, l. 12.

p. 20, l. 33. *parsimony:* 'frugality' (*Dict.*), good management of money or resources in a good or neutral sense.

p. 21, l. 14. *sciences:* branches or kinds of knowledge, learning. Cf. p. 98, l. 13; p. 113, l. 7; p. 123, l. 1.

p. 21, l. 15. *obliged:* put under an obligation, a sense that now exists only in legal usage.

p. 21, l. 27. *Surat.* 'An important port of India. . . . Founded at the beginning of the eighteenth century, and soon rising to the rank of chief commercial city . . . it was probably the most populous city of India during the eighteenth century' (Emerson, p. 152).

p. 22, l. 4. *pleasing terrour.* Cf. Burke's *Philosophical Enquiry into the Origin of our Ideas of the Sublime and Beautiful* (1757): 'When danger or pain press too nearly, they are incapable of giving any delight, and are simply terrible; but at certain distances, and with certain modifications, they may be, and they are delightful, as we every day experience' (1776 edn., p. 60). Cf. note to p. 26, l. 10.

p. 22, l. 24. *for show:* for the look of the thing, to save appearances.

p. 22, l. 27. *admiration:* wonderment, inclination to marvel (at something), a sense that is now obsolete. Cf. p. 40, l. 18.

p. 23, l. 20. *Agra.* 'The chief city of the Mogul empire, founded by Akbar the great in the sixteenth century. It remained the provincial capital till the mutiny of 1857, although its prestige had long before passed to Surat, Bombay, and other cities' (Emerson, p. 152).

p. 23, l. 21. *the great Mogul.* It is interesting to note that this term, first applied to Akbar the Great, had become a mere name as a result of the Mohammedan conquest of Hindustan, which occurred twenty years before *Rasselas* was written.

p. 24, l. 17. *accommodations:* 'conveniencies, things requisite to ease or refreshment' (*Dict.*) Cf. p. 50, l. 24.

p. 24, l. 18. *The Persians* . . . Cf. John Harris's *Navigantium atque Itinerantium Bibliotheca; or, A Complete Collection of Voyages and Travels,* rev. John Campbell, ii. (1748), 892: 'As they [i.e. the Persians] were observed anciently to be of all Men the most civil and obliging, they retain the same Disposition to this Day, especially toward Foreigners, who admire their Hospitality and Benevolence.'

p. 24, l. 24. *and who* . . . v. note to p. 91, l. 12.

p. 25, l. 4. *I found that Poetry* . . . Mrs. Piozzi (formerly Johnson's friend Mrs. Thrale) writes: 'His idea of poetry was magnificent indeed, and very fully was he persuaded of its superiority over every other talent bestowed by heaven on man. His chapter upon that particular subject in his *Rasselas*, is really written from the fulness of his heart' (*Anecdotes*, p. 130). According to William Maxwell, Johnson observed that 'every nation derived their highest reputation from the splendour and dignity of their writers' (*Life*, ii. 125). C. R. Tracy suggests that Johnson 'is doing something quite different from outlining his own aesthetic creed', that 'the difference between Imlac's views and Johnson's could hardly be exaggerated' (*Yale Review*, xxxix, 1949, 307, 308). It could, however, be argued that Imlac outlines the knowledge of 'nature' and 'life' which, in Johnson's view, was indispensable to the *complete* poet. Cf. the praise of Shakespeare in his famous *Preface*, and his description, in the *Life of Milton*, of the 'powers' required by the epic poet (*Lives*, i. 170–71).

p. 25, l. 7. *And it yet* . . . Cf. *Preface to Shakespeare*: 'The reverence due to writings that have long subsisted arises therefore not from any credulous confidence in the superior wisdom of past ages, or gloomy persuasion of the degeneracy of mankind, but is the consequence of acknowledged and indubitable positions, that what has been longest known has been most considered, and what is most considered is best understood' (Raleigh, p. 10).

p. 25, l. 14. *Nature and Passion* . . . Cf. *Adventurer* 95: 'Writers of all ages have had the same sentiments, because they have in all ages had the same objects of speculation. . . . [The] influence [of the passions] is uniform, and their effects nearly the same in every human breast' (Yale, ii. 425, 426–7); *Adventurer* 99: 'Human nature is always the same' (*ib.* p. 431).

p. 25, l. 15. *the first writers* . . . Cf. *Rambler* 86: 'One of the old poets congratulates himself that he has the untrodden regions of Parnassus before him, and that his garland will be gathered from plantations which no writer had yet culled. But the imitator treads a beaten walk, and, with all his diligence, can only hope to find a few flowers or branches untouched by his predecessor'; *Rambler* 143: 'Bruyere declares, that we are come into the world too late to produce any thing new, that nature and life are preoccupied, and that description and sentiment have been long exhausted. . . . The same ideas and combinations of ideas have been long in the possession of other hands'; *Rambler* 169: 'It has often been inquired, why . . . we fall below the ancients in the art of composition. . . . Some advantage they might gain merely by priority, which put them in possession of the most natural sentiments, and left us nothing but servile repetition or forced conceits'; Joseph Warton's *Essay on the Genius and Writings of Pope* (which Johnson reviewed in the *Literary Magazine* for 1756): 'St. Jerom relates, that his preceptor Donatus, explaining that sensible passage in Terence, "Nihil est dictum quod non sit dictum prius," railed severely at the ancients, for taking from him his best thoughts; "Pereant qui ante nos, nostra dixerunt"' (1762, 2nd revised edn., p. 88). Boswell reports Johnson as saying: 'Modern writers are the moons of literature; they shine with reflected light, with light borrowed from the ancients' (*Life*, iii. 333).

p. 25, l. 21. *that the first* . . . This was a distinction commonly made between Homer and Virgil. Johnson said that 'the dispute as to the comparative excellence of Homer or Virgil was inaccurate', adding: 'We must consider whether Homer was not the greatest poet, though Virgil may have produced the finest poem. Virgil was indebted to Homer for the whole invention of the structure of an epick poem' (*Life*, iii. 193–4). Cf. *Life of Dryden*: 'In the comparison of Homer and Virgil the discriminative excellence of Homer is elevation and comprehension of thought, and that of Virgil is grace and splendor of diction' (*Lives*, i. 447–8).

p. 25, l. 25. *suspended*. 'It was an Arab custom to suspend in some public place, as a mosque, works which had received the highest praise at the festival of Okad. Seven of these, belonging to the sixth century, were designated Muallakat "suspended" and became a sort of standard for Arabic poetry in after times' (Emerson, p. 154).

p. 25, l. 26. *no man was* . . . Cf. *Rambler* 153: 'No man ever yet became great by imitation'; *Life of Cowley*: 'No man could be born a metaphysical poet, nor assume the dignity of a writer, by descriptions copied from descriptions, by imitations borrowed from imitations, by traditional imagery and hereditary similes (*Lives*, i. 21).

p. 25, l. 28. *to nature and to life*. Cf. *Life of Dryden*, where Johnson complains that poets too infrequently derive their material 'from nature or from life' (*Lives*, i. 430). As an eighteenth-century critical term, *nature* usually included both 'nature' (external nature) and 'life' (human nature). Cf. Pope's famous dictum 'First follow Nature', and Johnson's praise of Shakespeare as 'the poet of nature' (Raleigh, p. 11). With the references to 'nature' and 'life' later in this chapter cf. Johnson's review of Warton's *Essay on Pope* (*Literary Magazine*, i. 36), *Preface to Shakespeare* (Raleigh, p. 39), *Life of Cowley* (*Lives*, i. 19), and *Life*, ii. 86.

p. 26, l. 10. *Whatever is beautiful* . . . It has been variously pointed out—by S. H. Monk, *The Sublime: A Study of Critical Theories in 18th-Century England* (1935), p. 100, n.47, by Scott Elledge, *PMLA*, lxii (1947), 157, and by J. H. Hagstrum, *Samuel Johnson's Literary Criticism* (1952), pp. 130–31—that Johnson is here indebted to Burke's *Philosophical Enquiry*. Cf. Hagstrum, p. 131: 'The careful distinction between the dreadful and the beautiful, between the "awfully vast" and the "elegantly little", is the Burkean antithesis. In this passage appear those familiar natural phenomena that Burke and others after him regularly cited as means of evoking the sublime (mountains and deserts, crags and pinnacles) as well as those that aroused the agreeable and milder pleasures of the beautiful (trees and flowers, rivulets and clouds).'

p. 26, l. 28. *The business* . . . Johnson always welcomed in poetry 'the grandeur of generality', claiming that 'all the power of description is destroyed by a scrupulous enumeration; and the force of metaphors is lost when the mind by the mention of particulars is turned more upon the original than the secondary sense, more upon that from which the illustration is drawn than that to which it is applied' (*Lives*, i. 45). Cf. *Rambler* 36: 'Poetry cannot dwell upon the minuter distinctions, by which one species differs from another, without departing from that simplicity of grandeur which fills the imagination; nor dissect the latent qualities of things, without losing its general power of gratifying every mind, by recalling its conceptions.' Arguably Johnson, who showed a marked tendency towards visualization in reading poetry, would have objected not to a streaked tulip but to any attempt to *number* its streaks.

p. 27, l. 7. *His character:* his role as a poet.

p. 27, l. 16. *transcendental:* 'general, pervading many particulars' (*Dict.*).

p. 27, l. 20. *the legislator of mankind*. Cf. Warton's *Essay on Pope*: 'I have lately seen a manuscript ode, entitled, "On the Use and Abuse of Poetry", in which Orpheus is considered . . . as the first legislator and civilizer of mankind' (1762 edn., p. 58). As already stated, Johnson had reviewed Warton's volume.

p. 28, l. 4. *enthusiastic*. In the eighteenth century 'enthusiasm' most often denoted extravagant, ill-regulated emotion.

p. 28, l. 25. *By what means* . . . During a journey with Boswell in June 1781, Johnson, having never looked at *Rasselas* since the year of its publication, seized upon a copy Boswell had with him and read it with concentration. Boswell adds: 'He pointed out to me the following remarkable passage ["By what means . . . Supreme Being"]. He said, "This, Sir, no man can explain otherwise"' (*Life*, iv. 119).

p. 28, l. 29. *natural:* 'having a certain relative status by birth, natural-born' (*OED*), a sense that is now obsolete. Johnson gives as one meaning of the substantival form *natural* 'native, original inhabitant' (*Dict.*).

p. 29, l. 7. *and mingle with* . . . Cf. 'the full tide of human existence' which Johnson associated with London's Charing Cross (*Life*, ii. 337).

p. 29, l. 12. *to which* . . . 'The *Abyssins* were much addicted to Pilgrimages into the Holy-Land' (Lobo, p. 254). Yet Imlac's subsequent remarks on pilgrimage, despite the fact that Lobo had censured as 'superstitious' the brand of Christianity practised by the Abyssinians (p. 47), clearly have a general applicability.

p. 29, l. 14. *visitants:* 'those who visit a place, shrine, etc. from religious motives' (*OED*).

p. 30, l. 1. *That the* . . . When Boswell wrote claiming that he derived a 'peculiar satisfaction' from 'celebrating the festival of Easter in St. Paul's cathedral', Johnson replied: 'It may be dangerous to receive too readily, and indulge too fondly, opinions, from which, perhaps, no pious mind is wholly disengaged, of local sanctity and local devotion. You know what strange effects they have produced over a great part of the Christian world. I am now writing, and you, when you read this, are reading under the Eye of Omnipresence. To what degree fancy is to be admitted into religious offices, it would require much deliberation to determine.

I am far from intending totally to exclude it. . . . Fancy is always to act in subordination to Reason. We may take Fancy for a companion, but must follow Reason as our guide. We may allow Fancy to suggest certain ideas in certain places; but Reason must always be heard, when she tells us, that those ideas and those places have no natural or necessary relation. When we enter a church we habitually recall to mind the duty of adoration, but we must not omit adoration for want of a temple; because we know, and ought to remember, that the Universal Lord is every where present; and that, therefore, to come to Iona or to Jerusalem, though it may be useful, cannot be necessary (*Life*, ii. 276–7).

p. 30, l. 3. *that some places* . . . Cf. Johnson's own reaction to Iona; 'We were now treading that illustrious Island, which was once the luminary of the *Caledonian* regions, whence savage clans and roving barbarians derived the benefits of knowledge, and the blessings of religion. To abstract the mind from all local emotion would be impossible, if it were endeavoured, and would be foolish, if it were possible. Whatever withdraws us from the power of our senses; whatever makes the past, the distant, or the future predominate over the present, advances us in the dignity of thinking beings. Far from me and from my friends, be such frigid philosophy as may conduct us indifferent and unmoved over any ground which has been dignified by wisdom, bravery, or virtue. That man is little to be envied, whose patriotism would not gain force upon the plain of *Marathon*, or whose piety would not grow warmer among the ruins of *Iona*' (*Journey*, pp. 346–7).

p. 30, l. 16. *Knowledge is* . . . Johnson remarked to Boswell: 'All knowledge is of itself some value. There is nothing so minute or inconsiderable, that I would not rather know it than not' (*Life*, ii. 357). In the last year of his life he wrote to Susannah Thrale: 'All knowledge is pleasing in its first effects, and may be subsequently useful. Of whatever we see we always wish to know, and congratulate ourselves when we know that of which we perceive another to be ignorant' (*Letters*, iii. 144). One day, when on the Thames with Boswell, Johnson asked the boy who was rowing them: '"What would you give, my lad, to know about the Argonauts?" "Sir (said the boy), I would give what I have."' Boswell continues: 'Johnson was much pleased with his answer, and we gave him a double fare. Dr. Johnson then turning to me, "Sir (said he), a desire of knowledge is the natural feeling of mankind; and every human being whose mind is not debauched, will be willing to give all that he has to get knowledge"' (*Life*, i. 458).

p. 30, l. 24. *we grow more happy* . . . Johnson said: 'A peasant and a philosopher may be equally *satisfied*, but not equally *happy*. Happiness consists in the multiplicity of agreeable consciousness. A peasant has not capacity for having equal happiness with a philosopher' (*Life*, ii. 9).

p. 30, l. 33. *policy:* 'the art of government' (*Dict.*).

p. 31, l. 6. *I envy none* . . . When he wrote this, Johnson was perhaps thinking of the letters that were then passing between London and Lichfield, where his mother lay dying.

p. 31, l. 9. *Human life is* . . . On the authority of William Maxwell, Boswell reports it as Johnson's frequent observation 'that there was more to be endured than enjoyed, in the general condition of human life' (*Life*, ii. 124). When it was debated whether life 'was upon the whole more happy or miserable, Johnson was decidedly for the balance of misery' (*ib*. iv. 300). He once wrote to Mrs. Thrale: 'Philosophers there are who try to make themselves believe that this life is happy, but they believe it only while they are saying it, and never yet produced conviction in a single mind' (*Letters*, i. 366). Cf. *Rambler* 32: 'So large a part of human life passes in a state contrary to our natural desires, that one of the principal topicks of moral instruction is the art of bearing calamities'; *Rambler* 165: 'The utmost felicity which we can ever attain will be little better than alleviation of misery'; *Adventurer* 120: 'There is, indeed, no topic on which it is more superfluous to accumulate authorities, nor any assertion of which our own eyes will more easily discover, or our sensations more frequently impress the truth, than, that misery is the lot of man, that our present state is a state of danger and infelicity' (Yale, ii. 466); *Life of Collins:* 'Man is not born for happiness' (*Lives*, iii. 337).

p. 31, l. 15. *the choice of life*. The 'choice of life' (βίων αἱρεσις, *vitarum electio*) was, in one context or another, a frequent topos in classical literature. Of most relevance for *Rasselas* is its occurrence in Cicero's *De Officiis*, i. 32–33 (115, 117, 119): 'ipsi . . . gerere quam personam velimus, a nostra voluntate proficiscitur. itaque se alii ad philosophiam, alii ad ius civile, alii ad eloquentiam applicant . . .

in primis . . . constituendum est, quos nos et quales esse velimus et
in quo genere vitae, quae deliberatio est omnium difficillima.
ineunte enim adulescentia, cum est maxima imbecillitas consilii,
tum id sibi quisque genus aetatis degendae constituit, quod maxime
adamavit; itaque ante implicatur aliquo certo genere cursuque
vivendi, quam potuit, quod optimum esset, iudicare . . . illud autem
maxime rarum genus est eorum, qui aut excellenti ingenii magni-
tudine aut praeclara eruditione atque doctrina aut utraque re ornati
spatium etiam deliberandi habuerunt, quem potissimum vitae
cursum sequi vellent.' ('What role we ourselves may choose to
sustain is decided by our own free choice. And so some turn to
philosophy, others to the civil law, and still others to oratory. . . .
Above all we must decide who and what manner of men we wish
to be and what calling in life we would follow; and this is the most
difficult problem in the world. For it is in the years of early youth,
when our judgment is most immature, that each of us decides that
his calling in life shall be that to which he has taken a special liking.
And thus he becomes engaged in some particular calling and career
in life, before he is fit to decide intelligently what is best for him . . .
There is one class of people that is very rarely met with: it is composed of those who are endowed with marked natural ability, or
exceptional advantages of education and culture, or both, and who
also have time to consider carefully what career in life they prefer
to follow.' Loeb edn., trans. Walter Miller, 1913, pp. 119, 121).
Cf. also Lucian's Dialogue in which Zeus and Hermes offer various
philosophic lives for sale; Plato, *Republic*, ix. 7 (581C), x. 15
(617D); Aristotle, *Ethics*, i. 5; Cicero, *Tusculanae Disputationes*, v. 3
(8–9); Macrobius, *Commentariorum in Somnium Scipionis*, ii. 17; the
Judgment of Paris (which may be interpreted as a choice between
pleasure, power and wisdom). Johnson originally intended that
'The Choice of Life' should appear as the title of his book.

p. 31, l. 21. *My children should* . . . When he wrote this, Johnson
was perhaps thinking of his own dying mother, who seems to have
taken care to give her son a very early grounding in religion. Cf.
Yale, i. 10; *Life*, i. 38, 40; *Anecdotes*, pp. 21–22.

p. 31, l. 26. *glide quietly away*. Cf. *The Vanity of Human Wishes*,
ll. 293–4:

> An age that melts with unperceiv'd decay,
> And glides in modest innocence away (Yale, vi. 105).

p. 31, l. 29. *specious:* 'showy, pleasing to the view; superficially, not solidly right' (*Dict.*), a sense that as applied to material things is now rare.

p. 32, l. 3. *At last . . .* Cf. *Idler* 43: 'The man of business, wearied with unsatisfactory prosperity, retires to the town of his nativity, and expects to play away the last years with the companions of his childhood, and recover youth in the fields where he once was young' (Yale, ii. 136).

p. 32, l. 22. *secrecy of solitude.* Cf. Boswell's remarks on London: 'In London, a man may live in splendid society at one time, and in frugal retirement at another, without animadversion. There, and there alone, a man's own house is truly his *castle*, in which he can be in perfect safety from intrusion whenever he pleases' (*Life*, iii. 378–9).

p. 32, l. 31. *But I was . . .* In a letter to his friend Joseph Baretti written in July 1762, Johnson describes his first return to his native Lichfield after a long absence in London: 'Last winter I went down to my native town, where I found the streets much narrower and shorter than I thought I had left them, inhabited by a new race of people, to whom I was very little known. My play-fellows were grown old, and forced me to suspect that I was no longer young. My only remaining friend has changed his principles, and was become the tool of the predominant faction' (*Letters*, i. 139).

p. 33, l. 10. *addressed:* paid addresses to, courted (cf. *OED*), a sense that is now obsolete.

p. 35, l. 24. *perturbation:* 'disquiet of mind; restlessness of passions' (*Dict.*), in this instance resulting from excitement rather than anxiety, for Johnson goes on to say: 'Much of his uneasiness was now removed.'

p. 36, l. 10. *knowledge is . . .* Cf. *Ecclesiastes*, ix. 16: 'Then said I, Wisdom is better than strength.'

p. 36, l. 17. *It has been . . .* Cf. *Pope's Essay on Man*, iii. 169–78:
> See him from Nature rising slow to Art!
> To copy Instinct then was Reason's part;
> Thus then to Man the voice of Nature spake—
> "Go, from the Creatures thy instructions take:
> Learn from the birds what food the thickets yield;

> Learn from the beasts the physic of the field;
> Thy arts of building from the bee receive;
> Learn of the mole to plow, the worm to weave;
> Learn of the little Nautilus to sail,
> Spread the thin oar, and catch the driving gale."

For previous instances of this topos v. *The Poems of Alexander Pope*, gen. ed. John Butt (Twickenham edn.), III. i: *An Essay on Man*, ed. Maynard Mack (1964, reprinted), pp. 110–11 n.

p. 37, l. 11. *Great works are* . . . G. L. Barnett points out that this passage is reminiscent of Cicero's *De Senectute*, vi. 17: 'Non viribus aut velocitate aut celeritate corporum res magnae geruntur, sed consilio, auctoritate, sententia . . .' (*NQ*, cci, 1956, 485–6). Cf. *Rambler* 25: 'Labour vigorously continued has not often failed of its reward.'

p. 37, l. 13. *He that shall walk* . . . Boswell writes of Johnson: 'He was all his life fond [of computation], as it fixed his attention steadily upon something without, and prevented his mind from preying upon itself' (*Life*, i. 72). Mrs. Piozzi writes: 'When Mr. Johnson felt his fancy, or fancied he felt it, disordered, his constant recurrence was to the study of arithmetic; and one day that he was totally confined to his chamber, and I enquired what he had been doing to divert himself; he shewed me a calculation which I could scarce be made to understand, so vast was the plan of it, and so very intricate were the figures: no other indeed than that the national debt, computing it at one hundred and eighty millions sterling, would, if converted into silver, serve to make a meridian of that metal, I forget how broad, for the globe of the whole earth, the real *globe*' (*Anecdotes*, p. 53). Hill points out, on the basis of the figures in the text, that Johnson 'must have reckoned vigorous walking at the rate of a little over three miles an hour' (p. 74).

p. 37, l. 22. *a prey to superstition.* Boswell writes of Johnson: 'He was prone to superstition, but not to credulity. Though his imagination might incline him to a belief of the marvellous and the mysterious, his vigorous reason examined the evidence with jealousy' (*Life*, iv. 426; v. 17–18).

p. 37, l. 25. *Many things* . . . Cf. *Adventurer* 81: 'There is scarce any man but has found himself able at the instigation of necessity, to do what in a state of leisure and deliberation he would have concluded impossible' (Yale, ii. 401–2).

p. 38, l. 9. *to repose on:* 'to confide or place one's trust in, to rely on, a thing or person' (*OED*), a sense that is now obsolete. Cf. *Rambler* 144: 'His hearers repose upon his candour and veracity.'

p. 39, l. 29. *dreary:* 'gloomy, dismal, horrid' (*Dict.*) in a stronger sense than is now current.

p. 40, l. 12. *eat*. Johnson gives both *ate* and *eat* as the preterite forms of *to eat* (*Dict.*). Cf. p. 90, l. 16.

p. 40, l. 23. *frighted*. Johnson records both *to fright* and *to frighten* (*Dict.*).

p. 40, l. 30. *dignity:* elevated rank.

p. 40, l. 33. *the ruggedness of the commercial race.* Johnson defines 'ruggedness' in this sense as 'roughness' (*Dict.*). Cf. his remarks on the booksellers of Dryden's age: 'The general conduct of traders was much less liberal in those times than in our own; their views were narrower, and their manners grosser. To the mercantile ruggedness of that race the delicacy of the poet was sometimes exposed' (*Lives*, i. 407). He once said that he had found mankind 'worse in commercial dealings, more disposed to cheat, than I had any notion of' (*Life*, iii. 236). For Johnson's more favourable attitude towards the 'commercial race' of his own age v. J. H. Middendorf, *Johnson, Boswell*, p. 60.

p. 41, l. 15. *prosperous:* without untoward incident or mishap, propitious.

p. 41, l. 22. *You will here . . .* Hill quotes (p. 175) from William Lithgow's *Travels* (1692 edn.): 'This incorporate World of *Grand Cairo* is the most admirable and greatest City, seen upon the Earth, being thrice as large of bounds as *Constantinople*, and likewise so populous, but not so well builded, being situate in a pleasant Plain, and in the heart of *Egypt,* kissing *Nilus* at some parts. . . . There is a great Commerce here with exceeding many Nations, for by their concurring hither, it is wonderfully peopled with infinite Numbers' (pp. 291–2, 293).

p. 41, l. 31. *offended*. This word may here contain some vestige of its early, now obsolete, meaning 'to strike so as to hurt' (*OED*).

p. 42, l. 4. *the vulgar:* the common people.

p. 42, l. 11. *acquaintance.* 'Originally a collective noun, with both sing. and pl. sense, but now normally *singular*, with pl. *acquaintances*' (*OED*). Cf. p. 62, l. 30; p. 107, l. 14.

p. 42, l. 14. *could make no discovery of:* could not reveal.

p. 42, l. 26. *the voluptuous:* those inclined to ease and luxury.

p. 43, l. 16. *to shun myself.* Johnson himself sought company as a means of escaping from his own melancholy thoughts. On one occasion he affirmed: 'I am very unwilling to be left alone, Sir, and therefore I go with my company down the first pair of stairs, in some hopes that they may, perhaps, return again' (*Life*, i. 490).

p. 43, l. 18. *Every man* . . . Cf. *Adventurer* 138: 'In estimating the pain or pleasure of any particular state, every man, indeed, draws his decisions from his own breast, and cannot with certainty determine, whether other minds are affected by the same causes in the same manner. Yet by this criterion we must be content to judge, because no other can be obtained; and, indeed, we have no reason to think it very fallacious, for excepting here and there an anomalous mind, which either does not feel like others, or dissembles its sensibility, we find men unanimously concur in attributing happiness or misery to particular conditions, as they agree in acknowledging the cold of winter and the heat of autumn' (Yale, ii. 493). Later in the same paper Johnson refers to 'the movements of the human passions . . . of which every man carries the archetype within him' (*ib.* p. 496). Cf. also *Adventurer* 95: '[The] influence [of the passions] is uniform, and their effects nearly the same in every human breast' (*ib.* pp. 426–7).

p. 43, l. 19. *when you feel* . . . Cf. *Adventurer* 20: 'Who is there of those who frequent these luxurious assemblies, that will not confess his own uneasiness, or cannot recount the vexations and distresses that prey upon the lives of his gay companions? The world, in its best state, is nothing more than a larger assembly of beings, combining to counterfeit happiness which they do not feel, employing every art and contrivance to embellish life, and to hide their real condition from the eyes of one another' (Yale, ii. 467–8); *Idler* 18: 'The public pleasures of far the greater part of mankind are counterfeit. . . . To every place of entertainment we go with expectation, and desire of being pleased; we meet others who are brought by the same motives; no one will be the first to own the disappointment; one face reflects the smile of another, till each believes the rest delighted, and endeavours to catch and transmit the circulating rapture. In time, all are deceived by the cheat to which all contribute' (*ib.* pp. 57–58).

p. 44, l. 3. *The causes of*... Cf. *Rambler* 63: 'To take a view at once distinct and comprehensive of human life, with all its intricacies of combination, and varieties of connexion, is beyond the power of mortal intelligences.... The good and ill of different modes of life are sometimes so equally opposed, that perhaps no man ever yet made his choice between them upon a full conviction, and adequate knowledge.'

p. 44, l. 13. *Very few*... Johnson wrote to Boswell: 'Life is not long, and too much of it must not pass in idle deliberation how it shall be spent; deliberation, which those who begin it by prudence, and continue it with subtilty, must, after long expence of thought, conclude by chance. To prefer one future mode of life to another, upon just reasons, requires faculties which it has not pleased our Creator to give us' (*Life*, ii. 22). Cf. *Idler* 55: 'Choice is more often determined by accident than by reason' (Yale, ii. 172); *Idler* 101: '"Young man," said Omar, "it is of little use to form plans of life. ... With an insatiable thirst for knowledge I trifled away the years of improvement; with a restless desire of seeing different countries, I have always resided in the same city; with the highest expectation of connubial felicity, I have lived unmarried; and with unalterable resolutions of contemplative retirement, I am going to dye within the walls of Bagdat"' (*ib.* pp. 309, 311).

p. 44, l. 24. *young men of spirit*. Cf. the account by 'Misargyrus' of his own youth in *Adventurer* 34 (Yale, ii. 339–44).

p. 45, l. 3. *images*. Johnson defines *image* in this sense as 'an idea, a representation of any thing to the mind, a picture drawn in the fancy' (*Dict.*). The rest of Johnson's sentence suggests he meant that their laughter was unmotivated by any idea or image in the mind.

p. 45, l. 11. *Happiness*... Cf. *Rambler* 53: 'To make any happiness sincere, it is necessary that we believe it to be lasting; since whatever we suppose ourselves in danger of losing, must be enjoyed with solicitude and uneasiness.'

p. 45, l. 18. *The first years . . .* Cf. *Ecclesiastes*, xii. 1: 'Remember now thy Creator in the days of thy youth, while the evil days come not, nor the years draw nigh, when thou shalt say, I have no pleasure in them.'

p. 46, l. 5. *the horrour of derision.* Cf. Johnson's retort to Boswell about the respective happiness of boyhood and manhood: 'Ah! Sir, a boy's being flogged is not so severe as a man's having the hiss of the world against him' (*Life*, i. 451).

p. 46, l. 13. *auditory:* 'audience' (*Dict.*).

p. 46, l. 14. *the government of the passions.* G. J. Kolb points out that this episode reflects, 'in thought and diction', seventeenth- and eighteenth-century restatements of 'classical stoic philosophy' (*MLN*, lxviii, 1953, 439–47). He cites such sources for the 'government' metaphor, the sage's comparison of 'reason' and rational conduct to the 'sun', his insistence on the importance of 'precepts', his assertion that 'happiness' results from man's 'conquest of passion', his enumeration of 'examples', his advice to cultivate 'patience', Imlac's later reference to 'angels', and personal bereavement as the supreme test of fidelity to stoical principles. Cf. *Rambler* 6: 'That man should never suffer his happiness to depend upon external circumstances is one of the chief precepts of the stoical philosophy; a precept, indeed, which that lofty sect has extended beyond the condition of human life. . . . Such *sapientia insaniens*, as Horace calls the doctrine of another sect, such extravagance of philosophy, can want neither authority nor argument for its confutation; it is overthrown by the experience of every hour, and the powers of nature rise up against it'; *Rambler* 32: '. . . the stoicks, or scholars of Zeno, whose wild enthusiastick virtue pretended to an exemption from the sensibilities of unenlightened mortals, and who proclaimed themselves exalted . . . above the reach of those miseries which embitter life to the rest of the world.'

p. 48, l. 13. *Young man . . .* Hill cites (pp. 177–8) a comparable episode in *Joseph Andrews*, iv. chap. 8, though he notes that Johnson had never read Fielding's novel (v. *Life*, ii. 174). Emerson suggests (p. 160) that Johnson might have had in mind the following passage from Cicero's *Tusculanae Disputationes*, iii. 28 (71): 'Oïleus ille apud Sophoclem, qui Telamonem antea de Aiacis morte consolatus esset, is, cum audivisset de suo, fractus est; de cuius commutata mente sic dicitur:

> Nec vero tanta praeditus sapientia
> Quisquam est qui aliorum aerumnam dictis adlevans
> Non idem, cum fortuna mutata impetum
> Convertat, clade subita frangatur sua,
> Ut illa ad alios dicta et praecepta excidant'.

('The hero Oïleus in Sophocles, though he had previously consoled Telamon for the death of Ajax, yet broke down when he heard of his own son's death. His change of mind is thus described:

> And there is none of wisdom so possessed,
> Who with mild words has soothed another's woes,
> But does not, when a turn of fortune comes,
> Fall broken by his own calamity;
> So words, for others wise, his own need fail.'

Loeb edn., trans. J. E. King, 1950 reprint, p. 309.)

p. 48, l. 19. *truth and reason* . . . Cf. *Life of Cowley*: 'Truth . . . is always truth, and reason is always reason; they have an intrinsick and unalterable value, and constitute that intellectual gold which defies destruction' (*Lives*, i. 59).

p. 49, l. 4. *the lowest cataract*. 'This is at Assuan in Upper Egypt, over 400 miles in direct line from Cairo and 580 miles by river. Yet the party reached it in a leisurely journey of three days. It is evident that Johnson could have had no conception of the distance' (Emerson, p. 161).

p. 49, l. 21. *they were* . . . Johnson later wrote of the Scottish Highlanders: 'They have inquired and considered little, and do not always feel their own ignorance. They are not much accustomed to be interrogated by others; and seem never to have thought upon interrogating themselves' (*Journey*, p. 272).

p. 49, l. 27. *malevolence*. In *Idler* 71 'Dick Shifter' has his illusions of pastoral simplicity shattered by malevolence of a more active kind when he is cheated on all sides by the rustics. Cf. also *Rambler* 46.

p. 50, l. 4. *She hoped* . . . Cf. *Life of Gay*: 'There is something in the poetical Arcadia so remote from known reality and speculative possibility, that we can never support its representation through a long work. A Pastoral of an hundred lines may be endured; but who will hear of sheep and goats, and myrtle bowers and purling rivulets, through five acts? Such scenes please barbarians in the dawn of literature, and children in the dawn of life; but will be for the most part thrown away as men grow wise, and nations grow learned' (*Lives*, ii. 284–5).

p. 50, l. 8. *without care:* without having anything cause anxiety or trouble.

p. 50, l. 16. *The shrubs were* . . . Johnson is here describing certain features of contemporary landscape-gardening. In the *Life of Shenstone* he mentions the poet's disposition 'to point his prospects, to diversify his surface, to entangle his walks, and to wind his waters . . . to make water run where it will be heard, and to stagnate where it will be seen' (*Lives*, iii. 350). Almamoulin of *Rambler* 120, in laying out his gardens, 'opened prospects into distant regions . . . and rolled rivers through new channels'. B. H. Bronson remarks that Johnson's 'description here seems more appropriate to Vauxhall Gardens than to Egyptian scenery' ('*Rasselas*', *Poems and Selected Prose*, 1964 reprint, p. 548, n.11).

p. 51, l. 1. *The laws of eastern hospitality.* 'When a Stranger comes to a Village, or to the Camp, the People are obliged to entertain him and his Company according to his Rank. . . . This practise is so well establish'd, that a Stranger goes into a House of one he never saw, with the same Familiarity, and Assurance of Welcome, as into that of an intimate Friend, or near Relation' (Lobo, pp. 55–56).

p. 51, l. 18. *Bassa.* '*Bashaw*, a title of honour and command among the Turks, the viceroy of a province' (*Dict.*). The form given in the text is used in Johnson's translation of Lobo.

p. 51, l. 25. *riot:* 'revel' (*Dict.*), a sense that is now rare.

p. 52, l. 2. *The happiness of solitude.* Johnson wrote of Cowley in *Rambler* 6: 'He so strongly imaged to himself the happiness of leisure and retreat, that he determined to enjoy them for the future without interruption, and to exclude for ever all that could deprive him of his darling satisfactions. He forgot, in the vehemence of desire, that solitude and quiet owe their pleasures to those miseries which he was so studious to obviate: for such are the vicissitudes of the world, through all its parts, that day and night, labour and rest, hurry and retirement, endear each other.'

p. 52, l. 21. *saluted:* 'greeted' (*Dict.*). Cf. p. 107, l. 13.

p. 53, l. 1. *enthusiasm:* 'a vain belief of private revelation' (*Dict.*), and one of the main targets of Swift's satire in *A Tale of a Tub*. Cf. note to p. 28, l. 4.

p. 53, l. 7. *To him that* . . . Cf. *Rambler* 63: 'Life allows us but a small time for inquiry and experiment, and he that steadily endeavours at excellence, in whatever employment, will more benefit mankind than he that hesitates in choosing his part till he is called to the performance.'

p. 53, l. 15. *professed arms:* became a soldier.

p. 53, l. 29. *the pleasure of novelty.* v. note to p. 20, l. 23.

p. 54, l. 3. *I am sometimes* . . . Johnson said: 'It is as unreasonable for a man to go into a Carthusian convent for fear of being immoral, as for a man to cut off his hands for fear he should steal. . . . I said to the Lady Abbess of a convent, "Madam, you are here, not for the love of virtue, but the fear of vice." She said, "She should remember this as long as she lived"' (*Life*, ii. 434–5).

p. 54, l. 7. *My fancy riots* . . . Cf. *Idler* 32: 'It is not much of life that is spent in close attention to any important duty. Many hours of every day are suffered to fly away without any traces left upon the intellects. We suffer phantoms to rise up before us, and amuse ourselves with the dance of airy images, which after a time we dismiss for ever, and know not how we have been busied. Many have no happier moments than those that they pass in solitude, abandoned to their own imagination, which sometimes puts sceptres in their hands or mitres on their heads, shifts the scene of pleasure with endless variety, bids all the forms of beauty sparkle before them, and gluts them with every change of visionary luxury' (Yale, ii. 101); *Rambler* 8: 'Such is the importance of keeping reason a constant guard over imagination, that we have otherwise no security for our own virtue, but may corrupt our hearts in the most recluse solitude, with more pernicious and tyrannical appetites and wishes than the commerce of the world will generally produce.'

p. 54, l. 11. *the advantages of society*. Cf. *Rambler* 44 (written by
Mrs. Elizabeth Carter): 'In social, active life, difficulties will perpetually be met with; restraints of many kinds will be necessary;
and studying to behave right in respect of these is a discipline of the
human heart, useful to others, and improving to itself'; *Rambler* 104:
'The apparent insufficiency of every individual to his own happiness
or safety, compels us to seek from one another assistance and
support.'

p. 54, l. 12. *The life of* . . . Cf. *Adventurer* 126: 'There are [some]
whose passions grow more strong and irregular in privacy; and
who cannot maintain an uniform tenor of virtue, but by exposing
their manners to the public eye, and assisting the admonitions of
conscience with the fear of infamy' (Yale, ii. 475); *Rambler* 89:
'Solitude is a dangerous state to those who are too much accustomed
to sink into themselves.' Mrs. Piozzi reports Johnson as saying:
'Solitude is dangerous to reason, without being favourable to
virtue. . . . Solitude is the surest nurse of all prurient passions'
(*Anecdotes*, pp. 70, 71).

p. 54, l. 17. *hid*. Johnson gives both *hid* and *hidden* as forms of the
past participle of *to hide* (*Dict.*).

p. 54, l. 21. *The happiness* . . . Johnson said of Rousseau (who had
maintained that man in a savage state of nature was better and
happier than man in a state of advanced civilization): '"Rousseau
knows he is talking nonsense, and laughs at the world for staring at
him." BOSWELL. "How so, Sir?" JOHNSON. "Why, Sir, a man who
talks nonsense so well, must know that he is talking nonsense"'
(*Life*, ii. 74). R. B. Sewall discusses Johnson's satire on the view of
primitivism expounded by Rousseau in his *Discourses*, of which the
words of the 'philosopher' in this chapter are a pastiche (*PQ*, xvii,
1938, 105–11). I am indebted to Sewall for the passages from
Rousseau quoted below.

p. 54, l. 23. *an assembly of learned men*. Emerson notes that 'literary
clubs were a characteristic feature of eighteenth-century life in
London' (p. 162).

p. 55, l. 8. *perseverance:* 'Persistence in any design or attempt . . .
applied alike to good and ill' (*Dict.*).

p. 55, l. 10. *an hypocrite*. Cf. *Idler* 27: 'It is not uncommon to
charge the difference between promise and performance, between

profession and reality, upon deep design and studied deceit; but the truth is, that there is very little hypocrisy in the world; we do not so often endeavour or wish to impose on others as on ourselves' (Yale, ii. 85).

p. 55, l. 10. *Some talked of*... Boswell writes: 'A gentleman talked of retiring. "Never think of that", said Johnson. The gentleman urged, "I should then do no ill." JOHNSON. "Nor no good either. Sir, it would be a civil suicide"' (*Life*, iv. 223). Having been asked on another occasion whether a man might retire from the world, Johnson replied: 'Yes, when he has done his duty to society. In general, as every man is obliged not only to "love GOD, but his neighbour as himself" he must bear his part in active life. . . . Every season of life has its proper duties. I have thought of retiring . . . but I find my vocation is rather to active life' (*ib*. v. 62–63). Cf. *Rambler* 104: 'The apparent insufficiency of every individual to his own happiness or safety, compels us to seek from one another assistance and support. The necessity of joint efforts for the execution of any great or extensive design, the variety of powers disseminated in the species, and the proportion between the defects and excellencies of different persons, demand an interchange of help, and communication of intelligence, and by frequent reciprocations of beneficience unite mankind in society and friendship'; *Idler* 19: 'Mankind is one vast republick, where every individual receives many benefits from the labour of others, which, by labouring in his turn for others, he is obliged to repay; and . . . where the united efforts of all are not able to exempt all from misery, none have a right to withdraw from their task of vigilance, or to be indulged in idle wisdom or solitary pleasures' (Yale, ii. 59); *Idler* 38: 'Perhaps retirement ought rarely to be permitted, except to those whose employment is consistent with abstraction, and who, tho' solitary, will not be idle; to those whom infirmity makes useless to the commonwealth, or to those who have paid their due proportion to society, and who, having lived for others, may be honourably dismissed to live for themselves' (*ib*. pp. 119–20). In *Rambler* 7 Johnson recommends 'some stated intervals of solitude' for private meditation.

p. 55, l. 32. *The way*... 'Cf. Rousseau's praise of Geneva, in the Dedication of the *Discourse*, for governing its citizens in a manner "la plus approchante de la loi naturelle" and thus making for their happiness' (Sewall, *op. cit.* p. 108, n.41).

p. 55, l. 32. *in obedience to* . . . 'Rousseau describes man in his natural state, uncorrupted by society, as "un être agissant toujours par des principes certains & invariables" with a "céleste & majestueuse simplicité dont son Auteur l'avoit empreinte . . ." (Preface to the *Discours*, Amsterdam, 1755, p. lv)' (Sewall, p. 108, n.42).

p. 56, l. 3. *He that* . . . 'After describing the ills of society ("les veilles, les excès de toute espece, les transports immodérés de toutes les Passions, les fatigues & l'épuisement d'Esprit, les chagrins, & les peines sans nombre . . ."), Rousseau attributes them all to our failure to conserve "la maniére de vivre simple, uniforme, & solitaire qui nous étoit prescrite par la Nature" (p. 22). Throughout the *Discourse* his picture of man in the state of nature is of one who lives simply, vigorously, enduring hardships and asking for nothing that nature cannot supply him' (Sewall, p. 108, n.43).

p. 56, l. 8. *Let them* . . . 'Cf. Rousseau: "La Nature traite tous les animaux abandonnés à ses soins avec une prédilection, qui semble montrer combien elle est jalouse de ce droit. Le Cheval, le Chat, le Taureau, l'Ane même ont la plûpart une taille plus haute, tous une constitution plus robuste, plus de vigueur, de force & de courage dans les forêts que dans nos maisons. . . . Il en est ainsi de l'homme même: en devenant sociable & Esclave, il devient foible, craintif, rampant . . ." (p. 25)' (Sewall, p. 109, n.45).

p. 56, l. 28. *to the fitness* . . . Johnson here glances at the philosophy of Leibniz, who had maintained that God had created the best world possible ('en produisant l'Univers il a choisi le meilleur plan possible'), adjusting it according to a principle of fitness ('du principe de la convenance') so as to produce a system containing as much order and harmony as possible ('avec autant d'ordre et de correspondance qu'il est possible'). Cf. *Principes de la nature et de la grace* (1714), sects. 10ff.

p. 57, l. 11. *as he was yet young.* 'Rasselas by this time was about thirty-two. He is in his twenty-sixth year at the opening of the story; he passes twenty months "in visionary bustle"; and four months "in resolving to lose no more time in idle resolves". Ten months he spent in "fruitless researches" for a means of escape; and a year with the inventor of the wings. Some months, perhaps a year, must be given to his conversations with Imlac, to digging the outlet, and to the journey to Cairo. In that town they studied the language two years before they began their "experiments upon life". That Shakespeare makes Hamlet thirty years old often raises wonder. It is more surprising that Rasselas should be represented as thirty-two' (Hill, pp. 181–2).

p. 58, l. 17. *Yet, since* . . . Johnson said: 'I agree with Mr. Boswell that there must be a high satisfaction in being a feudal Lord; but we are to consider that we ought not to wish to have a number of men unhappy for the satisfaction of one' (*Life*, ii. 178).

p. 58, l. 20. *popular:* belonging to the people.

p. 59, l. 1. *every tongue was* . . . Cf. Johnson's description of the fall of Wolsey in *The Vanity of Human Wishes*, ll. 109–13:

At length his sov'reign frowns—the train of state
Mark the keen glance, and watch the sign to hate.
Where-e'er he turns he meets a stranger's eye,
His suppliants scorn him, and his followers fly;
At once is lost the pride of aweful state . . . (Yale, vi. 96).

revocation: 'the action of recalling; recall (of persons). Now *rare* or *obs*. In 17–18th cent. esp. the recall of a representative or ambassador from abroad; also in *Letters of revocation*' (*OED*).

p. 59, l. 4. *Constantinople.* Egypt became a province of the Turkish empire after being conquered by the Ottoman Turks in 1517.

p. 59, l. 13. *Janisaries:* (ultimately an adaptation of Turkish *yenitsheri*, 'new soldiery'), 'a former body of Turkish infantry, constituting the Sultan's guard and the main part of the standing army' (*OED*).

p. 59, l. 18. *insinuated herself:* pushed herself gently into favour or regard (*Dict.*).

p. 59, l. 21. *airy:* 'gay, sprightly, full of mirth' (*Dict.*). Johnson described Mrs. Cholmondely as 'a very airy lady' (*Life*, v. 248).

p. 60, l. 10. *countenance:* 'patronage, appearance of favour' (*Dict.*).

p. 60, l. 21. *Answer, said she* . . . Johnson later ridiculed a similar apostrophe in Gray's *Ode on a Distant Prospect of Eton College*: 'His supplication to father Thames, to tell him who drives the hoop or tosses the ball, is useless and puerile. Father Thames has no better means of knowing than himself' (*Lives*, iii. 434–5).

p. 60, l. 28. *provinces*. Johnson defines *province* in this sense as 'the proper office or business of anyone' (*Dict.*).

p. 60, l. 32. *I did not* ... In his review of Soame Jenyns's *Free Enquiry into the Nature and Origin of Evil* (1757) Johnson challenged the view that poverty has its positive compensations. 'This author and Pope', he writes, 'perhaps never saw the miseries which they imagine thus easy to be borne. The poor, indeed, are insensible of many little vexations, which sometimes imbitter the possessions, and pollute the enjoyments, of the rich ... but this happiness is like that of a malefactor, who ceases to feel the cords that bind him, when the pincers are tearing the flesh.' Cf. *Rambler* 49: 'Poverty is, indeed, an evil from which we naturally fly'; *Rambler* 53: 'There is scarcely among the evils of human life any so generally dreaded as poverty.'

p. 61, l. 1. *Poverty has* ... Boswell reports Johnson as saying: 'There is no place where economy can be so well practised as in London ... You cannot play tricks with your fortune in a small place; you must make an uniform appearance. Here a lady may have well-furnished apartments and elegant dress, without any meat in her kitchen' (*Life*, iii. 378).

p. 61, l. 3. *It is the* ... Cf. *Idler* 17: 'To be idle and to be poor have always been reproaches, and therefore every man endeavours with his utmost care to hide his poverty from others, and his idleness from himself' (Yale, ii. 54).

p. 61, l. 8. *Yet some* ... Cf. Johnson's own attitude as an undergraduate at Oxford. According to Boswell, he was in the habit of going to Christ Church, to get lectures second-hand from a friend, 'till, his poverty being so extreme that his shoes were worn out, and his feet appeared through them, he saw that this humiliating circumstance was perceived by the Christ Church men, and he came no more. He was too proud to accept of money, and somebody having set a pair of new shoes at his door he threw them away with indignation' (*Life*, i. 76). Johnson, however, was 'sincerely grateful' when, a little over a year before he died, his friend William Gerard Hamilton offered to provide for his medical expenses out of his own pocket (v. *Letters*, iii. 100, 102, 113, 119). Johnson had no need to avail himself of the offer.

p. 61, l. 11. *and others* ... Cf. *Rambler* 87: 'There are minds so impatient of inferiority that their gratitude is a species of revenge, and they return benefits, not because recompense is a pleasure, but because obligation is a pain.'

p. 61, l. 21. *In families* . . . Mrs. Piozzi writes: 'Many of the severe reflections on domestic life in Rasselas, took their source from its author's keen recollections of the time passed in his early years' (*Anecdotes*, p. 8). Cf. *Rambler* 18: 'There is no observation more frequently made by such as employ themselves in surveying the conduct of mankind, than that marriage, though the dictate of nature, and the institution of providence, is yet very often the cause of misery.'

p. 61, l. 23. *a family* . . . Cf. *Rambler* 148: 'As Aristotle observes, ἡ οἰκονομικὴ μοναρχία, *the government of a family is naturally monarchical.'*

p. 61, l. 25. *the love of parents*. Replying to a question of Boswell's, Johnson said: 'Why, Sir, I think there is an instinctive natural affection in parents towards their children' (*Life*, ii. 101). On another occasion, however, he said: 'Sir, natural affection is nothing: but affection from principle and established duty is sometimes wonderfully strong' (*ib*. iv. 210).

p. 61, l. 27. *in a short time* . . . Cf. *Rambler* 55, in which 'Miss Maypole' relates the feeling of rivalry she engenders in her mother: '[I] am unhappily a woman before my mother can willingly cease to be a girl. I believe you would contribute to the happiness of many families, if, by any arguments or persuasions, you could make mothers ashamed of rivalling their children.' Boswell reports Johnson as saying: 'There must always be a struggle between a father and son, while one aims at power and the other at independence' (*Life*, i. 427).

p. 61, l. 28. *allayed*. Johnson defines *to allay* in this sense as 'to join any thing to another, so as to abate its predominant qualities' (*Dict.*). Boswell reports him as saying 'unalloyed' (v. note to p. 117, l. 19) which is not recorded in *Dict.*, but, as Hill suggests, Boswell probably here 'uses the form of the word to which he himself was accustomed' (p. 185).

p. 62, l. 7. *are naturally opposite*. Cf. *Rambler* 50: 'It has been always the practice of those who are desirous to believe themselves made venerable by length of time, to censure the new comers into life, for want of respect to grey hairs and sage experience, for heady confidence in their own understandings, for hasty conclusions upon partial views, for disregard of counsels, which their fathers and grandsires are ready to afford them.'

p. 62, l. 9. *The colours of life* . . . Cf. *Rambler* 69: 'So different are the colours of life as we look forward to the future, or backward to the past, and so different the opinions and sentiments which this contrariety of appearance naturally produces, that the conversation of the old and young ends generally with contempt or pity on either side.'

p. 62, l. 17. *The old man* . . . Cf. Johnson's remark to Boswell: 'Young men have more virtue than old men; they have more generous sentiments in every respect' (*Life*, i. 445).

p. 62, l. 21. *candour:* 'sweetness of temper, purity of mind, openness, ingenuity, kindness' (*Dict.*). The sense 'sweetness of temper' is now obsolete, and the word has come to mean 'openness' in the sense of 'frankness', 'outspokenness'.

p. 62, l. 25. *scrupulosity.* This was 'a favourite word with Johnson' (Hill, p. 185). Cf. *Life*, iv. 5, n.2; v. 29; *ante*, p. 113, l. 13.

p. 62, l. 27. *the torments of each other.* The subject of *Rambler* 148 is 'the cruelty of parental tyranny'.

p. 63, l. 4. *even the virtuous* . . . Johnson remarked to Boswell: 'Enmity takes place between men who are good different ways' (*Life*, iv. 530).

p. 63, l. 31. *to be fortunate* . . . Cf. Johnson's concluding remarks in the *Preface to the Dictionary* (published three years after his wife's death): 'If the embodied criticks of France, when fifty years had been spent upon their work, were obliged to change its oeconomy, and give their second edition another form, I may surely be contented without the praise of perfection, which, if I could obtain, in this gloom of solitude, what would it avail me? I have protracted my work till most of those whom I wished to please have sunk into the grave, and success and miscarriage are empty sounds.'

p. 64, l. 1. *Marriage has* . . . Johnson thought that 'even ill assorted marriages were preferable to cheerless celibacy' (*Life*, ii. 128). On another occasion Boswell reports him as saying:

'Marriage is the best state for man in general' (*ib.* ii. 457). Cf. *Rambler* 115: 'I am so far from thinking meanly of marriage, that I believe it able to afford the highest happiness decreed to our present state.' Johnson wrote to Baretti: 'A woman we are sure will not be always fair; we are not sure she will always be virtuous: and man cannot retain through life that respect and assiduity by which he pleases for a day or for a month. I do not however pretend to have discovered that life has any thing more to be desired than a prudent and virtuous marriage' (*Letters*, i. 146).

p. 64, l. 18. *whoever has many* . . . On William Maxwell's authority, Boswell reports Johnson as saying: 'The inseparable imperfection annexed to all human governments consisted in not being able to create a sufficient fund of virtue and principle to carry the laws into due and effectual execution. Wisdom might plan, but virtue alone could execute. And where could sufficient virtue be found?' (*Life*, ii. 118).

p. 64, l. 22. *If he gratifies* . . . Hill quotes (p. 186) the words of Louis XIV from Voltaire's *Siècle de Louis XIV*, chap. 26: 'Toutes les fois que je donne une place vacante, je fais cent mécontents et un ingrat.' Johnson once quoted this saying in a conversation with Boswell (*Life*, ii. 167).

p. 65, l. 2. *which indigence* . . . Cf. Johnson's *London*, l. 177:

> Slow rises worth, by poverty depress'd (Yale, vi. 56).

p. 65, l. 16. *bribery of flattery.* Boswell writes: 'When I boasted, at Rasay, of my independency of spirit, and that I could not be bribed, he [i.e. Johnson] said, "Yes, you may be bribed by flattery"' (*Life*, v. 305–6). Cf. Gay's *Fables*, i. 7–8:

> Learn to contemn all praise betimes,
> For flattery's the nurse of crimes.

p. 66, l. 2. *But this* . . . Cf. *Adventurer* 120: 'Affliction is inseparable from our present state; it adheres to all the inhabitants of this world in different proportions indeed, but with an allotment which seems very little regulated by our own conduct. It has been the boast of some swelling moralists, that every man's fortune was in his own power, that prudence supplied the place of all other divinities, and that happiness is the unfailing consequence of virtue. But surely, the quiver of Omnipotence is stored with arrows, against which the shield of human virtue, however adamantine it has been boasted, is held up in vain: we do not always suffer by our crimes; we are not always protected by our innocence' (Yale, ii. 468); *Ecclesiastes*, ix. 11: 'I returned, and saw under the sun, that the race is not to the swift, nor the battle to the strong, neither yet bread to the wise, nor yet riches to men of understanding, nor yet favour to men of skill; but time and chance happeneth to them all.'

p. 66, l. 8. *All that virtue* . . . Cf. *Rambler* 203: 'It is not . . . from this world that any ray of comfort can proceed. . . . But futurity has still its prospects; there is yet happiness in reserve, which, if we transfer our attention to it, will support us in the pains of disease, and the langour of decay. This happiness we may expect with confidence, because it is out of the power of chance, and may be attained by all that sincerely desire and earnestly pursue it.' Johnson wrote to Boswell: 'There is but one solid basis of happiness; and that is, the reasonable hope of a happy futurity' (*Life*, iii. 363). Cf. Locke's last words to Anthony Collins: 'This world . . . affords no solid satisfaction but the consciousness of well doing, and the hopes of another life' (quoted, *ib.* n.3).

p. 66, l. 18. *in books*. Johnson said: 'Many things which are false are transmitted from book to book, and gain credit in the world' (*Life*, iii. 55). He himself disliked 'exaggeratory declamation'.

p. 66, l. 19. *horrid:* 'hideous, dreadful, shocking' (*Dict*.). Cf. p. 77, l. 8.

p. 66, l. 23. *Jerusalem*. In A.D. 70 Vespasian's son Titus besieged Jerusalem, and after fierce fighting the Temple was destroyed and the city became a heap of ruins.

p. 67, l. 2. *whether their kings* . . . Johnson said: 'I would not give half a guinea to live under one form of government rather than another. It is of no moment to the happiness of an individual. . . . The danger of the abuse of power is nothing to a private man' (*Life*, ii. 170).

p. 67, l. 3. *whether the armies* . . . Mrs. Piozzi reports Johnson as saying: 'Historians magnify events expected, or calamities endured . . . Among all your lamentations, who eats the less? Who sleeps the worse, for one general's ill success, or another's capitulation?' (*Anecdotes*, p. 56).

p. 67, l. 13. *It is our business* . . . Cf. notes to p. 16, l. 10; p. 54, l. 11.

p. 67, l. 17. *Marriage is* . . . Boswell reports Johnson as putting forward the opposite view: 'It is so far from being natural for a man and woman to live in a state of marriage, that we find all the motives which they have for remaining in that connection, and the restraints which civilized society imposes to prevent separation, are hardly sufficient to keep them together' (*Life*, ii. 165).

p. 67, l. 23. *the various forms* . . . For Johnson's account of some of these and their causes v. *Rambler* 18.

p. 67, l. 31. *that none* . . . Johnson said: 'It is not from reason and prudence that people marry, but from inclination' (*Life*, ii. 101).

p. 68, l. 8. *To the mind* . . . Cf. *Adventurer* 107: 'With regard to simple propositions, where the terms are understood, and the whole subject is comprehended at once, there is . . . an uniformity of sentiment among all human beings. . . . In questions diffuse and compounded, this similarity of determination is no longer to be expected. . . . As a question becomes more complicated and involved, and extends to a greater number of relations, disagreements of opinion will always be multiplied, not because we are irrational, but because we are finite beings, furnished with different kinds of knowledge, exerting different degrees of attention, one discovering consequences which escape another, none taking in the whole concatenation of causes and effects, and most comprehending but a very small part; each comparing what he observes with a different criterion, and each referring it to a different purpose' (Yale, ii. 441); *Rambler* 108: 'Of extensive surfaces we can only take a survey, as the parts succeed one another'; *Rambler* 125: 'It is impossible to impress upon our minds an adequate and just representation of an object so great that we can never take it into our view.' Boswell reports Johnson as saying: 'The human mind is so limited, that it cannot take in all the parts of a subject' (*Life*, i. 444).

p. 68, l. 10. *Where we see* . . . 'This sentence, in which the princess speaks in the style of *The Rambler*, is some justification for Macaulay's far too sweeping criticism—"No man surely ever had so little talent for personation as Johnson"' (Hill, p. 187). In *Rambler* 20, Johnson complains of such correspondents as write 'under characters which they cannot support', especially those who unconvincingly 'affect the style and the names of ladies'. Boswell, however, is justified in attributing the same fault to the author himself: 'Johnson's language [in *The Rambler*] must be allowed to be too masculine for the delicate gentleness of female writing. His ladies, therefore, seem strangely formal, even to ridicule' (*Life*, i. 223).

p. 68, l. 28. *will not the* . . . Cf. *Rambler* 45: 'Marriage is not commonly unhappy otherwise than as life is unhappy; and . . . most of those who complain of connubial miseries have as much satisfaction as their nature would have admitted, or their conduct procured, in any other condition. . . . Whether married or unmarried, we shall find the vesture of terrestrial existence more heavy and cumbrous the longer it is worn.' Before Boswell's marriage, Johnson said to him: 'Now that you are going to marry, do not expect more from life, than life will afford' (*Life*, ii. 110).

p. 69, l. 15. *The general folly* . . . Cf. the instances of unhappy marriages depicted in *Rambler* 18; *Rambler* 45, in which, after considering various foolish motives that lead to matrimony, Johnson continues: 'I am not so much inclined to wonder that marriage is sometimes unhappy, as that it appears so little loaded with calamity. . . . By the ancient custom of the Muscovites, the men and women never saw each other till they were joined beyond the power of parting. . . . If we observe the manner in which those converse, who have singled out each other for marriage, we shall, perhaps, not think that the Russians lost much by their restraint.' Johnson once said: 'I believe marriages would in general be as happy, and often more so, if they were all made by the Lord Chancellor, upon a due consideration of characters and circumstances, without the parties having any choice in the matter' (*Life*, ii. 461).

p. 70, l. 3. *The daughter* . . . Cf. note to p. 61, l. 27.

p. 70, l. 14. *collect:* 'infer as a consequence, gather from premises' (*Dict.*), a sense that is now rare and is supplied by 'gather' (*OED*).

p. 70, l. 20. *suffrages:* opinions, especially (as here) those on any controverted question.

They have generally . . . On William Maxwell's authority, Boswell reports Johnson's opinion as follows: 'He did not approve of late marriages, observing, that more was lost in point of time, than compensated for by any possible advantages' (*Life*, ii. 128).

p. 72, l. 14. *as we approach* . . . Cf. *Rambler* 162: 'As the attention tends strongly towards one thing, it must retire from another.'

p. 73, l. 1. *while you are* . . . v. note to p. 53, l. 7.

p. 73, l. 8. *civil:* 'civilised, not barbarous' (*Dict.*), a sense Johnson illustrated from Spenser's *A View of the Present State of Ireland*: 'England was very rude and barbarous, for it is but even the other day since England grew civil' (v. *Spenser's Prose Works*, ed. Rudolf Gottfried, 1949, p. 118). Boswell writes: 'I found him busy (23 March 1772), preparing a fourth edition of his folio Dictionary. . . . He would not admit *civilization*, but only *civility*. With great deference to him, I thought *civilization*, from to *civilize*, better in the sense opposed to *barbarity*, than *civility*; as it is better to have a distinct word for each sense, than one word with two senses, which *civility* is, in his way of using it' (*Life*, ii. 155). Four years later Johnson was to say, humorously, at Boswell's expense: 'I lately took my friend Boswell and shewed him genuine civilised life in an English provincial town. I turned him loose at Lichfield, my native city, that he might see for once real civility: for you know he lives among savages in Scotland, and among rakes in London' (*ib.* iii. 77). Cf. p. 91, l. 26.

p. 73, l. 16. *my business* . . . Cf. *Idler* 97: 'He that would travel for the entertainment of others, should remember that the great object of remark is human life' (Yale, ii. 300). Mrs. Piozzi writes that Johnson was a somewhat 'tiresome' travelling-companion in that he failed to appreciate 'prospects'. When Mr. Thrale wished to point these out to him, Johnson was disposed to reply: 'Let us if we *do* talk, talk about something; men and women are my subjects of enquiry; let us see how these differ from those we have left behind' (*Anecdotes*, p. 66). Johnson liked biography, describing it, in *Idler* 84, as 'that which is most eagerly read, and most easily applied to the purposes of life' (Yale, ii. 261). For the same reason he preferred 'the history of manners, of common life' (*Life*, iii. 333).

p. 73, l. 20. *The things* . . . Cf. *Paradise Lost*, viii. 192–4:

> to know
> That which before us lies in daily life,
> Is the prime Wisdom.

As a moralist Johnson took this sentiment very seriously (v. esp. *Rambler* 24, 180). Mrs. Piozzi writes: 'All his conversation precepts tended towards the dispersion of romantic ideas, and were chiefly intended to promote the cultivation of "That which before thee lies in daily life"' (*Anecdotes*, p. 128).

p. 74, l. 12. *There is no* . . . Johnson's usual predilection was for 'the history of manners, of common life' (*Life*, iii. 333). On one occasion he agreed with the opinion of Lord Monboddo that 'the history of manners is the most valuable' (*ib.* v. 79).

p. 74, l. 22. *Example is* . . . Cf. Seneca, *Epistles*, vi. 5: 'longum iter est per praecepta, breve et efficax per exempla.'

p. 75, l. 6. *pompous:* 'splendid, magnificent, grand' (*Dict.*), a sense Johnson illustrated by a quotation from Pope's *Epistle to Mr. Jervas*, ll. 23–24:

> What flatt'ring scenes our wand'ring fancy wrought;
> Rome's pompous glories rising to our thought!

p. 75, l. 8. *the pyramids.* Emerson writes: 'A description of the pyramids by John Greaves, Professor of Astronomy at the University of Oxford, is given in Churchill's *Collection of Voyages and Travels*, vol. ii. In Richard Pococke's *Description of the East* (1743) is an abstract of Mallet's account of the great pyramid, and similarity of expression seems to imply that one or both of these may have been known to Johnson' (p. 167).

p. 76, l. 2. *concussion:* tremor or earthquake ('agitation, tremefaction', *Dict.*).

p. 76, l. 18. *That the dead* . . . Johnson said: 'It is wonderful that five thousand years have now elapsed since the creation of the world, and still it is undecided whether or not there has ever been an instance of the spirit of any person appearing after death. All argument is against it; but all belief is for it' (*Life*, iii. 230). Of apparitions he observed: 'A total disbelief of them is adverse to the opinion of the existence of the soul between death and the last day; the question simply is, whether departed spirits ever have the power of making themselves perceptible to us' (*ib.* iv. 94).

p. 76, l. 21. *rude:* 'uneducated, unlearned; ignorant; lacking in knowledge or book-learning; uncivilized' (*OED*).

p. 77, l. 22. *marble.* Cf. Greaves, who writes of the 'rich and spacious chamber' beyond 'the end of the second gallery': "The floor, the sides, the roof of it, are all made of vast and exquisite tables of *Thebaick* marble' (Churchill's *Voyages*, 1732, ii. 664). Emerson, while pointing out that none of the chambers is lined with marble, also cities (p. 167) *Purchas his Pilgrimage*, where the chambers are said to be 'all of well wrought Theban marble'.

p. 77, l. 22. *chest*. Emerson quotes (pp. 167–8) from Pococke's *Description of the East* (i. 239): 'This *chest*, no doubt, contained the body of the king inclosed in three or four chests of fine wood.' Charles Peake ('*Rasselas' and Essays: Johnson*, Routledge English Texts, p. 188) quotes from George Sandys's *A Relation of a Journey* (1615), a book which Johnson had recommended to a friend (v. *Life*, iv. 311): 'In this no doubt lay the body of the builder' (p. 130).

p. 77, l. 27. *the wall of China*. Boswell writes of Johnson: 'He talked with an uncommon animation of travelling into distant countries; that the mind was enlarged by it, and that an acquisition of dignity of character was derived from it. He expressed a particular enthusiasm with respect to visiting the wall of China. I catched it for the moment, and said I really believed I should go and see the wall of China had I not children, of whom it was my duty to take care. "Sir, (said he,) by doing so, you would do what would be of importance in raising your children to eminence. There would be a lustre reflected upon them from your spirit and curiosity. They would at all times be regarded as the children of a man who had gone to view the wall of China. I am serious, Sir"' (*Life*, iii. 269).

p. 78, l. 12. *that hunger of imagination* . . . In a letter to Mrs. Thrale, Johnson, referring to Boswell's desire to see Wales, remarked: '. . . what is there in Wales? What that can fill the hunger of ignorance, or quench the thirst of curiosity' (*Letters*, ii. 205). Cf. *Rambler* 41: 'So few of the hours of life are filled up with objects adequate to the mind of man, and so frequently are we in want of present pleasure or employment, that we are forced to have recourse, every moment, to the past and future for supplemental satisfactions, and relieve the vacuities of our being, by recollection of former passages, or anticipation of events to come'; *Rambler* 207: 'Such is the emptiness of human enjoyment, that we are always impatient of the present. . . . Few moments are more pleasing than those in which the mind is concerting measures for a new undertaking.'

p. 78, l. 14. *Those who* . . . Cf. *Adventurer* 119: 'It seems to be the great business of life, to create wants as fast as they are satisfied' (Yale, ii. 462); *Idler* 30: 'The desires of man encrease with his acquisitions. . . . No sooner are we supplied with every thing that nature can demand, than we sit down to contrive artificial appetites' (*ib.* ii. 92).

p. 78, l. 22. *is compelled* . . . Johnson considered that the building of 'grand houses' and the making of 'fine gardens' were 'only struggles for happiness' (*Life*, iii. 198–9).

p. 81, l. 20. *sunk.* Johnson gives the preterite form as '*sunk*, anciently *sank*' (*Dict.*). Cf. note to p. 10, l. 12.

p. 82, l. 15. *How comfortless* . . . Johnson said: 'If the cause of our grief is occasioned by our own misconduct, if grief is mingled with remorse of conscience, it should be lasting' (*Life*, iii. 136–7).

p. 83, l. 17. *condition:* 'rank' (*Dict.*), a sense Johnson illustrated by a quotation from *The Tempest*, III. i. 59–60:

> I am in my condition
> A prince, Miranda.

p. 83, l. 20. *convenience:* 'opportune occasion, opportunity' (*OED*), a sense that is now obsolete.

p. 83, l. 26. *excursions:* 'digressions, rambles from a subject' (*Dict.*).

p. 84, l. 15. *to retire* . . . Cf. notes to p. 52, l. 2; p. 54, l. 3; p. 55, l. 10.

p. 84, l. 22. *Do not entangle* . . . Cf. Cowley's *Ode: Upon Liberty*, ll. 95–99, a passage quoted by Johnson and said to contain 'just and noble thoughts' (*Lives*, i. 60):

> Where honour or where conscience does not bind,
>   No other law shall shackle me;
>   Slave to myself I ne'er will be;
> Nor shall my future actions be confin'd
> By my own present mind.

Johnson wrote to Mrs. Thrale: 'All unnecessary vows are folly, because they suppose a prescience of the future which has not been given us. They are, I think, a crime because they resign that life to chance which God has given us to be regulated by reason; and superinduce a kind of fatality, from which it is the great privilege of our Nature to be free' (*Letters*, i. 325). Mrs. Piozzi writes: 'Much of his eloquence, and much of his logic have I heard him use to prevent men from making vows on trivial occasions' (*Anecdotes*, p. 144).

p. 84, l. 24. *the weariness of retirement*. In *Adventurer* 102, 'Mercator' describes the 'gloomy inactivity' that characterized his retirement.

p. 84, l. 33. *wealth is nothing*. Boswell writes: 'Although upon most occasions I never heard a more strenuous advocate for the advantages of wealth, than Dr. Johnson, he this day [3 June 1781], I know not from what caprice, took the other side. "I have not observed (said he) that men of very large fortunes enjoy any thing extraordinary that makes happiness"' (*Life*, iv. 126).

p. 85, l. 11. *obsequiousness*: 'obedience, compliance' (*Dict.*); 'eagerness to serve or please, dutiful service' (*OED*), a sense that is now obselete. Cf. p. 94, l. 6.

p. 85, l. 16. *who, when* . . . E. E. Duncan-Jones points out that this supposed reaction on the part of primitive man is mentioned in Manilius's *Astronomicon*, i. 66–70, and Statius's *Thebaid*, iv. 282–4, mocked at by Lucretius in *De Rerum Natura*, v. 973–6, and alluded to in Marvell's *The First Anniversary of the Government under O.C.*, ll. 337–40 (*TLS*, 3 April 1959, p. 193).

p. 85, l. 30. *Do not suffer* . . . Cf. Rambler 165: 'The stream of life, if it is not ruffled by obstructions, will grow putrid by stagnation.'

p. 85, l. 32. *commit yourself again* . . . Cf. Johnson's observations to Mrs. Thrale on the death of her husband: 'A mind occupied by lawful business, has little room for regret'; 'I think business the best remedy for grief as soon as it can be admitted' (*Letters*, ii. 415, 418).

p. 86, l. 1. *diffuse yourself*: diversify your attention. Cf. *Rambler* 190: 'He afterwards determined to avoid a close union with beings so discordant in their nature, and to diffuse himself in a larger circle.'

p. 86, l. 20. *She rejoiced* . . . When Dr. John Taylor mentioned a gentleman who, on the death of his wife, 'had endeavoured to *retain* grief' but been unable to make it 'lasting', Johnson replied: 'All grief for what cannot in the course of nature be helped, soon wears away' (*Life*, iii. 136).

p. 86, l. 30. *avocation:* 'the business that calls, or the call that summons away' (*Dict.*).

p. 88, l. 15. *monastry of St. Anthony.* 'Saint Anthony (c. A.D. 250–350), the first Christian monk, was born in middle Egypt. At the age of 20 he began to practise an ascetic life, and after 15 years of this life, he withdrew for solitude to a mountain by the Nile. . . . In the early years of the 4th century, he emerged from his retreat to organize the monastic life of the monks who imitated him. After a time he again withdrew to the mountain by the Red sea, where now stands the monastery that bears his name' (*Ency. Brit.*, ii. 30). Emerson suggests (p. 170) that Johnson 'had in mind the "convent of St. Anthony" mentioned by Pococke in describing his "voyage of Upper Egypt"'. Emerson continues: 'This is about fifty miles from Cairo, on the east bank of the Nile. . . . He [i.e. Pococke] says, "The country is very little inhabited above the convent of St. Anthony, and those that are on the east side are mostly Arabs, who submit to no government" (*Description of the East*, i. 70–71, 128).' St. Anthony is mentioned by Lobo (pp. 386, 389).

p. 89, l. 19. *pleasant meadow.* 'Johnson was thinking of English not of Egyptian scenery' (Hill, p. 191).

p. 90, l. 7. *irritate:* 'provoke' (*Dict.*).

p. 91, l. 12. *The sons of Ishmael.* Cf. *Genesis*, xvi. 12, xxi. 9–21 ; Gibbon's *Decline and Fall*, chap. 50: 'The separation of the Arabs from the rest of mankind has accustomed them to confound the ideas of stranger and enemy; and the poverty of the land has introduced a maxim of jurisprudence which they believe and practise to the present hour. They pretend that, in the division of the earth, the rich and fertile climates were assigned to the other branches of the human family; and that the posterity of the outlaw Ismael might recover, by fraud or force, the portion of inheritance of which he had been unjustly deprived.'

p. 91, l. 27. *pasport:* 'permission of egress' (*Dict.*).

p. 91, l. 28. *punctuality:* 'nicety, scrupulous exactness' (*Dict.*); 'scrupulousness' (*OED*), a sense that is now archaic. Cf. *Rambler* 201: 'The chief praise to which a trader aspires is that of punctuality, or an exact and rigorous observance of commercial engagements.'

p. 92, l. 7. *officious:* 'eager to serve or please, dutiful' (*OED*), a sense that is now obsolete. Cf. p. 5, l. 10 and note.

p. 92, l. 24. *erratick.* 'wandering from place to place, vagrant, nomadic' (*OED*), a sense that is now obsolete.

p. 92, l. 25. *passenger:* 'traveller, wayfarer' (*Dict., OED*).

p. 92, l. 29. *Walls supply stones* . . . Johnson wrote of the cathedral at Elgin that it was 'at last not destroyed by the tumultuous violence of Knox, but more shamefully suffered to dilapidate by deliberate robbery and frigid indifference', adding: 'Those who had once uncovered the cathedrals never wished to cover them again; and being thus made useless, they were first neglected, and perhaps, as the stone was wanted, afterwards demolished' (*Journey*, pp. 47, 49).

p. 94, l. 14. *river-horses:* hippopotamuses. D. M. Lockhart suggests that Johnson's paragraph is indebted to a reference to 'Crocodiles', 'Sea-Horses', 'Sirens', and 'Tritons' in the history (published 1660) of Balthazar Telles (*PMLA*, lxxviii, 1963, 524). Lobo describes the Nile as full of '*Hippotames*, or River-Horses, and Crocodiles' (p. 96).

p. 95, l. 15. *sensitive:* 'having sense or perception, but not reason' (*Dict.*), a sense that is now obsolete.

p. 96, l. 8. *intercepting:* 'interrupting' (*OED*), a sense, now obsolete, that Johnson illustrated from *Titus Andronicus*, III. i. 39–40:

> Yet in some sort they are better than the tribunes,
> For that they will not intercept my tale.

p. 96, l. 22. *the tediousness of life.* Johnson himself was always ready to acknowledge 'the *taedium vitae*' (cf. *Life*, i. 394), and for this reason sought 'novelty' in both life and literature. With Pekuah's remark cf. Imlac's to Rasselas p. 30, ll. 19–21: 'Ignorance is mere privation, by which nothing can be produced: it is a vacuity in which the soul sits motionless and torpid for want of attraction.' Mrs. Piozzi writes: 'The vacuity of life had at some early period of his life struck so forcibly on the mind of Mr. Johnson, that it became by repeated impression his favourite hypothesis, and the general tenor of his reasonings commonly ended there, wherever they might begin' (*Anecdotes*, p. 99). In *Rambler* 6, Johnson refers to 'the burden of life'.

p. 98, l. 31. *vacation:* freedom from business, 'leisure' (*Dict.*).

p. 99, l. 17. *charity.* The importance of this prime Christian virtue was constantly stressed by Johnson. For example, in *The Vanity of Human Wishes* (l. 361), he exhorts his reader to pray
For love, which scarce collective man can fill (Yale, vi. 108).

p. 99, l. 17. *To man* ... Cf. note to p. 73, l. 20; *Rambler* 180: 'Raphael, in return to Adam's enquiries into the courses of the stars and the revolutions of heaven, counsels him to withdraw his mind from idle speculations, and employ his faculties upon nearer and more interesting objects, the survey of his own life, the subjection of his passions, the knowledge of duties which must daily be performed, and the detection of dangers which must daily be incurred'; *Life of Milton:* 'The knowledge of external nature, and the sciences which that knowledge requires or includes, are not the great or the frequent business of the human mind. ... We are perpetually moralists, but we are geometricians only by chance' (*Lives*, i. 99, 100).

p. 99, l. 23 *sublime:* 'of lofty bearing or aspect' (*OED*).

p. 99, l. 28. *condition:* 'state, circumstances' (*Dict.*), way of life.

p. 100, l. 14. *emersion:* 'The time when a star, having been obscured by its too near approach to the sun, appears again' (*Dict.*); '*Astron.* The reappearance of the sun or moon from shadow after eclipse, or of a star or planet after occultation' (*OED*).

p. 100, l. 24. *imbecility:* 'weakness, feebleness of mind or body' (*Dict.*).

p. 101, l. 3. *the rage of the dog-star.* Cf. Pope's *Epistle to Dr. Arbuthnot*, l. 3:
The dog-star rages ...;
Horace, *Odes*, III. xiii. 9–10:
te flagrantis atrox hora Caniculae
nescit tangere.

'Dog-star' was the name given to the constellation Sirius, which in Homer is represented as the dog of Orion, the hunter. Setting with the sun in August, it was therefore associated with that period of greatest heat which was commonly regarded as a cause of madness.

p. 101, l. 4. *the fervours of the crab.* Cf. Ovid, *Metamorphoses,* x. 126–7:

> aestus erat, mediusque dies; solisque vapore
> concava litorei fervebant bracchia Cancri;

Paradise Lost, x. 675:

> . . . the *Tropic* Crab.

p. 101, l. 5. *the elemental powers.* 'The powers, that is to say, of any of the four elements, usually so called, earth, fire, air and water, of which the world was thought to be composed' (Hill, p. 192).

p. 101, l. 17. *obscurity:* 'darkness, want of light' (*Dict.*).

p. 102, l. 8. *rain on the southern mountains.* '*Abyssinia* where the *Nile* rises, and Water's [sic] vast Tracts of Land, is full of Mountains, and in its natural Situation much higher than *Egypt*; . . . all the Winter, from *June* to *September*, no Day is without Rain; . . . the *Nile* receives in its course all the Rivers, Brooks and Torrents which fall from those Mountains; these necessarily swell it above the Banks, and fill the Plains of *Egypt* with the Inundation' (Lobo, p. 107). Lobo had previously dismissed as fanciful other explanations of this annual flooding.

p. 102, l. 9. *raise the Nile* . . . 'This [inundation] comes regularly about the Month of *July*, or three weeks after the beginning of a rainy Season in *Æthiopia*' (Lobo, *loc. cit.*).

p. 102, l. 25. *I cannot prove* . . . Johnson recognized the limitations of subjective 'proof', maintaining that 'a man who thinks he has seen an apparition, can only be convinced himself; his authority will not convince another' (*Life*, iv. 94).

p. 103, l. 9. *to whom he* . . . Cf. the following couplet from those added by Johnson to Goldsmith's *The Traveller*:

How small of all that human hearts endure,
That part which laws or kings can cause or cure (Yale, vi. 356).
Cf. note to p. 67, l. 2.

p. 103, l. 15. *and formed* . . . Cf. *Adventurer* 45: 'Some philosophers have been foolish enough to imagine, that improvements might be made in the system of the universe, by a different arrangement of the orbs of heaven' (Yale, ii. 360).

p. 103, l. 17. *but I have* . . . Cf. *Idler* 43: 'The natural advantages which arise from the position of the earth which we inhabit with respect to the other planets, afford much employment to mathematical speculation, by which it has been discovered, that no other conformation of the system could have given such commodious distributions of light and heat, or imparted fertility and pleasure to so great a part of a revolving sphere' (Yale, ii. 134–5).

p. 103, l. 22. *administration:* management.

p. 104, l. 10. *Of the uncertainties* . . . Boswell writes: 'To Johnson, whose supreme enjoyment was the exercise of his reason, the disturbance or obscuration of that faculty was the evil most to be dreaded. Insanity, therefore, was the object of his most dismal apprehension; and he fancied himself seized by it' (*Life*, i. 66). Mrs. Piozzi writes: 'He had studied medicine diligently in all its branches; but had given particular attention to the diseases of the imagination, which he watched in himself with a solicitude destructive of his own peace, and intolerable to those he trusted' (*Anecdotes*, p. 52). With reference to this episode of the mad astronomer, Sir John Hawkins writes: 'It cannot but excite the pity of all those who gratefully accept and enjoy Johnson's endeavours to reform and instruct, to reflect that the peril he describes he believed impending over him' (*The Life of Samuel Johnson, LL.D.* (1787, 2nd revised edn.), p. 370. With Collins in his mind, Johnson wrote to Joseph Warton: 'The moralists all talk of the uncertainty of fortune, and the transitoriness of beauty; but it is yet more dreadful to consider that the powers of the mind are equally liable to change, that understanding may make its appearance and depart, that it may blaze and expire' (*Letters*, i. 90).

p. 104, l. 13. *recollected:* brought back to a state of composure. Johnson defines *recollect* in this sense as 'recover reason or resolution' (*Dict.*). Since a fondness for balance is a notable feature of his style, Emerson suggests that this unusual passive (instead of the reflexive 'recollected herself') may have been due to the following passive 'was abashed' (p. xlviii).

p. 104, l. 18. *prevalence.* D. J. Greene points out that 'prevalence', as used here, 'is derived from the verb "prevail", to overcome', adding that 'Johnson is talking about . . . the danger ensuing when an individual's fantasy prevails over his contact with reality' (*Johnson, Boswell*, p. 157).

p. 104, l. 19. *Disorders of intellect* . . . Johnson said: 'Madness frequently discovers itself merely by unnecessary deviation from the usual modes of the world' (*Life*, i. 397); 'Many a man is mad in certain instances, and goes through life without having it perceived:—for example, a madness has seized a person of supposing himself obliged literally to pray continually—had the madness turned the opposite way and the person thought it a crime ever to pray, it might not improbably have continued unobserved' (*ib.* iv. 31). At Dunvegan Johnson said of himself: 'I inherited a vile melancholy from my father, which has made me mad all my life, at least not sober' (*ib.* v. 215). Boswell, noting that some ancient philosophers considered 'all deviations from right reason . . . madness', writes of Johnson: 'When he talked of madness, he was to be understood as speaking of those who were in any great degree disturbed, or as it is commonly expressed, "troubled in mind"' (*ib.* iii. 175).

p. 104, l. 26. *airy:* 'without reality, without any steady foundation in truth or nature, vain, trifling' (*Dict.*). With Johnson's usage and sentiment cf. *Idler* 32: 'We suffer phantoms to rise up before us, and amuse ourselves with the dance of airy images. . . . All this is a voluntary dream, a temporary recession from the realities of life to airy fictions; and habitual subjection of reason to fancy' (Yale, ii. 101); *The Vanity of Human Wishes*, ll. 7 ff.:

> Where wav'ring man . . .
> As treach'rous phantoms in the mist delude,
> Shuns fancied ills, or chases airy good (*ib.* vi. 92).

p. 104, l. 27. *All power of* . . . Johnson thought madness 'occasioned by too much indulgence of imagination' (*Life*, iv. 208). Cf. Swift, *A Tale of a Tub*, chap. 9 ('A Digression on Madness'): 'But when a Man's Fancy gets *astride* on his Reason, when Imagination is at Cuffs with the Senses, and common Understanding, as well as common Sense, is Kickt out of Doors; the first Proselyte he makes, is Himself' (ed. A. C. Guthkelch and D. Nichol Smith, 2nd edn., 1958, p. 171).

p. 105, l. 2. *comes:* becomes.

apparently: 'evidently, openly' (*Dict.*), manifestly.

p. 105, l. 6. *When we are alone* . . . Cf. *Idler* 32: 'Many have no happier moments than those that they pass in solitude, abandoned to their own imagination, which sometimes puts sceptres in their hands or mitres on their heads, shifts the scene of pleasure with endless variety, bids all the forms of beauty sparkle before them, and gluts them with every change of visionary luxury' (Yale, ii. 101).

p. 105, l. 13. *and culls from* . . . With this passage, and the 'fictions' which Pekuah, Nekayah and Rasselas later admit to having entertained, cf. *Rambler* 2: 'When the knight of La Mancha gravely recounts to his companion the adventures by which he is to signalize himself in such a manner that he shall be summoned to the support of empires, solicited to accept the heiress of the crown which he has preserved, have honours and riches to scatter about him, and an island to bestow on his worthy squire, very few readers, amidst their mirth or pity, can deny that they have admitted visions of the same kind; though they have not, perhaps, expected events equally strange, or by means equally inadequate. When we pity him, we reflect on our own disappointments; and when we laugh, our hearts inform us that he is not more ridiculous than ourselves, except that he tells what we have only thought.'

p. 105, l. 20. *In time some* . . . The editor of the 1825 edn. of Johnson's *Works* points out that 'Dr. Willis [i.e. Francis Willis, who attended George III] defined, in remarkable accordance with this case in *Rasselas*, insanity to be the tendency of a mind to cherish one idea, or set of ideas, to the exclusion of others' (i. 293 n.).

p. 105, l. 21. *the mind . . . feasts* . . . Cf. *Preface to Shakespeare*: 'The mind, which has feasted on the luxurious wonders of fiction, has no taste of the insipidity of truth' (Raleigh, p. 32).

p. 106, l. 19. *fantastick:* 'unreal' (*Dict.*), 'proceeding merely from imagination' (*OED*), a sense that is now obsolete.

p. 106, l. 21. *image:* 'copy by the fancy, imagine' (*Dict.*). Cf. p. 117, l. 22.

a perfect government. The prince was clearly indulging in fantasy. v. note to p. 64, l. 18.

p. 107, l. 14. *prattled:* engaged in light conversation, chatted. (This word is now used to refer to either the talk of children or childish talk.)

p. 107, l. 23. *qualities:* 'properties' (*Dict.*).

p. 107, l. 26. *contemplation:* matter for contemplation.

p. 107, l. 27. *dignity.* 'The word means not "worthiness" but "advancement, high place" in knowledge' (Emerson, p. 174).

p. 108, l. 3. *disputed:* 'contended by argument, debated' (*Dict.*).

the annual overflow of the Nile. Lobo mentions this as a subject of debate in earlier times (pp. 106–7). Cf. note to p. 102, l. 8.

p. 108, l. 4. *I cast* . . . Cf. *Idler* 103 : 'Succession is not perceived but by variation. . . . It is only by finding life changeable that we are reminded of its shortness' (Yale, ii. 315).

p. 108, l. 6. *I have ceased* . . . Even in old age Johnson's own curiosity remained lively. Boswell reports him as saying: 'It is a man's own fault, it is from want of use, if his mind grows torpid in old age' (*Life*, iii. 254). Yet as a Christian humanist he always prized 'self-knowledge' above 'star-knowledge'; cf. *Rambler* 24: 'The great praise of Socrates is, that he drew the wits of Greece, by his instruction and example, from the vain persuit of natural philosophy to moral inquiries, and turned their thoughts from stars and tides, and matter and motion, upon the various modes of virtue, and relations of life.'

p. 108, l. 9. *recreate:* 'amuse or divert in weariness' (*Dict.*), 'refresh with some agreeable occupation or pastime' (*OED*).

p. 108, l. 13. *I have neither* . . . Cf. note to p. 63, l. 31. Johnson's mother probably died on 20 or 21 January 1759, when he had almost finished *Rasselas*. Cf. *Idler* 41 (published 27 January 1759): 'What is success to him that has none to enjoy it? Happiness is not found in self-contemplation; it is perceived only when it is reflected from another' (Yale, ii. 130).

p. 108, l. 24. *My retrospect of life* . . . Cf. notes to p. 10, l. 28; p. 11, l. 27; *Idler* 44: 'Few can review the time past without heaviness of heart. He remembers many calamities incurred by folly, many opportunities lost by negligence' (Yale, ii. 139). On 'Easter Eve, 1757' Johnson thus petitioned God: 'Pardon my sins, remove the impediments that hinder my obedience. Enable me to shake off Sloth, and to redeem the time mispent in idleness and Sin by a diligent application of the days yet remaining to the duties which thy Providence shall allot me' (*ib*. i. 63).

p. 108, l. 27. *vacancy:* 'listlessness, emptiness of thought' (*Dict.*), 'inactivity' (*OED*), a sense that is now rare or obsolete.

p. 109, l. 11. *age was querulous.* In *Rambler* 50, Johnson refers to 'the querulousness and indignation which is observed so often to disfigure the last scene of life'.

p. 110, l. 24. *All imposture* . . . Johnson said: 'Truth should never be violated, because it is of the utmost importance to the comfort of life, that we should have a full security by mutual faith' (*Life*, iv. 305); 'Without truth there must be a dissolution of society. . . . Society is held together by communication and information; and I remember this remark of Sir Thomas Brown's, "Do the devils lie? No; for then Hell could not subsist"' (*ib.* iii. 293). Cf. *Adventurer* 50: 'When Aristotle was once asked, what a man could gain by uttering falsehoods; he replied, "not to be credited when he shall tell the truth". . . . I cannot but think that they who destroy the confidence of society, weaken the credit of intelligence, and interrupt the security of life . . . might very properly be awakened to a sense of their crimes, by denunciations of a whipping post or pillory' (Yale, ii. 361, 366). J. D. Fleeman points out that Johnson's 'insistence upon truthfulness, and his abhorrence of all forms of deception, are primary features of all his writings' (*Johnsonian Studies*, ed. Magdi Wahba, 1962, p. 109).

p. 111, l. 15. *auditress.* Cf. *Paradise Lost*, viii. 51:

> *Adam* relating, she sole Auditress.

p. 111, l. 24. *stay:* remain inactive, 'wait' (*Dict.*), a sense that is now obsolete.

p. 111, l. 31. *recollected:* 'recovered to memory, gathered what was scattered' (*Dict.*).

p. 113, l. 11. *commerce:* 'intercourse' (*Dict.*).

p. 113, l. 13. *fear, disquiet, and scrupulosity.* The astronomer's subsequent confession to Imlac amply illustrates his state of mind. Imlac's reply contrasts the sage's 'scruples' with his 'lucid moments'. This whole episode has an unmistakable relevance for Johnson himself (v. note to p. 104, l. 10). The advice, 'fly to business' or company, was such as seemed to him most effectual in combating those scruples of conscience which arose from his own sense of guilt, and contributed to his own melancholy.

p. 114, l. 9. *I am like* . . . Cf. note to p. 8, l. 6.

p. 115, l. 2. *when scruples* . . . Johnson wrote to Boswell: 'Let me warn you very earnestly against scruples. . . . Do not . . . hope wholly to reason away your troubles; do not feed them with attention, and they will die imperceptibly away. Fix your thoughts upon your business, fill your intervals with company, and sunshine will again break in upon your mind' (*Life*, ii. 423). Mrs. Piozzi writes of Johnson: 'Those teachers had more of his blame than praise, I think, who seek to oppress life with unnecessary scruples: "Scruples would (as he observed) certainly make men miserable, and seldom make them good. Let us ever (he said) studiously fly from those instructors against whom our Saviour denounces heavy judgments, for having bound up burdens grievous to be borne, and laid them on the shoulders of mortal men"' (*Anecdotes*, p. 74). Hill quotes (pp. 197–8) from the conclusion of Burton's *Anatomy of Melancholy*: 'Only take this for a corollary and conclusion, as thou tenderest thine own welfare in this and all other melancholy, good health of body and mind, observe this short precept, give not way to solitariness and idleness. "Be not solitary, be not idle."'

p. 115, l. 15. *in secret.* Referring to his own melancholy, Johnson said that he 'had been obliged to fly from study and meditation, to the dissipating variety of life' (*Life*, i. 446).

p. 115, l. 29. *when we have* . . . Cf. *Rambler* 6: 'Such are the changes that keep the mind in action; we desire, we pursue, we obtain, we are satiated; we desire something else and begin a new pursuit.'

p. 116, l. 3. *Variety* . . . Cf. *Preface to Shakespeare:* '. . . upon the whole, all pleasure consists in variety' (Raleigh, p. 17); *Life of Butler:* 'The great source of pleasure is variety. Uniformity must tire at last, though it be uniformity of excellence' (*Lives*, i. 212).

p. 116, l. 16. *Their time is* . . . Johnson wrote to Baretti: 'I have not, since the day of our separation, suffered or done any thing considerable. . . . I have hitherto lived without the concurrence of my own judgment; yet I continue to flatter myself, that, when you return, you will find me mended. I do not wonder that, where the monastick life is permitted, every order finds votaries, and every monastery inhabitants. Men will submit to any rule, by which they may be exempted from the tyranny of caprice and of chance. They are glad to supply by external authority their own want of constancy and resolution, and court the government of others, when long experience has convinced them of their own inability to govern themselves. If I were to visit Italy, my curiosity would be more attracted by convents than by palaces' (*Letters*, i. 134–5).

p. 116, l. 25. *converses*: 'cohabits with, holds intercourse with, is a companion to' (*Dict.*).

p. 117, l. 3. *if he cannot*... Johnson was prepared to allow religious retirement to 'those who cannot resist temptations, and find they make themselves worse by being in the world, without making it better' (*Life*, v. 62). On another occasion he said: 'If convents should be allowed at all, they should only be retreats for persons unable to serve the publick, or who have served it. It is our first duty to serve society, and, after we have done that, we may attend wholly to the salvation of our own souls' (*ib.* ii. 10). Mrs. Piozzi writes: 'The votaries of retirement had little of Mr. Johnson's applause, unless that he knew that the motives were merely devotional, and unless he was convinced that their rituals were accompanied by a mortified state of the body, the sole proof of their sincerity which he would admit, as a compensation for such fatigue as a worldly life of care and activity requires' (*Anecdotes*, p. 163). Cf. note to p. 54, l. 3.

p. 117, l. 11. *Those retreats of*... Johnson said: 'I never read of a hermit, but in imagination I kiss his feet; never of a monastery, but I could fall on my knees, and kiss the pavement. . . . I have thought of retiring, and have talked of it to a friend; but I find my vocation is rather to active life' (*Life*, v. 62–63).

p. 117, l. 14. *to close his life* . . . Cf. Johnson's remark to Boswell: 'I have sometimes thought that I would wish to die quite alone, and have the whole matter transacted between God and myself, sometimes that I would have a friend with me; for we all think death less terrible when we have company with us' (*Life*, iii. 498).

p. 117, l. 19. *using*. This word retains the sense 'enjoying' from Latin *utor*.

harmless pleasures. In his *Life of Smith*, Johnson writes of the death of his friend David Garrick: 'I am disappointed by that stroke of death, which has eclipsed the gaiety of nations, and impoverished the publick stock of harmless pleasure' (*Lives*, ii. 21). Boswell objected to this as an 'anticlimax of praise', asking: '"Is not *harmless pleasure* very tame?"' JOHNSON: "Nay, Sir, harmless pleasure is the highest praise. Pleasure is a word of dubious import; pleasure is in general dangerous, and pernicious to virtue; to be able therefore to furnish pleasure that is harmless, pleasure pure and unalloyed, is as great a power as man can possess"' (*Life*, iii. 388).

p. 117, l. 25. *probatory:* 'serving for trial' (*Dict.*); 'testing' (*OED*). This word is now rare or obsolete.

p. 117, l. 27. *Mortification is not* . . . Cf. *Rambler* 110: 'Austerities and mortifications are means by which the mind is invigorated and roused, by which the attractions of pleasure are interrupted, and the chains of sensuality are broken. . . . Austerity is the proper antidote to indulgence; the diseases of mind as well as body are cured by contraries.'

p. 117, l. 29. *In the state* . . . Johnson said: 'The happiness of Heaven will be, that pleasure and virtue will be perfectly consistent' (*Life*, ii. 292).

p. 118, l. 7. *catacombs.* 'The term "catacomb" was originally used only for the subterranean burial places of Christians at Rome, but was later extended, first to similar Christian cemeteries in other places and then to those of other people. There are no catacombs in the immediate vicinity of Cairo, but Pococke, in describing the catacombs of Saccara about ten miles from Gizeh, says the common way of reaching them is from Cairo, so that this may account for Johnson's reference' (Emerson, p. 177).

p. 118, l. 11. *I know not* . . . Hill suggests (p. 199) that Johnson would not himself have gone into the catacombs, citing as evidence his reaction to the bones exposed at the ruined chapel of Raasay. Boswell writes: 'Dr. Johnson would not look at the bones. He started back from them with a striking appearance of horrour' (*Life*, v. 169).

p. 118, l. 27. *What reason* . . . 'Throughout the period of more than 30 centuries during which mummification was practised in Egypt, the embalmers had two definite objects in view: first, the preservation of the body from decay; and second, the perpetuation of the personal identity of the deceased' (*Ency. Brit.*, xv. 925–6). 'The whole idea of the tomb seems originally to have resulted simply from the passionate desire to deny the existence of death.

... The Egyptians, a cheerful, merry people, loathed the idea of death and did their best to persuade themselves that the dead were not actually dead at all, but continuing to live in the underworld of the tomb' (*ib*. viii. 55).

p. 119, l. 3. *original*. Johnson brackets *origin* and *original* as exactly equivalent in use (*Dict.*). Regarding the origin of this practice v. *Ency. Brit.* viii. 55: 'Originally the bodies of the dead no doubt dried fortuitously in their graves in the desert sand; some may have been smoked. It was seen to be possible in Egypt to preserve the dead from dissolution, and gradually the practice of mummification grew up.'

p. 119, l. 24. *some yet say* . . . La Mettrie, echoing Aristotle's *De Anima* (412, a) concerning 'the most far-reaching difference' between philosophers, wrote in 1747: 'Je réduis à deux, les Systêmes des Philosophes sur l'ame de l'Homme. Le premier, & le plus ancien, est le Systême du Matérialisme; le second est celui du Spiritualisme' (*L'Homme Machine*, ed. Aram Vartanian, 1960, p. 149). In regarding man as a mechanical entity, La Mettrie singles out for special comment Claude Perrault and Thomas Willis, the latter of whom, as Vartanian points out, distinguished in his *De Anima brutorum*, or *Two Discourses concerning the Soul of Brutes*, 'two souls in man: a higher soul that was rational, immaterial, immortal, and remained peculiar to him alone; and a lower soul, possessed in common with the beasts, which performed all involuntary acts of a sensory, motor, and vital nature'. Vartanian adds: 'Describing this animal soul concretely as a "sulphureous, fiery component of the blood," Willis imagined it to be "généralement répandue par tout le corps." As such, it represented (except for its being restricted to a subintellectual level) a chemiatric version of the Epicurean "subtle atoms" theory' (p. 243). Hobbes had declared not only that God was a 'most pure and most simple corporeal spirit', but that spirit was a 'thin, fluid, transparent, invisible body' (*The English Works of Thomas Hobbes*, ed. W. Molesworth, 1839–45, reprinted 1962, iv. 306, 309). Even Descartes could not deny interaction between an immaterial soul and a material body. Hume pronounced 'the question concerning the substance of the soul . . . absolutely unintelligible' (*A Treatise of Human Nature*, ed. L. A. Selby-Bigge, 1949 reprint, p. 250).

p. 119, l. 33. *that cogitation* . . . By saying, however, that we 'possibly shall never be able to know whether any mere material being thinks or no' (*Essay concerning Human Understanding*, iv. 3, sect. 6), Locke had given rise to some confusion on this point. Cf. Vartanian, *op. cit.* p. 204.

p. 121, l. 17. *idea:* mental image, picture in the mind. Boswell writes: 'Johnson was at all times jealous of infractions upon the genuine English language, and prompt to repress colloquial barbarisms. . . . He was particularly indignant against the almost universal use of the word *idea* in the sense of *notion* or *opinion*, when it is clear that *idea* can only signify something of which an image can be formed in the mind. We may have an *idea* or *image* of a mountain, a tree, a building; but we cannot surely have an *idea* or *image* of an argument or *proposition*' (*Life*, iii. 196).

p. 121, l. 22. *impassive:* 'not susceptible of physical impression or injury' (*OED*).

indiscerptible: 'incapable of being broken or destroyed by dissolution of parts' (*Dict.*).

p. 121, l. 27. *That it will not perish* . . . Cf. Plato, *Republic*, x. 9–10 (609 ff.), where the argument runs as follows. Everything has its own special or proper evil, and if this does not destroy it nothing else will. Injustice, licentiousness, cowardice and ignorance are evils proper to the soul, but none of these destroys it in the same way as disease destroys the body, none of these corrupts and withers it and causes death. If the soul's natural vice and proper evil cannot destroy it, still less will the evil that brings destruction on another thing destroy it. Since it is not destroyed by any evil whatever, it must exist always, and if it always exists, it is immortal.

p. 121, l. 29. *That it will not be annihilated* . . . Johnson said: 'No wise man will be contented to die, if he thinks he is to fall into annihilation. . . . There is no rational principle by which a man can die contented, but a trust in the mercy of God, through the merits of Jesus Christ' (*Life*, v. 180). He refused to regard the prospect of annihilation with indifference, refused (in his own words) to confound 'annihilation, which is nothing, with the apprehension of it, which is dreadful' (*ib.* iii. 296). Boswell writes: 'I told him that David Hume said to me, he was no more uneasy to think he should *not be* after this life, than that he *had not been* before he began

to exist. JOHNSON: "Sir, if he really thinks so, his perceptions are
disturbed; he is mad"' (*ib.* ii. 106); 'I said, I had reason to believe
that the thought of annihilation gave Hume no pain. JOHNSON: "It
was not so, Sir. He had a vanity in being thought easy. It is more
probable that he should assume an appearance of ease, than that so
very improbable a thing should be, as a man not afraid of going (as,
in spite of his delusive theory, he cannot be sure but he may go), into
an unknown state, and not being uneasy at leaving all he knew.
And you are to consider, that upon his own principle of annihilation he had no motive to speak the truth"' (*ib.* iii. 153).

p. 121, l. 32. *collected.* Johnson defined *to collect himself* as 'to
recover from surprise, to gain command over his thoughts, to
assemble his sentiments' (*Dict.*), a sense he illustrated from *The
Tempest*, I. ii. 15–16:

> Be collected,
> No more amazement.

p. 122, l. 10. *I hope hereafter* . . . Cf. *The Vanity of Human Wishes*,
ll. 343–68:

> Where then shall Hope and Fear their objects find?
> Must dull Suspence corrupt the stagnant mind?
> Must helpless man, in ignorance sedate,
> Roll darkling down the torrent of his fate?
> Must no dislike alarm, no wishes rise,
> No cries attempt the mercies of the skies?
> Enquirer, cease, petitions yet remain,
> Which heav'n may hear, nor deem religion vain.
> Still raise for good the supplicating voice,
> But leave to heav'n the measure and the choice,
> Safe in his pow'r, whose eyes discern afar
> The secret ambush of a specious pray'r.
> Implore his aid, in his decisions rest,
> Secure whate'er he gives, he gives the best.
> Yet when the sense of sacred presence fires,
> And strong devotion to the skies aspires,
> Pour forth thy fervours for a healthful mind,
> Obedient passions, and a will resign'd;
> For love, which scarce collective man can fill;
> For patience, sov'reign o'er transmuted ill;

For faith, that panting for a happier seat,
Counts death kind Nature's signal of retreat:
These goods for man the laws of heav'n ordain,
These goods he grants, who grants the pow'r to gain;
With these celestial wisdom calms the mind,
And makes the happiness she does not find (Yale, vi. 107–9);

Rambler 7: 'The great task of him who conducts his life by the precepts of religion, is to make the future predominate over the present, to impress upon his mind so strong a sense of the importance of obedience to the divine will, of the value of the reward promised to virtue, and the terrours of the punishment denounced against crimes, as may overbear all the temptations which temporal hope or fear can bring in his way, and enable him to bid equal defiance to joy and sorrow, to turn away at one time from the allurements of ambition, and push forward at another against the threats of calamity.' Cf. note to p. 66, l. 8.

p. 122, l. 28. *disgust:* dissatisfaction bordering on vexation.

American Literature

British and Irish Literature

Children's Literature

Classics and Ancient Literature

Colonial Literature

Eastern Literature

European Literature

History

Medieval Literature

Oxford English Drama

Poetry

Philosophy

Politics

Religion

The Oxford Shakespeare

A complete list of Oxford Paperbacks, including Oxford World's Classics, Oxford Shakespeare, Oxford Drama, and Oxford Paperback Reference, is available in the UK from the Academic Division Publicity Department, Oxford University Press, Great Clarendon Street, Oxford OX2 6DP.

In the USA, complete lists are available from the Paperbacks Marketing Manager, Oxford University Press, 198 Madison Avenue, New York, NY 10016.

Oxford Paperbacks are available from all good bookshops. In case of difficulty, customers in the UK can order direct from Oxford University Press Bookshop, Freepost, 116 High Street, Oxford OX1 4BR, enclosing full payment. Please add 10 per cent of published price for postage and packing.

The Oxford World's Classics Website

www.worldsclassics.co.uk

- Information about new titles
- Explore the full range of Oxford World's Classics
- Links to other literary sites and the main OUP webpage
- Imaginative competitions, with bookish prizes
- Peruse the Oxford World's Classics Magazine
- Articles by editors
- Extracts from Introductions
- A forum for discussion and feedback on the series
- Special information for teachers and lecturers

www.worldsclassics.co.uk

A SELECTION OF   OXFORD WORLD'S CLASSICS